Praise for Weddings by Bella

"*Fools Rush In* is a charming tale about stumbling upon love and finding a bit of your true self along life's journey. This fun read makes you grateful for the truly important things in life."

Megan DiMaria, author, *Searching for Spice*
and *Out of Her Hands*

"I fell in love with the Rossi clan, who feel as passionately about their pizza as Texans do about chili. Add a hunky cowboy with a slow Southern drawl, and you've got a recipe for one terrific story."

Virginia Smith, author, *Stuck in the Middle*

"Janice Thompson is a master storyteller who draws her readers into the tale along with the characters. From page one of *Fools Rush In*, I felt as if I were Bella's best friend."

Ane Mulligan, editor, Novel Journey

"If you enjoy weddings, Italian cuisine, and stories filled with humor and romance, you're going to love *Swinging on a Star*."

Anita Higman, award-winning author,
Love Finds You in Humble, Texas

"*Swinging on a Star* has more layers of love than Aunt Rosa's lasagna. A large, loving family creates a healthy stock for the sweet romance that sizzles and simmers on every page—all of it flavored with God's grace. Janice Thompson effortlessly mixes cowboys and operas with a dash of Hollywood to create a tasty treat of a tale."

Allison Pittman, autho

Books by Janice Thompson

WEDDINGS BY BELLA

Fools Rush In

Swinging on a Star

Weddings BY *Bella*

BOOK TWO

SWINGING ON A STAR

A NOVEL

JANICE THOMPSON

Revell

a division of Baker Publishing Group
Grand Rapids, Michigan

© 2010 by Janice Thompson

Published by Revell
a division of Baker Publishing Group
P.O. Box 6287, Grand Rapids, MI 49516-6287
www.revellbooks.com

Printed in the United States of America

Library of Congress Cataloging-in-Publication Data
Thompson, Janice A.
    Swinging on a star : a novel / Janice Thompson.
        p.   cm. — (Weddings by Bella ; bk. 2)
    ISBN 978-0-8007-3343-8 (pbk.)
    1. Single women—Fiction. 2. Weddings—Planning—Fiction. I. Title.
PS3620.H6824S85 2010
813'.6—dc22   2009030560

Scripture used in this book, whether quoted or paraphrased by the characters, is taken from the King James Version of the Bible.

Published in association with MacGregor Literary Agency.

10   11   12   13   14   15   16   7   6   5   4   3   2   1

To Phil and Leslie Nott. Your beautiful Renaissance-themed wedding inspired me to write this fun medieval tale.

1

High Hopes

If Aunt Rosa hadn't landed that gig on the Food Network, I probably wouldn't have ended up on the national news. And if their pesky camera crew hadn't shown up at our house on one of the most important days of my life, I'm pretty sure I wouldn't have been hauled off to the Galveston County jail. Unlike my brother Armando, I'd never aspired to get arrested or have my face plastered across the television screen on the evening news. But thanks to Aunt Rosa's homemade garlic bread, I found myself facing both of these things . . . and in exactly that order.

When the call came last Tuesday from the powers that be at the Food Network, the entire Rossi family went into a tailspin. Aunt Rosa's recipe had been chosen from among thousands to be featured in an upcoming episode titled *Italian Chefs from Coast to Coast*. This was a great honor, of course, but the timing couldn't have been worse. After all, I was right in the middle of coordinating my first-ever medieval-themed wedding at Club Wed, our family's wedding facility. I was up to my earlobes in castles and moats. Who had the time—or patience—for television crews?

I pointed out my concerns to my mother just a week and a half before the big day as she prepared to leave for the opera house. She'd only just started applying her makeup, a process that usually took a good hour or more, so I knew I had plenty of time. Pacing around her oversized bathroom, I spoke my mind.

"Mama, you know what I'm up against. This wedding is so important. Everything has to be perfect. The bride has had this one planned out since she was a little girl, and the best man is coming all the way from California. It's a huge deal, and if I can manage to pull it off, it'll be a great promotion for Club Wed."

"You've coordinated weddings before, Bella," Mama said with a wave of her hand. "What's so different about this one?"

"It's a *themed* wedding, Mama. Medieval. I've never done one of those before, so I'm nervous."

"You worry too much, honey." She squirted lotion into her hand and then smeared it on her face, working it into every pore. "Remember how you fretted over the country-western themed wedding, and it came off without a hitch?"

"You call Uncle Laz's parrot stealing a toupee from one of our guests 'without a hitch'?" I sighed, not even trying to hide my frustration. "And what about the part where our caterer's eyebrows got burned off while he was barbecuing the beans?" After a pause, I added, "Besides, I'm not *trying* to worry, but there's so much to think about. I'm transforming the whole gazebo area into a medieval wonderland. The bridesmaids and groomsmen are wearing Renaissance costumes and dressing up as ladies-in-waiting and knights in shining armor. Doesn't that sound awesome?"

"Of course."

"We're even having horses and trumpeters and a court jester—the whole thing. And Laz, Jenna, and Nick are serving authentic foods from the Middle Ages. I've put a ton of work into this. It's a really big deal."

My mama's perfectly sculpted eyebrows arched, and I could sense a lecture coming on. I'd gotten pretty good at reading her thinly plucked eyebrows. "Well, I hate to burst your bubble," she said, "but Aunt Rosa's debut on national television is a pretty big deal too. I'm surprised you're not more excited for her." As she pulled her dark hair back in a cloth headband, the tiny wrinkles around her eyes lifted. With rehearsed flair, she reached for a bottle of liquid foundation and gave it a good shake.

"I am excited for her," I said. "But, you realize the camera crew is set to arrive the day before the wedding, right? This is going to be a fiasco of major proportions!" Surely she could see my point. After all, we would be smack-dab in the middle of the wedding rehearsal at that time, and I didn't want any disruptions. If the street happened to be filled with Food Network trucks and the like, it would, at the very least, spoil the ambience. My clients had paid good money to have this wedding come off without a hitch. I couldn't let them down.

"I, for one, think it's perfect." My mother poured a dollop of foundation into her open palm. "It's a great way to promote the family business *and* give Rosa the attention she needs." Mama jabbed her slender, beautifully manicured index finger into the gooey liquid, then began to place dots of the flesh-colored stuff all over her face. Soon my polka-dotted mother turned my way. "I think you're missing a great opportunity here, Bella. Think about it."

"I guess I'm just not seeing it." I closed the lid on the toilet and sat down, feeling defeated. "It's going to be a huge distraction—a great way to draw attention *away* from the wedding facility. I'm afraid that's what's going to happen, not the other way around."

"Don't be silly. And remember, this isn't about you, Bella Bambina," she chastened me. "This is about your aunt. She's worked all her life for a moment like this. We can't rob her of this chance to shine like the star she is."

"No, of course not," I said. "It's just that . . ." I sighed, unsure of what to say next.

In the next room, Guido—the parrot my uncle had adopted from his mob friend Sal—began to sing "Amazing Grace." I'd grown accustomed to his morning ritual, but it was starting to get a little old. Or maybe my patience was just wearing thin. Living in a house with so many relatives could do that to a person, particularly when there was so much work to be done. Still, I needed the grace that Guido was singing about—and I needed it now.

A rap at the bathroom door caught my attention. Aunt Rosa stuck her head inside and flashed a shy smile when I looked her way. She wore her hair pulled up in a loose bun. Her housedress was the same one she'd worn a hundred times before over the past several years. So was the apron, which was covered in flour. Unlike Mama, Rosa didn't believe in wasting money on new things. Or makeup. Unless she had a man to impress, of course. Lately I'd begun to suspect she'd found one. I'd caught her wearing lipstick on at least three occasions.

"Bella, there's someone at the front door for you." My aunt brushed her palms against her apron. "He says he's with the Stages Set Design Company."

"Ah." The guy we'd hired to turn the gazebo area into a castle and moat for the big day. The bride's father had instructed me to spare no expense, and I wasn't taking his words lightly. The construction of the castle would cost over ten grand. Oh, but how glorious it would look! I could almost picture it now . . . minus the Food Network trucks in the background, of course. The upcoming medieval evening would draw a whole new clientele to the wedding facility. I hoped.

I looked at my Aunt Rosa—standing there with her face still beaming from the news about her television opportunity—and immediately felt shame and remorse for voicing any complaints. If anyone deserved this, she did.

Lord, I'm sorry. I'm letting my worries about this wedding spoil my aunt's once-in-a-lifetime opportunity. Forgive me?

As he whispered a gentle "Of course," I reached to hug Rosa, who flashed an embarrassed smile. "We're so proud of you, Rosa," I whispered in her ear. "If anyone deserves a chance to strut her stuff, it's you. You're the best cook in the world."

"Thank you." She giggled like a schoolgirl. "But I can still hardly believe they picked *me*! This is the most exciting thing that's happened to me since I got off the plane from Napoli. I'm going to be on my favorite channel of all—the Food Network." She reached for her St. Christopher medal and began to praise all of the saints at once. I couldn't help but smile as her chorus ushered heavenward in lyrical Italian.

In the meantime, I slipped past her and down the stairs. My aunt had a cooking career to build. Me? I'd better get busy building a castle.

2

Lost in the Stars

I spent the next two hours tagging along on the set designer's heels as he measured the area behind the wedding facility for the incoming castle. The inside space would accommodate 150 people, he assured me, and would have a dance floor and stage for the musicians, the juggler, the court jester, and the sword-swallower. My throat hurt just thinking about that last one.

As we talked things through, I could almost picture the space filled with guests, instrumentalists, and caterers. Not to mention the bride and groom dressed as queen and king.

By the time he left, I'd had all my questions answered. Well, most anyway. I still couldn't quite figure out the whole moat thing. Was he planning to put in a river? In our backyard? Fill it with faux crocodiles, perhaps?

I pondered all of these things as I made my way inside the wedding facility. Traveling through the large ballroom where so many lovely receptions had taken place, I paused for a moment to reflect on God's goodness. Over the past few months, he'd certainly made me feel like a princess at the ball. Given me the family business to run. Sent me the man of my dreams . . .

I released a happy sigh as I thought about D.J. Neeley, my honey. What had I ever done to deserve him? Surely if I behaved myself for the rest of my mortal life, I still couldn't earn such a gift. No, only the Lord could have accomplished this—bringing together an Italian girl from Galveston Island with a handsome country boy from Splendora, Texas. A cowboy, no less.

I glanced at my watch, surprised by the time. D.J. had promised to pick me up for lunch. We were going to Parma John's, of course, my uncle's pizzeria on the Strand. It was our favorite hangout, and the food was fantabulous. D.J. should be here within the hour, and I could hardly wait.

When I arrived in my office, I made my way through the ever-growing stack of papers on the desk. How had things gotten so out of control? I'd better get busy—pronto. I began to organize everything in tidy piles—bills in one and letters of agreement in another. That left me with a large miscellaneous pile. No problem. I could shove that stack in my desk drawer to be dealt with later.

I looked out of the window, noticing Eugene, our UPS guy, getting out of his big brown truck next door. He carried a package to the front door of our house. I knew what would happen, of course. Rosa would meet him there with a bright smile. Laz would peek through the window, watching as she took the package from Eugene. As was so often the case, he wouldn't look happy.

All of this transpired just as I'd guessed. Then Rosa invited Eugene in for a glass of tea, her usual gesture of thanks for his deliveries. Oh, I couldn't hear her asking from the window, but that didn't matter. The routine was always the same. Eugene would come in. Rosa would flirt. Laz would get miffed. And Guido would take to singing "Amazing Grace."

Life never changed much at the Rossi house. Nor did I want it to. No, with only a couple of minor exceptions, we Rossis lived a pretty comfortable, predictable life.

Now if only I could keep the family business from going under. Maybe then we could go on with our comfortable, predictable life.

I dove into my work, paying a couple of bills and then calling vendors. After that, I listened to voice mails, delighted to find one from a potential client. I made a note to call her tomorrow morning. In the meantime, I needed to reword some things in the Club Wed contract. Since we'd decided to take on themed weddings, the old wording didn't exactly work. I turned to the computer and pulled up the file, then started making adjustments.

When the phone rang a few minutes later, I was so focused on my work that it startled me. I reached for it without taking the time to look at the caller ID.

"Thank you for calling Club Wed, Galveston Island's premier wedding facility." I answered in my usual chipper voice, doing my best to sound professional. Didn't want potential clients to figure out that I'd only been managing the facility for a few months, after all. And if I came across as confident, maybe I'd start to feel that way.

"Bella?" I heard Marian Jarvis's cheerful voice over the phone line. "Are you there?"

I grinned, thankful this bride-to-be was always so upbeat and excited. "I'm here. What's up?"

"Just wanted you to know that Rob and I are on our way

to pick up the best man from the airport." Her voice had a lilt to it beyond the norm. Almost as if she had something up her sleeve.

"The wedding isn't for ten days," I said, taken aback by her words. "Why so early?"

She giggled, and I knew something was up. "Oh, hon, do I have a lot to tell you! Are you sitting down?"

"Yes, I'm sitting down. Let me have it." I drew in a breath, anxious to hear her news.

"Okay, you know how I told you that Rob's best man—er, first knight—was from Los Angeles?"

"Sure." I'd heard about this elusive best man in snatches only. For some reason, Marian's stories about him were a little vague.

"Well, there's more to the story than that. You've heard of Brock Benson, right?"

"The actor?" I leaned back against the chair, instantly transported to a scene in Brock's latest action-adventure set aboard a pirate ship on the high seas. "Of course. Who hasn't? But what does he have to do with your wedding?"

"Oh, Bella, I've been dying to tell you this, but it's top secret information. Brock is Rob's best friend. They've known each other since they were kids in grade school together on the West Coast. Brock is flying in early so that he and Rob can spend some time together before the wedding."

"W-wait." I sat straight up, my heart going a thousand miles an hour. "A-are you telling me that Brock Benson, three-time Academy Award–winning Hollywood superstar, is the best man in this wedding, and that he's coming to Texas?"

Another giggle traveled across the phone line. "Well, technically he's already in Texas. He's been shooting a movie in the Austin area but is joining Rob for the next week and a half until the big day. But yes, he's the best man. That's where you come in."

"Where I come in?" Suddenly I could hardly breathe. Brock Benson was coming to Galveston Island to play the role of best man in the wedding I was coordinating? Was I dreaming this? If so, someone had better pinch me—quick!

"We're going to need a place for him to stay where the paparazzi won't catch up with him," Marian said. "I know it's hurricane season, so the reporters are out in full force as soon as they hear there's any sign of a storm. They usually stay at the bigger hotels down there, right?"

"R-right." Storm? Hotels? She'd lost me at Brock Benson—tall, dark, and handsome movie hero.

"Rob and I were thinking maybe you could help us find someplace more secluded, where reporters wouldn't happen to show up at a moment's notice. You know? Maybe a smaller hotel or even a bed-and-breakfast. Someplace like that."

"How long are we talking?" I asked, finally coming to my senses. "I mean, how long will he be on the island?"

"We're coming down in Rob's car tomorrow, and the guys will stay till the wedding. Now, we won't need a place for all of that time. Rob's dad has a yacht, and the groomsmen wanted to take a little fishing trip a few days before the wedding. In fact, my ladies-in-waiting are coming to the island a couple of days before the ceremony too. We'll be staying in a condo that I've rented. That way we'll all be close by for the big day. But I'm worried about hiding Brock from the media. He's pretty hot right now."

Um, yeah. Hot didn't even begin to describe it. Try sizzling. Like the proverbial cat on a tin roof. I felt a heat wave coming on even now as I thought about his gorgeous brown eyes and chiseled features.

Just as quickly, my thoughts shifted to the real man of my dreams—D.J. Neeley—my boot-wearin', country-western-song-lovin' honey. My knight in shining armor.

Determined to stay focused, I made a suggestion. "Let's put the guys up at the Tremont. Have you ever been there?"

"No."

"I think you would like it. It's a high-end hotel built in the 1800s. Reporters don't often stay there because it's a little on the pricey side. They usually pick one of the newer, bigger places on the seawall. If we put him at the Tremont, he'll be close to the wedding facility—just a few blocks away, in fact."

The realization suddenly had my head spinning. Brock Benson, king of Hollywood, would soon take up residence just a few blocks from both my home and my place of business. How could I keep my sister Sophia—his biggest fan—from shouting the news from one end of the island to the other?

That would be a tricky one. I tried to picture her reaction to Brock's arrival. Surely she'd faint dead away at his feet. After all, she'd spent over an hour standing in line to get tickets to his latest movie, insisting she had to see it the very night it came out. The girl simply couldn't get enough of the Hollywood hunk. Would her enthusiasm blow his cover? Just one more thing to add to my ever-growing list of things to worry about.

Just then, another call came through. *Ooo, D.J.* Switching over to him proved to be problematic, however, since Marian continued to talk a mile a minute about the role Brock Benson would play in her wedding. Several seconds into her chatter, I heard a *click* and realized D.J. must've given up. No problem. He would be here soon, anyway.

"We can talk more about all of this later, Bella," Marian said with a giggle. "I just thought it was time to let you know all of this. Didn't want to spring Brock on you at the last minute."

"O-okay."

We ended the call, and I looked down at the blueprint for the castle, feeling a little like Cinderella—caught in my ragged gown and completely unprepared for my night at the ball. The prince was coming! I'd better sweep out the chimney and measure my feet for glass slippers.

Ironically, the thought had no sooner flitted through my mind than the Lord—in his ever-perfect timing—shifted my attention out the window. I grinned as I saw D.J.'s truck pulling into the driveway. So much for Hollywood princes. Here was the real deal. And talk about a chariot! His Dodge 4x4 glistened in the afternoon sunlight, a true testament to the power of love. Well, love between a cowboy and his truck, anyway.

A wave of excitement washed over me. Oh, how I wanted to tell D.J. everything I'd just learned. Would I be breaking confidence to share the news of Brock's impending arrival?

Hmm. A moral dilemma. I'd never been very good with those. Seemed I always just wanted to blab whatever I felt like blabbing with little thought to consequences. Maybe I'd better keep this particular story to myself until I'd prayed about it. On the other hand, I could trust D.J., even if I did decide to tell him. I'd never met a more trustworthy guy.

I paused to think about the first time I'd met D.J. Neeley. Due to a slight miscommunication—mine, not his—I'd thought he was a deejay. In fact, I'd hired him sight unseen to handle the music for the country-western themed wedding I was coordinating. Turned out he wasn't a deejay. His *name* was D.J. He was Dwayne Neeley Jr. from Splendora, Texas. Thank goodness he knew a little something about country tunes. He'd swept in and saved the day, no doubt about that, and in the process had left a lasting impression on my heart. And I knew I could count on him to make the medieval reception spectacular as well, which was exactly why I needed to give him my undivided attention today.

I watched as my broad-shouldered cowboy ambled up the driveway. He'd just come from a construction job, so the sawdust-covered image in front of me made me smile. Sometimes I wondered if D.J. had sawdust in his blood. Not that I minded. He was a true-blue Southern gentleman. I'd take the sawdust any day. Besides, there was something about a Jesus-lovin' cowboy that did my heart good. And talk about handsome! This boy was good-looking from the tips of his cowboy boots all the way up to that sandy-colored hair. Yep, real swashbuckling hero material here.

I paused a moment at the mirror in the front hallway to check my appearance before stepping out onto the porch. I'd pulled my long, dark curls into a ponytail today. Mama always frowned on that, but D.J. never seemed to mind. Of course, I'd have to look more professional tomorrow when I met with Rob and Marian, but I didn't need to worry about that right now.

Once outside, I rushed into D.J.'s arms. He planted a tender kiss on my forehead, then tipped my chin with his index finger to look into my eyes.

"You're a sight for sore eyes," he said with that thick east-Texas drawl of his. "I've been missing you somethin' fierce today, Bella Rossi."

Okay, I loved the man. But I still had to laugh at the way he pronounced my name: *Bay*-luh. D.J. Neeley wasn't the quintessential Italian boy my mama had planned for me to marry, but he was the man of my dreams, the one God had brought all the way to Galveston Island just for me.

After a little smooching on the front porch, I grabbed D.J.'s hand and pulled him inside. "You've got to look at this, baby." Pointing at the blueprint for the castle, my heart raced with excitement. "Isn't this the most amazing thing you've ever seen?"

"Sure is." He let out a whistle. "I still can't believe that girl's father is going to pay ten grand for this setup. You sure there's room for it out back?"

"Yes. We measured today. There's even a moat going in. It's going to be amazing, just like a real medieval ball."

"And you'll be the princess." He kissed the tip of my nose.

"Hardly. It's all about the bride on her special day. Not me."

"Well, the bride wouldn't be having a special day if not for you," D.J. said. "So I'm stickin' with what I said. You can be the damsel in distress, and I'll be the one to rush in and rescue you. Your knight in shining armor. How's that?"

"Sounds yummy. And fitting, since you've already rescued me a couple thousand times over the past three months."

"I'd fight dragons for you, Bella." He planted a convincing kiss on my lips, and I felt myself swoon. Oh, how I loved this man. He always knew just what to say—no fear of Hollywood writers going on strike here. My honey came up with his own lines.

"You hungry?" D.J. asked, forcing my thoughts back to the matters at hand. When I nodded, he said, "Let's shake this place. I'm ready for some pizza. What about you?"

"Yeah, I'm ready." A little giggle escaped my throat as I reached for my key. With this guy by my side, I was ready for just about anything.

3

All or Nothing at All

D.J. and I prepared to leave for Parma John's, my Uncle Lazarro's restaurant . . . and my favorite place on Planet Earth, next to the wedding facility. A sense of pride came over me every time I thought about my uncle. He had come to Texas in the '80s with the dream of opening a pizzeria. That dream had been fulfilled in short order. I'd come to Texas as a young girl, never knowing I would one day manage our family's wedding facility. And now it was the driving force of my life. Funny how much Laz and I had in common, both of us willing to go the distance for the businesses we loved.

Our family has always lived by the old saying *"Val più la pratica della grammatica."* Translation: "Experience is more important than theory." I thought about that as D.J. and I drove to the restaurant. With every fiber of my being, I longed to prove myself to him and to others in the family by making a success out of the wedding facility. Sure, I'd only been managing Club Wed for three months, but what I lacked in experience, I made up for in enthusiasm. That had to count for something. Right? I would prove myself. But in the meantime, D.J. and I had some pizza to consume.

As we drove to Parma John's, D.J. kept me entertained by telling a story about something going on at one of his construction sites. I did my best to stay focused but found it difficult. My thoughts kept gravitating to Brock Benson.

We arrived at Parma John's less than five minutes after leaving Club Wed. The lunch crowd was already there in force, and the place was hopping. I searched through the mob of tourists for my best friend, Jenna, and found her at the counter, taking an order. She looked up at me with a crooked grin. "What's up with you lovebirds? Hungry?"

"Yep." D.J. and I spoke the word in unison, then laughed.

"It's Wednesday." She gave me a wink. I knew what that meant—the Simpatico Special, a large hand-tossed pizza split down the middle with toppings of choice on either side. D.J.'s first-ever trip to Parma John's nearly three months ago was made on a Wednesday. We'd shared the half-and-half pizza then, and we'd share it now, for old time's sake. Or maybe just because we were hungry. I was a little bit pepperoni. He was a little bit Canadian bacon. Simpatico!

"Gotta love Wednesdays," D.J. said with a wink. Oy, what he could do to my heart!

I plopped down on an empty barstool and watched my best friend as she worked. Her freckles seemed more pronounced than ever this late in the summer. And she'd done something different with her hair. What was it? Ah, she must be experimenting with a lighter shade of red. Not bad, not bad. Then again, she was in love, and women in love tended to live on the edge.

22

Jenna chattered a mile a minute about her latest date with Bubba Neeley, D.J.'s younger brother. I tried to listen, really tried, but my thoughts were elsewhere. I was dying to tell her about Brock Benson, though I knew I shouldn't. This would be a true test of my ability to keep a secret—keeping it from Jenna.

And Sophia. I turned as I heard my younger sister's voice. She exited the kitchen with my older brother Nick on her heels.

Nick was the oldest of the Rossi siblings. He and his wife, Marcella, were parents to Deany-boy and Frankie, the world's most obnoxious elementary-aged kids. And Sophia—God bless her—had watched those boys all summer long. No wonder she was in such a bad mood all the time.

Nick and Sophia were going at it, guns blazing. Nothing new there. D.J. and I watched their exchange with amusement.

"Those boys need some discipline, Nick," Sophia said, putting her finger in his face. "You and Marcella let them walk all over you."

He turned back to his work. "Marcella's still having a lot of morning sickness. This pregnancy has been harder on her than the last two."

I paused to think about his words. My sister-in-law was expecting a baby in the early spring. Everyone in the family was praying for a girl this time around. Not that we didn't love the boys, but man, were they ever a handful!

"She's too tired to spend a lot of time disciplining right now," Nick said. "And I'm overworked. Besides, what difference does it make? School has started again. They'll be fine."

D.J. snorted and I jabbed him with my elbow.

The tips of Sophia's ears turned red, a sure sign she was about to blow. "Deany-boy's teacher is a friend of mine, and she's ready to yank her hair out after only a few weeks. That kid pulls too many pranks."

"Boys will be boys." Nick shrugged and then joined Laz in the kitchen. He nodded in our direction as he passed by.

D.J. managed to keep his thoughts inside his head. I had to wonder if my honey was mesmerized by my family . . . or horrified. He never commented on their heated conversations, always smiled instead. I knew for a fact that the Rossis were the polar opposite of his clan out in the piney woods of east Texas. The Neeleys doted on each other round the clock and never raised their voices. That I knew of, anyway.

Lord, I know it's possible. Could some of that spill over on my family?

Just then, my younger brother Joey passed by me on his way to wait on a table. He paused to give me a kiss on the cheek and then shook D.J.'s hand. "What, no one offered you drinks?" He looked at the empty spot in front of us on the bar. "Want the usual?"

"Yep. I'll take a Dr Pepper," D.J. said with a nod.

"Same for me," I added.

Within seconds there were two Dr Peppers on the bar. Just one more thing my sweetie and I had in common. With a wink, Joey disappeared in the crowd.

Thank you, Lord. There is hope for the Rossi clan!

As I followed his movements across the room, I noticed his fiancée, Norah, seated at a nearby table, and gave a little wave. She responded with a nod, then went back to reading a book. Norah was different from most of the girls I knew—quiet, and not so into the hair and makeup thing. And brilliant. Sometimes she startled me with her brilliance. Then again, she would have to be brilliant to choose my brother. Joey was the sweetest, most caring man I knew. Next to Pop, of course.

Though we hadn't yet talked about Norah and Joey's upcoming wedding, I knew it would be wonderful. They deserved a special day. Hopefully they wouldn't mind waiting awhile, though. I couldn't stop to think about their wedding just yet. Not with a Hollywood hottie on his way.

I took a sip of the cold beverage, nerves all atwitter as I thought about my upcoming meeting with Brock Benson. What would it be like to meet a Hollywood star for the first time? Would I act like a silly schoolgirl? What would I say? I struggled to come up with an opening line.

"A penny for your thoughts."

I looked over at D.J. as he spoke, doing my best to shake off my distraction.

"Oh, I've got work on my brain." Sort of. Truth be told, I couldn't stop thinking about the incoming best man. My cheeks heated up and I did my best to shift gears. Today was all about D.J.

My sweetie turned to me with an encouraging smile. "Big wedding coming up. Are you excited?"

"Y-yeah. Lots going on, though. It's complicated." I paused, choosing my words carefully. "But let's go back to what you were talking about on the way over here," I prodded, eager to steer the conversation away from further comment about what had me so distracted. "What's up? Something going on at work?"

"I've been really busy." D.J. sighed. "The house we're rebuilding was really hit hard during the hurricane. Took ages even to get the work started due to an insurance glitch. But anyway, I've been getting to know the owner. He's a pastor of a small church on the west end of the island. His church was completely destroyed too. Wish there was something I could do to help—other than construction work, I mean."

"Oh, wow."

Since the hurricane, D.J. had worked more hours than ever. Thankfully, the island was finally getting back into shape, though certain pockets would be a long time in seeing total restoration. It did my heart good to know my softhearted cowboy was helping other people repair both their homes and their lives. This was one of the things I loved best about him. He always put others first. I had the feeling it came naturally to him, though I knew his parents and brother had the same undying love for people. It was really a God-ordained kind of love for people, the kind you couldn't be taught.

"I feel really bad for this guy." The worry lines in D.J.'s brow deepened. "Insurance wouldn't pay to rebuild—the house or the church. It's zapping him just to get the house up again, but the church . . . well, it looks like it's a wash. Literally."

I groaned at that news. So many of the people who'd lost their homes and businesses had been told their flood policies were useless. "So, what's he going to do?"

"Don't know. Right now he's just depending on his little congregation to raise funds, but so many of them have been hard hit. It's tough, that's for sure."

"Maybe we could do something to help," I said. "After I'm done with this wedding, I mean."

"That would be great, Bella. Let's talk about that when you're ready, okay?"

"Mm-hmm."

D.J. took a swig of his soda. "So, what did you do today?"

26

"Oh, I, um . . ." I wanted to tell him everything! Surely it wouldn't hurt for him to know, right? D.J. Neeley was the most reliable man I'd ever met in my life. "Well, as a matter of fact . . ." I leaned in to whisper when Nick rushed by, bumping into my drink and spilling it all over my lap.

I let out a yelp, and D.J. jumped back to avoid being splashed. Then he sprang into action, tossing me a handful of napkins.

I took this as a sign from above that I'd already said too much. I sopped up the mess in total silence.

A familiar voice rang out, causing me to look up from my damp jeans. Mama buzzed through the door of the pizzeria with Bubba on her heels. Jenna's face lit up as it always did when she saw her sweetheart. Bubba gave her a wink, never slowing his pace behind Mama, who approached the counter and took a seat on an empty barstool. All the while she talked a mile a minute.

"You did a fine job at rehearsal today, Bubba," she said. "But I can't understand why you're giving the people in the wardrobe department such fits." She plopped her purse—an authentic Dolce and Gabbana—down on the bar and nodded at Jenna to bring her a glass of Diet Coke. Jenna flew into action. Within seconds, Mama had her lips pursed around a straw. Diet Coke always had a calming effect on her. I hoped today would be no different.

Bubba offered up a woeful shrug. "I ain't never worn stuff like that before. Never thought I'd see the day when someone wanted to dress me up like a girl."

D.J. snorted, and Dr Pepper came shooting out of his nose. I slipped him a napkin, and he remedied the situation before Mama could see. She had a tendency to frown on such things. Still, I found the whole thing hilarious. And I could certainly see Bubba's point. What guy—especially one unfamiliar with theatrical productions—wanted to stand on stage in tights? And at the Galveston Grand Opera, no less.

"It's not a girl's costume," Mama said, looking more than a little perturbed. "It's authentic to the time period. We're talking *The Marriage of Figaro* here. Did you look up those websites I sent you?"

"Yeah."

"You saw the costumes?"

"Yeah." His countenance hadn't lifted at all, so I decided I'd better cheer him on.

"You can't exactly wear your jeans and cowboy boots for this one, Bubba," I said. "You'd stick out like a sore thumb. I know you don't want to draw attention to yourself."

"Exactly. Which is exactly why this costume idea won't work. I'm gonna look like a goober in those frilly getups they've made for me." Bubba sighed as he looked to Jenna for support. She flashed a warm smile and placed her hand on his. I heard him mutter, "And Mama's bringing all of our neighbors. I can just see the write-up in the *Splendora Daily* now." He groaned, then snapped closed the menu he'd been holding and put it on the bar.

Poor guy. His days as a barbecue aficionado and shade tree mechanic were behind him now that he'd been "discovered" by my mama. One minute the boy was singing country tunes at a Fourth of July picnic, the next he was standing on a stage at the Galveston Grand Opera, belting out "Figaro." With a slight country twang.

I glanced down the counter at my mother. She reached into her purse and came out with a compact, then touched up her lipstick and smacked her lips together. Maybe I'd better help her out this time. After all, the show opened in three days and would run for the better part of a month.

"*The Marriage of Figaro* is a romantic comedy, Bubba," I said. "The costume is a part of the whole. You know? If people laugh, it will just add to the show."

"Mm-hmm." He didn't look convinced.

"He'll do it." Those three words from D.J. sealed the deal. He looked at his brother and added, "Won't ya?"

"Yeah." Bubba sighed. "But I won't like it."

One tragedy averted, thanks to my knight. He always managed to save the day. Just another one of his many talents.

Mama turned from her compact to look at D.J. and Bubba. "You boys still coming to our house for dinner tomorrow night? Rosa's cooking the same meal they're going to be featuring on the Food Network special, and she wants our input, especially on the bread. She's getting a little nervous, but having everyone there will serve to calm her nerves."

D.J.'s eyes sparkled with a new enthusiasm. I knew he loved my aunt's great cooking. Who didn't?

"I'll be there," he said. "Six, right?"

"Yes."

"What about you, Bubba?" I asked.

He nodded but didn't say anything. I had a feeling the boy was ready to head back to the piney woods of Splendora to avoid facing this whole costume fiasco. Not that D.J. would let that happen. No, the show would go on, and all would be well. And Bubba would come to dinner. He was, after all, a really amiable sort of guy. I'd never seen him worked up like this before, and I had a feeling it wouldn't last long, especially not with D.J. on the case.

"Oh, Bubba has to come." Mama reached for her glass once again. "His vocal coach has asked me to work with him

29

on his tone and inflection. We've got a lot of work ahead of us before the show opens on Saturday night."

Yes indeed. But they weren't the only ones who had a lot of work to do, were they? Bubba might be focused on memorizing his lines and Rosa might be gearing up for the Food Network, but what they were facing paled in comparison to my new job description. Not only did I have to pull off a full-blown medieval wedding, I had to hide the best man until it was over. Heaven help me!

4

Swinging on a Star

On Thursday afternoon at a quarter till five, I readied myself for the big meeting with the bride and groom and their best man. Hmm. Make that "first knight." I kept forgetting the terminology for this medieval event.

I always prided myself on dressing nicely and wearing makeup, but I must admit I spent a little more time in front of the mirror on this day than usual. I particularly focused on my long, dark curls, which seemed to have a mind of their own. No point in Brock Benson thinking Texas girls were careless with their looks.

Glancing down, I smiled as my gaze fell on my boots. Until a few months ago, I'd never worn boots. That was before D.J. But now . . . now I understood both the comfort of a good boot and a good guy. And I couldn't do without either one. Nor would I want to.

A sound from outside caught my attention. I looked through the open window to see Rob's Hummer pull into the driveway. I still laughed at the fact that my medieval couple traveled around in a vehicle that looked rather Trojan-horse-like. Seemed fitting.

Rob stepped out first, then went around to the passenger side to open the door for Marian. He was such a gentleman, always right there at his bride-to-be's side. But right now my eyes were searching out someone else, someone I'd been nervously anticipating all day. Squinting, I could almost see someone exiting the backseat passenger side. Not very well, though, with the bride and groom standing in the way.

Then the Red Sea parted . . . and I laid eyes on him.

Brock was taller than he looked on the big screen. Probably six feet or more. And those broad shoulders . . . mama mia! Be still my heart! Even from this distance, his white-toothed smile took my breath away. And I'd never seen clothing that fine outside of a magazine. Rodeo Drive, here we come! Along with his shockingly handsome attire, Brock wore dark, trendy sunglasses. Probably necessary when one was an easily recognized superstar. He pulled them off to look at the wedding facility. Now I could see the man in all his splendor, and what I saw dazzled me.

My younger brother's favorite pickup line came to mind right away: *"Fa cosi caldo qui o e la tua presenza?"*—"Is it hot in here, or is it just you?"

"Yowza!" I reached for a Club Wed brochure and began to fan myself, then snatched up my bottle of water, taking a big gulp. *Lord, help me. I don't want to act like one of those ridiculous groupies he probably sees every day of his life. Just let me be myself. And Lord, keep this conversation centered on the big day, nothing else.*

Still, I could hardly catch my breath. Might be problematic, since we had so much to discuss. Breathing was pretty critical to the equation. I practiced my slow, deep breathing techniques and tried to concentrate on the conversation ahead. "You can do this, Bella. You can. Just stay focused. Think of the family. Think of how much you need Club Wed to succeed."

That last line did it. Making a success of the wedding facility was the driving force in my life these days, a force stronger than any Hollywood hottie.

I paused at the mirror in the foyer of the wedding facility to check my appearance. Pushing back a loose hair, I noticed the trembling in my hands. *Stop it, Bella.*

I opened the door at the very moment Marian put her hand up to knock. It startled all of us, and we ended up laughing. Great icebreaker. Doing my best to focus on the bride-to-be, I stepped out onto the veranda, willing myself to calm down. Oh, but a quick glance at the tall movie star— truly first-knight material—and my knees nearly buckled. His dark brown hair was . . . perfect. Not too short. Not too long. And his deep brown eyes nearly took my breath away. *Who has eyes that color of brown? What would you call that? Cinnamon? Caramel?* I swallowed hard, wondering if he wore contacts.

Likely, but who cared? The man seemed to have a heavenly glow about him, kind of like those pictures of various saints hung on Aunt Rosa's bedroom wall.

Look away from the light, Bella. Look away from the light.

Marian made introductions right away, and Brock put me at ease with his relaxed smile. "Great to meet you, Bella. Thanks for all of your help to make my best friend's big day so special."

"You're welcome." I gave him a polite nod. Using my most

professional voice, I asked, "Would you like to start outside in the gazebo area? I can talk you through the layout of the castle. Then we can go inside to discuss the details."

"Sounds great!" Marian grabbed hold of my arm and gave it a squeeze. I patted her hand and led the way down the front steps and around the side of the facility to the courtyard out back.

Marian whispered in my ear, "What do you think, Bella? Isn't he heavenly?"

Looking back, I nodded. "Yeah, pretty heavenly. But remember, Marian, I've already got a star in D.J., so nothing else really comes close."

She patted my arm and nodded. "Oh, I know. I wasn't suggesting anything. It's just so exciting to have him here."

To say the very least.

When we arrived at the spot where the castle would be placed, Brock let out a whistle. "Wow, this is a great area. Kind of reminds me of the side yard at my house in Malibu."

Well, of course it does.

"Thanks," I managed. "Quite a few weddings have been performed out here. One of our most recent was a country-western themed one. It was a lot of fun." Boy, had it ever been! The night was forever engrained in my memory.

"Oh, that's ironic." Brock grinned. "The movie I've been shooting in Austin is sort of a twist on the old cowboy theme. They've had me wearing boots and jeans and speaking in a drawl." He dragged out the word *duh-rawl*, and I laughed. For a second there, he sounded just like D.J. Of course, that's where the similarities ended. Handsome as he was, Brock couldn't hold a candle to my honey. Sure, the voice was more polished. And yes, the clothes were more expensive—unbelievably so— but clothes didn't make the man.

"I think you'll be impressed with the set design people we've hired for this wedding," I told Brock as I snapped back to attention. "Very professional. And from what I can tell looking at the photographs from other events they've done, you actually feel like you've walked into a genuine medieval castle. A real step back in time." *Unless you count the Food Network trucks in the background. They're pretty modern looking, I'm sure.* Forcing a smile, I continued. "So, you should feel right at home."

"Especially in the costume you'll be wearing." Rob jabbed Brock in the ribs, and he groaned.

"Trust me, this will be the first time in my acting career I've worn tights." Brock grimaced at the word *tights*, which provoked a few guffaws from the rest of us. I hadn't thought about the costumes as being an issue for the groomsmen, but maybe so. And how funny. This was the second time in two days I'd heard some poor guy complain about a costume-related issue.

"C'mon now," Rob said with an encouraging smile. "They're not exactly tights. They're just, well, stretchy pants. Under a long shirt. And besides, you played a pirate in a movie once, right? You've worn stuff like this before."

Brock groaned again. "That was different. Those were real pants."

"Well, it might be different from what you're used to," I said, "but remember, you won't be the only one. All of the men in the ceremony—and all of the servers too—will be dressed in full-out medieval attire, so you'll be in good company."

"And half the guests are coming in medieval attire," Marian said. "You'd stick out more in regular clothes, trust me."

Hadn't I said the same thing to Bubba just yesterday?

35

"Still . . ." Brock shuddered. "I'm trying to imagine what'll happen if the paparazzi happen to wander in on us."

"They won't." Marian looked my way. "Bella's got this completely under control. Right?"

I swallowed hard and forced another smile. "Yes, but I think we need to go inside and talk through some security issues. I'm assuming you'll want to hire private security guards, right?"

"I don't think that's necessary." Brock shrugged. "I'll just keep an eye out for paparazzi and stay on the down-low." He went into a story about something that happened at the last private party he'd attended, and before long we all looked concerned.

"Let me know if you change your mind," I said. "Your safety is important to us." *So is the peace of mind of my bride and groom.*

Forcing myself to stay focused, I led the way through the wedding facility into my office, where I offered everyone a Pellegrino.

As my now-captive audience took their seats, my cell phone rang, and I gasped, horrified. "Oh, sorry. Meant to turn that off."

"No problem, Bella." Brock's punctuated speech sent my heart into a tailspin. I loved a man with great diction.

I silenced the ringer on my phone, noticing the missed call was from D.J. I would call him back later. He knew I was with clients. Besides, we'd see each other at dinner.

Minutes later, we were all hard at work, finalizing plans for the big day. Once I slipped into wedding-planning mode, my nerves dissipated. No longer did I spend time thinking about the fact that I had a Hollywood star in my office. No, only one thing mattered now—the bride-to-be.

I pulled out my notepad and began to cover the basics. First, the food. Laz, Jenna, and Nick, who'd agreed to cater the big event, had created an authentic menu, true to Renaissance times. It had been Nick's idea, really. Something he'd seen at a theater he'd gone to once in Dallas. Marian had already given her wholehearted approval, but I thought it would be fun to talk it through with the guys. Let them see just how seriously we were taking this medieval theme.

"A true medieval feast would have included things like turtledoves and partridge," I said. "And goose and venison. We've decided not to go that route."

"The turtledoves thank you for the reprieve." Brock gave me a wink, and my heart gravitated to my throat.

"We, um, have decided to do roast quail and fish, as well as a traditional beef kabob dish."

"And turkey legs," Rob said. He jabbed Brock in the ribs with his elbow. "That was my idea. I've never been to a Renaissance festival without getting a turkey leg. We don't want anyone to leave disappointed."

"Of course not," Brock agreed. "And I'll be the first in line for mine."

I laughed but made a point to get back to the subject at hand. "We'll have a variety of side dishes—potatoes and all sorts of fruits and cheeses. We were thinking pears, strawberries, apples, raspberries, and red currants. Afterward, along with the wedding cake, we will serve tarts and custards. All of this is appropriate to the time."

"You're making me hungry." Brock looked at his watch. "We skipped lunch, and I'm starved."

"We'll have to do something to remedy that," Rob said.

Marian turned my way. "Bella, is there someplace around here we could grab a bite to eat after this? Someplace secluded, I mean."

"Hmm." I thought of Parma John's but knew it was out of the question. "I do know a great seafood place with a private room. I could call ahead and see if the room is available."

"That might work." Brock gave me a grateful smile. "Didn't mean to interrupt your spiel about the wedding, though. Go ahead and finish."

"Oh, well, I was just about to finalize the flower order with Marian." I turned to her, trying to stay focused.

Marcella had recently taken over our local florist's shop. She had already presented the bride and groom with a delightful plan for wedding bouquets, so I knew we had that part squared away, but I needed to clarify a few things based on a phone call from her earlier today.

"You're still wanting to do Texas wildflowers, is that right?"

"Yes." Marian nodded. "Nothing too weddingish. I want the bouquets to look just like I went out into the yard and plucked the flowers myself. Besides, brides back in those days only carried flowers to keep from smelling."

Brock's eyebrows elevated at that one. He turned to her with a "Huh?"

"Well, traditionally people bathed only a couple times a year back in medieval times. So the original purpose of carrying flowers was to make the bride smell better." She turned to Rob with a wink.

"Yeah, that's one tradition I don't mind breaking," Rob said with a grin. "We can be authentic and clean at the same time." He nodded with a slight look of panic in his eyes, which tickled Marian.

"Nah, I think authentic is best. I'll stop bathing between now and then, just to add more realism to our special day." He wrinkled his nose, and she giggled. "Kidding!"

Rob turned to Brock and mumbled, "That was a close one!" and they laughed.

Marian jumped right back into the planning. "What about the musicians?" she asked. "Were you able to lock in that group I told you about? The ones I found at the Renaissance festival last year?"

"The madrigal group? Yes. They even sent me a sample CD of their work. Their harmonies are great. And they make the rounds to several festivals around the country each year, so they know their stuff." Thank goodness this part of the evening was locked up tight. We'd been lucky to get this group, though Marian's dad had to pay a pretty penny to do so.

"I guess we'd better get letters of commitment from them regarding my privacy," Brock said with a sigh. "We need to make sure no one involves the media."

"Ah." Letters of commitment? As in, legally binding? Would all of the guests have to sign one too?

A shudder ran down my spine as I thought about that. What a mess this was turning out to be. Why couldn't Brock Benson just be a normal best man? Why did this have to be so complicated?

We talked through the rest of the wedding plans, but I could tell the guys were distracted. I saw Rob mouth the word *hungry* to Brock, and I reached for the phone. "You guys must be starved. Let me call Landry's to see about getting their private room for you." I punched in the number and quickly asked for the most secluded place in the restaurant. They could accommodate the group in half an hour, so we needed to get this show on the road.

After ending the call, I turned to Rob and Brock. "Shouldn't be a big crowd tonight anyway. It's a Thursday night." Shifting my focus, I reached for a pen and paper. "While I'm thinking of it, let me give you the reservation information for the hotel. I think you'll like the Tremont. It's very private."

I started to write down the information, but the pen slipped out of my hand and clattered to the floor. Brock and I leaned down at the same time to pick it up, our hands touching for a microsecond. I pulled away, feeling my face warm with embarrassment. In that second, a very junior-highish thought flitted through my brain.

I am never washing this hand again.

5

Call Me Irresponsible

As my eyes met with Brock's, my heart flip-flopped. Man, did he ever smell yummy. What was he wearing? And those amazing cheekbones! Somehow being this close made me want to reach out and touch them just to see if they were real. *Has he had work done?*

Fortunately—or unfortunately—I didn't have time to think about it. My sister's voice rang out, startling me back to an upright position. "Bella," she called. "Are you in the office?"

"Oh no! Sophia!" I clamped a hand over my mouth and stared at Rob and Marian.

Brock immediately rose to his feet and slipped behind the door. When Sophia stepped inside, she saw only the bride and groom, who by now were playing it cool. I could tell from the heat in my cheeks that I was flushed, but I hoped she would write it off to the weather.

Though Sophia had sounded plenty impatient seconds

41

earlier, she smiled as she took in my guests. "Hi, everyone.
Didn't mean to interrupt." She turned to me, giving me super-
secret coded messages with her eyes, messages I could not
mistake. "Bella, I just wanted to let you know that Rosa's
getting anxious. Mama wants the whole family at the dinner table at six, and that includes you and D.J." She swept a
loose dark hair behind her ear and nodded, as if that settled
everything.

"Oh, well, I, um—"

"Oh, that's too bad!" Marian said. "We're actually headed
out to dinner, and Bella's going along for the ride."

"I—I am?" I looked at her, startled.

"Well, sure. We still have a few things to discuss pertaining
to the wedding. We can't do this without you."

Yikes. "I see." My thoughts shifted into overdrive. How
could I make this work? I'd have to call D.J., of course. He
would understand. But Rosa . . . now that was a different
story. I gave my sister what I hoped would be taken as a sor-
rowful look. "Sorry, but I guess I'll have to give Aunt Rosa
a rain check."

"She's going to murder you in your sleep." Sophia's eyes
narrowed. "You know how she is about her food. If you don't
show up . . ."

"Well, there's nothing I can do about it. Sorry. Business
before pleasure and all that."

"I guess you've got to do what you've got to do." My sister
gave me a curious look—probably due to my less than enthusiastic response—then took another step into the room,
smiling in Marian and Rob's direction. "So, how's the wedding planning coming? I heard all about this castle you're
getting married in. Sounds amazing. Are you two ready to
ride off into the sunset on white horses?"

"Y-yes." Marian nodded, then shifted her gaze to Brock, who stood tightly pressed behind the door. Probably by now the Hollywood hunk could barely breathe. Still, he managed to keep things under control. Looked like all of that on-the-set training was working to his advantage. Besides, these Hollywood types probably hid behind all sorts of doors to get away from flighty fans.

Just then—and I watched this in slow motion from the best seat in the house, so I got the full effect—Brock put his hand up to his nose and began that heaving motion that comes right before a person sneezes. I watched him bob his head three or four times in total silence. Then, when he blew . . . he blew. I'd never heard anyone sneeze that loudly before. The jolt caused the door to shoot back, knocking Sophia a good foot or two from where she'd started.

"W-what in the world?" She pulled the door forward. "Just what do you think you're—"

That was it. We lost her after that. Sophia took one look at Brock Benson and turned into a babbling idiot. She began to rant—in perfect Italian—about the man who now stood before her. To his credit, Brock stepped from behind the door, took her hand, and kissed it. I'd never actually seen anyone swoon before, but I'm pretty sure Sophia did. And then Brock did the unthinkable. He responded to her—in perfect Italian.

Oy, were we in trouble!

My sister's cheeks flushed, and she began to fuss with her long mane of hair. "What are you . . . ? I mean, how are you . . . ? And why are you . . . ?" She tried multiple times and multiple ways to get her questions out, but it just wasn't happening. Still, it was fun to watch her try. Made me wish I had a video camera going so I could replay it for her later.

"Brock Benson." He continued to hold her hand as he introduced himself.

I could see her hand shaking in his, but he didn't seem to mind. Likely he got this a lot. "Sophia Rossi," she managed. After a few more seconds of staring, she finally turned to me. "Th-this is like some sort of a miracle! But, h-how did it happen?" she whispered. "Do the others know?"

"I guess the cat's out of the bag," Rob said with a shrug. "Brock is the first knight in our wedding."

"First knight?" Sophia's brow wrinkled.

"Best man," Rob said. "But we'd planned to keep it a secret."

"We *will* keep it a secret," I echoed, giving Sophia a warning look. "We'll go to our graves with this secret."

She crossed her heart and held up two fingers. "Girl Scouts' honor." The whole room hung in suspended silence for a good thirty seconds while my sister stared at the handsome man in front of her. Thankfully, he seemed to take it in stride.

I wanted to ask the girl to close her mouth. To tell her that she looked a little silly. But I held my tongue.

"H-how are you going to do this?" she asked me at last. "Is he staying on the island?"

"Yes. We're putting both Rob and Brock up at the Tremont for the next week. It's a lovely hotel, and I really think they'll like it."

"The Tremont?" Sophia shook her head. "They can't stay there, Bella. You know that."

"Sure they can. They've already got a room waiting."

"But don't you remember?" My sister turned to Brock, batting her eyelashes. "The Grand Opera production of *The Marriage of Figaro* is this weekend, and most of our out-of-town guests are staying at the Tremont." Sophia turned back to me. "D.J.'s parents are coming down from Splendora and bringing several of their church ladies with them, remember? They're all staying at the same hotel because they want to be close to each other. And the Tremont is the closest hotel to the opera house."

"Oh man!" How could I have forgotten that half the town of Splendora was coming for Bubba's debut? His mama— Earline—would be there, along with half the congregation of Splendora's Full Gospel Chapel in the Pines. Likely the whole of east Texas would show up to support him. And they were all staying at the Tremont! How had I forgotten that teeny-tiny detail?

Easy. My mind was on a thousand other things.

"Opera?" Brock's eyes lit up. "I love the opera. And *The Marriage of Figaro* is one of my favorites."

Great. Wonderful. This was getting better by the minute. I dropped down into my chair, slapping myself in the head. "What are we going to do?"

"Oh, I'm sure we can find another place," Rob said with a wave of his hand. "Marian managed to find a condo for rent. There's got to be another one available. Or maybe we can rent a bed-and-breakfast somewhere."

"Or . . ." Sophia's eyes lit up, and her perfectly arched eyebrows elevated in anticipation. "You guys can stay at our place next door."

I looked at her like she'd lost her mind. "Our place?" A house already filled to overflowing with a large Italian family, a disobedient Yorkie-Poo, and a parrot that cursed at strangers in between verses of "Amazing Grace"? No way! I wouldn't wish that on my worst enemy, let alone a Hollywood star.

"Sure, why not?" Sophia said. "Nick's room is empty, and so is Armando's now that he's living in Houston again. Besides, Joey would probably love the company. He's always complaining about how there's too much estrogen in the house."

"Too much estrogen in the house." Rob shuddered as he repeated the words, then looked at Brock and laughed. What was up with that? Was the groom-to-be hoping to find a fair lady for his best man while here on the island? If so, he'd better look elsewhere! I was already taken. And Sophia . . .

Hmm. I looked at the hopeful expression on my sister's face and paused. She wasn't exactly taken, though my ex-boyfriend Tony certainly had his eye on her.

Still bubbling, Sophia looked my way. "Bella, you know they'll love Aunt Rosa's cooking." She turned to Brock and began to sing our aunt's praises, going on and on about her amazing Italian cuisine. I'm pretty sure we had him at the words *chicken parmesan.*

Not that I blamed him. There was something about the mention of Italian food that did most of us in, and I particularly loved it when Aunt Rosa cooked chicken parmesan. It made the whole house smell delicious and was incredibly tasty. Perfect for an evening like this, when the world was imploding.

"We've got plenty of room," Sophia added, clearly oblivious to my ponderings. "Besides, Mama's busy with the opera, so she'll hardly even notice they're there."

With a shake of my head, I began to explain all of the reasons this wouldn't work. However, I barely got three words into my dissertation before Brock looked my way with a nod. "Actually, Bella, it sounds good to me. I always feel safer staying in a home than in a hotel. There's less risk involved."

"Less risk?" Obviously Brock Benson hadn't met the Rossis. He had no idea what he was agreeing to. Nor did he seem to care.

Brock laughed. "The idea of a good home-cooked meal is almost too much to pass up. Do you have any idea how long it's been since I've had homemade Italian food?" He explained that his midday meals were most often brought in by caterers, and his evening meals were almost always in some swanky L.A. restaurant. Never good home cooking. Then he went off on a tangent about how much he missed sitting around the dinner table in a family environment. How could I argue with that?

"What do you think, Bella?" Marian gave me a hopeful look. "Is the Rossi bed-and-breakfast open for business? It's just a week and a half, after all."

"Just a week and a half," I echoed. "I . . . I . . ." Glancing into Brock's eyes, I found myself saying, "I'll ask Mama, but I'm sure it'll be fine."

"Awesome!" Brock said. He turned to Rob with a smile. "See, I told you this was going to work out."

"I guess I could stay at the Tremont," Rob said with a shrug. "And you could stay here."

"No way." Brock shook his head. "Skip the hotel, Rob. I came to Texas to hang out with my best friend. We'll both stay at their place."

"I . . . I guess." Rob's pursed lips let me know his take on this. Surely he hadn't planned to spend the week before his wedding living in a house with the rowdiest family on Galveston Island. I had a feeling he was going along with this to make Brock happy. In fact, I had a feeling Brock Benson usually got his way in things. He just schmoozed folks until he got what he wanted. Quite a talent. Had he learned that in Hollywood, or was it some sort of hereditary trait?

"Thank you, Bella." Brock reached for my hand and kissed it. After I caught my breath, I nodded. He then nodded in Sophia's direction.

My sister looked as if she'd died and gone to the Hollywood version of heaven. I half expected a piped-in audio of "The Hallelujah Chorus" to fill the room and 3-D angels to appear on the walls.

The bride-to-be turned to me with a look of pure contentment on her face. "Oh, Bella! How can I ever thank you? This is the perfect solution. I'll sleep so much better knowing Brock is under your roof for the next week."

She might, but I sure wouldn't. In fact, I doubted I'd sleep a wink. And how could I tell these fine folks that the Food Network crew would be pulling in with their trucks the day before the wedding? No, I'd better not broach that subject today.

6

Come Fly with Me

I cancelled our dinner plans at Landry's and geared myself up
for the Rossi-family-meets-Hollywood-star moment. Before
taking Brock, Rob, and Marian to our house, I gave them
the *Reader's Digest* version of the Rossis so they would be
psychologically prepared. It wouldn't be fair otherwise. There
would be too much to absorb too quickly.

"Mama and Pop retired from the wedding facility a few
months back," I said. "And I run it now. Uncle Laz—Pop's
older brother—has lived with us for years. He owns Parma
John's, a pizzeria and coffee shop on the Strand."

"Parma John's?" Brock smiled. "Great name."

"Thanks. It was his idea. And he's nuts about coffees, so
you'll find several varieties there. Now, about Aunt Rosa,
Mama's sister—you need to know she hates Uncle Laz."

"Why?" Brock's brow wrinkled.

"Long story. Goes back to their childhood in Napoli. Laz
once broke Rosa's heart. I don't think he realized it at the

time, so we can't hold it against him. And a lot has happened since. But to cut to the chase, I think they're secretly in love." Hence Rosa's current fascination with lipstick. "I tell you this because their bantering goes on all day long. They never quit."

"Ah. Love will do that to you," Brock said with a sigh. "Not that I've really experienced love in real life, but I once played a pirate who acted like he hated the leading lady, when in reality he loved her. If that counts." He flashed a Hollywood-esque smile.

"Oh my gosh, I saw that movie. *The Pirate's Lady*." Sophia clamped a hand over her mouth, and then released it with an exaggerated sigh. "You played Jean Luc Dumont, and you fell in love with the beautiful but badly behaved Genevieve Montecito. The whole thing was sort of a play on the old *Taming of the Shrew* theme. You spent half the movie trying to tame her."

"That's right." He turned to her. "I can't believe you remembered that. It was one of my earliest films and my very first pirate movie."

"Are you kidding? Of course I remember it!" Sophia gawked at him. "I can quote half the lines." She dove into a few just to prove herself, and Brock's handsome face lit with a broad smile. He began to quote some of Jean's lines, and she countered them with Genevieve's.

I watched all of this in rapt awe. For that matter, so did Marian and Rob, who occasionally glanced at me as if to ask, "Is this for real?"

Brock nodded at Sophia as their scene drew to an end. "Man, it feels good to run those old lines again. I love it."

"I can tell." Sophia flashed a coy smile. "Anytime you need a partner, think of me."

"Mm-hmm. You're a natural," he said, taking her hand and gazing deep into her eyes till she looked like she'd fallen under some sort of spell. "Have you ever considered coming to Hollywood?"

"M-me?" Sophia's eyelashes batted up and down in exaggerated motion.

Good grief. Perfect time for an interruption. Mama would kill me if someone I'd introduced Sophia to actually talked her into moving away. Then again, my sister was pretty flighty. I'd seen this side of her before. She fell hard and fast but usually recovered just as quickly. Hopefully this time wouldn't be any different.

"Maybe we should get back to explaining about Laz and Rosa," I said. "They're continually feuding over who is the better singer, Dean Martin or Frank Sinatra. They're always arguing about it, but no one ever wins."

Brock shook his head. "What's to argue about? Sinatra, of course. Ol' Blue Eyes."

A shiver ran down my spine as I contemplated the war *those* words would cause in the Rossi household. "Just don't let Laz hear you say that, okay?"

He laughed, then looked at me with disbelief in his eyes. "You're serious?"

"Oh yeah."

"Wow." Brock shrugged. "Sounds intense."

"Well, Laz has always been a little intense, but that's because he had a near-death experience that changed his life back in the '80s."

"Oh?"

"Yes, I should probably tell you about it. He calls it his Damascus Road experience. In reality, he was hit by a bus while walking home from a bar. Happened when we lived in Atlantic City."

Brock almost spit his Pellegrino across the room as his laughter erupted. "Sorry. I know that's not funny."

"Oh, I guess it is now. But I just wanted you to know, because it comes up a lot. He ended up at the Catholic hospital, and the nuns gave him quite a talking-to. His whole life turned around that night. In fact, our whole family ended up in Texas because of what happened that night."

"I'm not sure I even want to know what that means," Brock mumbled to Rob.

Nor did I want to tell him. There just wasn't time. Still, I hadn't exaggerated. When Laz gave his heart to the Lord, it really did change our family—for all eternity. And it didn't just change how we lived, it changed where we lived.

I proceeded to fill him in on the rest of my family, focusing on my three brothers—Nick, Armando, and Joey. Then I got to Sophia. When I mentioned her name, he turned to her and flashed an Academy Award–worthy smile. Her cheeks flushed crimson, and she batted her eyelashes once again. *Good grief, girl. Don't overdo it.*

Once I'd thoroughly explained our eccentric Italian family, we could avoid the inevitable no longer. I led the way across the lawn and up the stairs onto the veranda of the hundred-year-old Victorian home. As I did, I heard shouts coming from inside the house. Looked like Aunt Rosa and Uncle Laz were at it again. Would those two ever get along?

Just then the front door burst open, and Rosa chased Laz outside onto the veranda, shaking a broom in his face. "I've told you to stay out of the kitchen when I'm working, old man! Don't ever let me catch you touching my gravy again!"

Okay. We were off to a great start.

Rosa's anger dissipated when she saw us standing there. "I-I'm sorry, Bella. I didn't know you had guests." She sighed and put the broom down. "But that man is getting on my last nerve." Her gaze traveled from Marian to Rob to Brock to me. Then, just as quickly, her eyes darted back to Brock. "Oh." She put a hand to her mouth, her eyes widening. "Oh, oh, oh."

He extended his hand. "I'm Brock."

"I—I—I know." She turned all shades of red, then began to use her free hand to fuss with her hair. "You're Jean Luc Dumont, that heavenly pirate who saves women from the clutches of evil. I must look a sight."

"Oh, not in the least." A look of genuine tenderness came over Brock as he spoke to her. "There's something absolutely lovely about you. Reminds me of home."

"Are you Italian, boy?"

"Fourth generation. Benson is just a stage name. I was born Vincenzo DiMarco. My cousins still call me Vinny."

Go figure. Vinny, eh? This information put a whole new spin on things. I had to admit I preferred the stage name, but this certainly explained why he was so anxious to stay for dinner.

Uncle Laz gave a "humph" and shuffled inside.

Brock leaned my aunt's direction. "Just so you know, I'm a Sinatra fan. Can't get enough of him, in fact."

At once her face lit into a smile. Using the broom to push back the rest of us, she said, "Well, why didn't you say so? Come on in the house, young man. I'm making homemade chicken parmesan and the most divine garlic twists you've ever tasted, loaded with butter. Not margarine. Butter. Never use that fake stuff. If my arteries are going to be clogged, they're going to be clogged with the real thing. No point in risking your life over a substitute." Her voice faded away as she disappeared inside the foyer.

"Any fan of Frank Sinatra's is not welcome in this house," Laz yelled from inside the door. He glanced toward Rosa, a scowl on his face.

Alrighty then. Looked like things couldn't possibly get any better.

7

They All Laughed

I entered the house on Aunt Rosa's heels, with Brock—er, Vinny—directly behind me. Sophia tagged along on his heels, babbling endlessly, her voice laced with a nervous vibrato. Behind her, the bride- and groom-to-be entered arm in arm.

Once inside, I heard music coming from the living room. Mama and Bubba were hard at work, rehearsing. His huge voice filled the house from rafter to rafter. Very impressive.

I turned to say something to Sophia, only to discover she'd spirited away to some other place. Terrific. Leave me to take care of this on my own. No problem.

Precious, my Yorkie-Poo, chose that moment to greet us in attack mode. She directed her energies at Brock, who stared down at her with an amused look on his face.

"That's a lot of noise coming from such a tiny little thing." He tried to reach down to pet her, but she snapped at him. Pulling his hand up again, Brock shook his head. "Never mind."

I reached down and snatched up the little devil. "Come here, you. Settle down."

Once I had her sufficiently quieted, I slipped into the living room with my three guests on my heels. This was my first time to hear Bubba belt out Figaro's lines. I'd heard him sing country tunes before, but nothing like this. Wow. Turned out Mama had been right about him. He was the perfect choice. I could hardly believe the amazing operatic voice pouring out of him.

Brock looked at me with a stunned expression on his face, then mouthed the words, "Who is that? He's amazing."

I nodded in response. I'd known he was good, but not this good. And as for who Bubba was, well, I'd make introductions later. Disturbing Mama when she was in work mode was a huge no-no.

I heard Guido off in the distance, warbling a tune slightly more off-key. Mama stopped playing the piano and pounded on the keys in frustration. She shouted, "Somebody make that bird shut up!"

My uncle hobbled across the room, cane in hand, to the cage. Once there, he began to talk in a soothing voice to the ornery parrot. This all served to make Brock laugh, which he did in absolute silence, something I'd never witnessed before. In the Rossi house, nothing was silent. Ever.

Mama promptly went back to coaching Bubba. "Don't sing through your nose, please. No twang-twang at the opera, Bubba. Open up and sing from your heart, not your nostrils. This is the Galveston Grand Opera, not the Grand Ole Opry."

"Yes'm." He nodded, then tried again, sounding a little less like Brad Paisley and a little more like Andrea Bocelli.

"Bellissimo!" Mama shouted. She began to play with great

gusto, never even noticing we'd entered the room. On and on she went, her fingers flying across the keys.

I looked at Brock and groaned. "Welcome to my world." Then I took a few steps in the direction of the dining room, where I put Precious down on the floor. She did her usual jumping up and down thing but eventually retreated to the kitchen.

"I love your world, Bella." Brock gave me a look so warm it melted my heart. "Normal things happen here. Life isn't scripted. There's no way to tell how it might end."

"Well, that part's true, but you call this normal?"

Off in the distance, Aunt Rosa cried out, "Lazarro Rossi, if you don't get rid of that bird before my big day, I'm never speaking to you again."

"No skin off my teeth, woman," Laz snapped back. "I like my peace and quiet anyway."

Rosa's voice rang out again. "That bird is going to be the death of me yet!"

Laz countered with "I'm not that lucky!"

"Wow. They're like an old married couple," Brock observed, pulling out a chair for me.

I couldn't help but laugh at that one. "They're definitely not married." As I took my seat, I gestured for the others to do the same. Rob and Marian sat about midway down the table.

"Maybe they should be," he uttered in a dramatic stage whisper. "Maybe that's what's wrong with them."

"See? That just confirms what I've been thinking! I'm convinced they're a match made in heaven."

"Aha. I see." Brock's eyebrows elevated mischievously. "So, the plot thickens."

"What do you mean?"

"Well . . ." He leaned in to whisper. "I'm almost sure I caught Rosa making eyes at your Uncle Laz as she came through the door. I've gotten pretty good at discerning real emotion from acting. Been in this business awhile. All of this shouting sounds more like acting to me. It's a game they play, but it's not real."

"I totally agree."

"What's real is what's underneath—the look in his eyes, the tremor in her voice . . ." Brock held me captivated with his words. "The heart always gives the mouth away. Or maybe it's the other way around. But you know what I mean."

"Mm-hmm." I leaned close to him, the gentle scent of his manly cologne working wonders on my already overactive imagination. "But I can't believe you picked up on all of that stuff about Rosa and Laz after only a few seconds. See, I've often suspected . . ."

"Suspected what, Bella?" Rosa snapped a dish towel in my direction as she walked by.

"Suspected I will soon need to move to my own place if I tell you what I really said." I gave her a wink.

"If you want to stay put, then mind your manners. And don't be filling this boy's head with any nonsense about me. I need his head and his heart to be clean so he can better critique my food."

"Critique?" Brock looked stunned. "I thought we were here to eat."

"That too," she said. "But I need a good, honest critique from someone who isn't biased." She pointed at Brock. "And you're that someone."

"Oh. Okay."

"What are we critiquing?" I looked up as I heard D.J.'s familiar deep voice, a voice that captivated me every time.

He leaned over and kissed me on the top of the head, then looked around the room at the crowd with a puzzled look on his face. "You should've told me we were having company for dinner. I would've dressed up."

Granted, the boy was wearing jeans and a button-up over a white T-shirt. And yes, he had sawdust in his hair, as always. But his winning smile, along with that dark tan he'd acquired while working in the Galveston sun, made up for any wardrobe mishaps.

I smiled and gestured for him to take the seat next to me, wondering how long it would take before he figured out Brock's identity. "Hi, baby," I whispered. "Glad you could make it."

He took a seat and grinned, which only served to further complicate things. Brock quirked a brow my direction as if to ask, "Who have we here?" I'd better make introductions.

"Hey, everyone," I said. "This is D.J., my . . ." My voice trailed off as I almost made the mistake of calling him my fiancé. He wasn't. Not yet anyway. But I already pictured him as such in my mind, and in that moment I found myself wanting to say the word. However, the fact that I left the details of our relationship hanging midsentence did nothing to better my chances of getting a proposal anytime soon.

D.J. looked at me with a wrinkled brow and said, "Boyfriend. I'm her boyfriend." He glanced at the others and nodded. "Dwayne Neeley Jr. But everyone calls me D.J."

Coming to my senses, I made proper introductions. "D.J., this is Rob. He's the groom-to-be. And this is his beautiful fiancée, Marian."

"Pleased to meet you." D.J. nodded and smiled, pure kindness and hospitality oozing from every pore. "I've heard a lot about your big day. I know Bella's very excited."

"Yes." I paused, turning to the handsome movie star on my right. "And this is . . ." *Heaven help me.* "Brock Benson."

"Brock." D.J. nodded with absolutely no hint of recognition in his eyes.

A wave of relief washed over me. D.J. wasn't much of a moviegoer. That much I already knew. So maybe he didn't make the connection.

"Brock is their best man," I said.

"Great. I know y'all are looking forward to the big day." D.J. grabbed one of Rosa's famous garlic twists and took a bite, then turned to me. "Missed you today, baby." He grabbed my hand and gave it a squeeze.

"I missed you too."

Just as I relished the thought that I might get a reprieve, Sophia breezed into the room. Don't ask me how she'd done it, but the girl had somehow found the time to change into a new outfit and jazz up her long, dark hair. Even her makeup looked like it had been refreshed. How long had we been in the house? Ten minutes? Fifteen? The girl was a miracle worker—and clearly even faster with the lip liner than her mother.

D.J. took one look at her and whistled. "Who you trying to impress, girl?"

She slugged him in the arm, then muttered "Stop it" under her breath.

God bless D.J. At least the stunned look on his face was real. He had no idea what he'd done. And I wouldn't be filling him in anytime soon.

On the other hand . . .

My mother swept into the room with Bubba at her side. She took one look at Brock and began to fan herself. "Oh my. I . . ." She stared at him, speechless.

Likely Brock thought we were all incapable of articulating a single sentence.

Pop entered the room wearing his undershirt and a pair of slacks, holding a brown button-up shirt in his hand. He slipped it on in front of our guests, then pulled out Mama's chair with gentlemanly flair. When she didn't take her seat, he gave her a funny look and started buttoning his shirt. Eventually he took the empty chair beside her. "Something going on in here I need to know about?" My pop's gaze traveled the table, finally landing on Brock. He stuck a fork into a piece of chicken as he said, "Oh, hey. You're that actor Brock Benson, right? And you're sitting at our table. What's up with that?"

That was all she wrote. The whole place came alive. It was hard to distinguish who was saying what, now that everyone was talking on top of everyone else.

"Mama mia!" my mother shouted. She looked my way and gasped, then said, "You should tell a person." With an exaggerated smile, she turned back to our guests and greeted them. "Mr. Benson, how can we ever thank you for gracing our table? You've dined with some of the finest people around the globe, and now here you are at the Rossi family table. To what do we owe this honor?"

Before Brock could come up with a decent answer, D.J. looked my way, his eyes wide. "Wait a minute," he whispered. "Is that the guy who won best actor last year?" When I nodded, the strangest look crossed his face. "What's he doing here?" D.J. took another bite of garlic bread and leaned back in his seat, looking Brock over.

I somehow managed to get the noise to a dull roar and then gave a quick explanation, focusing my attention on my mother. After sharing the story, I managed to squeak out the important concern. "Brock and Rob need a place to stay till next weekend, Mama."

Sophia clutched her hands to her chest, an imploring look on her face. "I told them we would be honored to let them stay here."

"Stay here?" Laz, Pop, D.J., and Bubba spoke in unison, sounding just like one of those old-fashioned male quartets. D.J. sang bass, Bubba sang tenor. Pop and Laz, well, they joined right in there. Within minutes the Rossi and Neeley men were a mighty chorus, listing all the reasons why this would never work.

Of course, the womenfolk had different opinions.

"Oh, I think it's a marvelous idea!" Mama's eyelashes began to flutter, as they so often did when she was nervous. "And we certainly have the space, now that two of the boys have moved out."

"Where else can they get good food and a safe place to stay, away from the media?" Sophia threw in.

"Away from the media?" Laz looked at Rosa and shook his head. "What about the Food Network? Have you all forgotten that little tidbit?"

I hadn't planned to introduce this complication yet, but there it was, like a newspaper headline for all to read.

"The Food Network?" Brock shook his head. "What do they have to do with anything?"

"Well, there is this one little thing," I said. "Aunt Rosa has been selected to be in a special on the Food Network next weekend. They're sending a crew to film her—re-creating this meal, actually—the night of the wedding rehearsal."

Marian looked as if she might faint at this news. "Yikes." She shook her head, turning pale. "What can we do?"

"I'm sure if we all put our heads together, we'll come up with a plan," I said.

"Besides, on the night of the rehearsal, Brock will be at the wedding facility, not here," Mama reminded everyone. "So, that solves everything. We just need to keep him hidden until then."

Brock shrugged. "Sure. Why not? And in the meantime . . ." He extended his plate. "Could someone pass the chicken parmesan?"

8

Everybody Loves Somebody

On Friday morning, D.J.'s mom showed up at our front door unannounced. Now, I'd loved Earline Neeley for as long as I'd known her. All three months, in fact. She'd swept me into the fold and extended the love of Jesus time and time again. Best of all, she'd entrusted the heart of her son to me, a fact I did not take lightly. Still, I wasn't sure why she'd chosen to grace us with her presence today. Galveston was a far cry from Splendora.

I stood in the open doorway, trying to decide what to do. If I let her inside, she was sure to see Brock and give away our little secret. However, if I kept her standing on the veranda, she was sure to think I'd lost my mind and might encourage her son to have me committed. We certainly couldn't have that.

As I stood there toying with my decision, I tried to envision what Brock would make of Earline. She was a darling, no doubt about it, but the woman wasn't exactly Hollywood material.

Then again, maybe she was. At five foot two and two-hundred-plus pounds, she could easily be a character actor in a TV sitcom. And she certainly had the eclectic personality to warrant the role. Earline was a true-blue Southern lady. And where she came from—Splendora, Texas, just an hour and a half up Highway 59—*Full Gospel* meant *full figured.* In other words, all of the ladies in her little group were on the hefty side, and they all loved the Lord with full abandon. It's just that they had more to abandon than most.

I finally ushered Earline into the house and could tell right away that this was a woman on a mission.

Her face paled as she spoke, and her words were a little shaky. "Oh, honey . . . have you seen my boys today?"

I did my best to calm her by keeping my voice steady. "Which one are you looking for, Bubba or D.J.? Or does it matter?"

"Bubba would be best, I suppose." She fanned herself with her hand as she plopped down on the bench in our front hallway. "I need to talk to him about this opera thing."

"What about it?" Mama entered the room with a concerned look on her face. "Has something gone wrong? He isn't sick, is he?"

"Oh no. Nothing like that. This is about me, actually." She looked up at my mother with tears in her eyes.

Mama's expression softened. "What about you, honey?"

"Well . . ." Earline sighed. "See now, I don't get to fancy places much, and I'll need a dress to wear. I, um . . . well, I thought he might have some idea what sort of getup I'll need. The first performance is tomorrow, and I'm clueless!"

"Well, why didn't you say so!" My mama's face lit up, and

she slipped into Mother Teresa mode. "Earline, grab your purse. We're going to town."

Now, I knew Mama well enough to know that "going to town" meant going to Houston, about an hour north of the island. I listened in as my mother started her usual conversation about how the two of them were going to travel to Italy together someday. Earline, praise God, got swept up with the idea and linked arms with my mother, content to be heading to town. I breathed a huge sigh of relief, knowing a near-catastrophe had been averted. We'd somehow kept her from noticing Brock. His secret was safe with the Rossi clan.

Or so I thought.

Life has a funny way of playing tricks on you. Mama and Earline had just taken their first step through the front door when Brock's voice rang out. "Unhand her, you infidel, or I will take your head off!"

Earline turned—in slow motion, no less—her mouth hanging open.

Oblivious to us all, Brock continued, his voice ringing out from the balcony above the foyer. "What say ye to this, my man? Will you stand there, mouth agape, or free her to the one who loves her, body and soul?"

"F-free me . . . body and soul!" Earline whispered. She looked at me, her eyes scary-wide. "I . . . I know that voice. That's—"

Just then Brock came bounding down the stairs. Well, most of the way. He got to about the two-thirds point and stopped cold, staring at Earline. Her cheeks turned strawberry-sherbet pink, and she reached inside her purse for the fan she usually reserved for church. "Oh my stars! That's Jean Luc Dumont! I mean, B-B-Brock Benson!"

"Oops." Brock clamped a hand over his mouth, turned on his heels, and bounded back up the stairs.

Earline looked as if she might faint at any moment.

Mama took Earline by the arm and ushered her out to the veranda. "You know, honey, sometimes our eyes—and ears—deceive us. Happens to me all the time."

"But that was . . . I'm sure it was—"

"I have it on good authority that was Vinny DiMarco," Mama said, linking her arm through Earline's. "A friend from out of town who's come for a wedding. He's very convincing, isn't he? I daresay he could be in the movies."

"Yes, he could!" I could hear Earline singing his praises all the way to the car. As they pulled away, I sat on the front porch steps. Minutes later, Brock joined me.

"Sorry." He sighed. "I blew it, huh?"

"Close. But I can't blame you. I can say this is harder than I thought it would be."

"Who was that, anyway?" he asked.

"Earline Neeley. D.J.'s mom."

"No way."

"Yeah. I know they don't really resemble each other. And she's quite a character. But I love her."

"Well, it's a shame I couldn't just come downstairs and meet her. Maybe that would've been for the best."

"No, I really think we're better off not letting too many people know." I shook my head as I pondered all of the things that could go wrong. "Frankly, I don't know how you live in seclusion, hiding away from people. It would be impossible for me. I'm just too social." I offered up a sympathetic smile.

"Oh, I'm pretty social too." He laughed. "And it's not as hard as you think. In Hollywood, the movie stars are seen out in public a lot. It's not such a big news story there. But

I'm afraid if the reporters caught wind of the fact that I'm here, it would ruin the wedding. I don't want anything to ruin my best friend's big day."

"That's sweet." I sighed. "And I'll do my best to protect you from the masses. But I make no promises where my family is concerned."

"I love your family, Bella. I really do."

"Thanks. I'm assuming that's why you felt comfortable enough in my house to holler out all that stuff just now?"

"Oh, that." He shrugged, suddenly looking a little embarrassed. "Sometimes I challenge myself to remember lines from shows I was in years ago. My memorization skills aren't what they used to be, but I figure if I keep working on them, I'll get better with time. I like to try, anyway."

"I think it's pretty amazing that you can remember something from years gone by." I sighed again, thinking about it. "I can't even remember what I had for breakfast."

"Scrambled eggs with prosciutto and cheese," he said. "Tasty stuff. One of the best breakfasts I've had in quite a while, as a matter of fact."

"Yeah, Rosa's quite a cook."

"I watched her as she cooked. Looks like a hard worker."

"She's always been like that. I think it's a Rossi tradition. We just go, go, go—around the clock."

"I appreciate a good, strong work ethic. Someone who isn't afraid to get their hands dirty," Brock said. He held out his manicured nails, and I laughed. "Hey, I work hard." He gave me a pouting face.

"Oh, I believe you. And I do too. I come by it honestly. After all, I was raised by people who own their own businesses."

I paused to reflect on that. I'd watched for years as Mama and Pop ran the wedding facility, paying particular attention to the hours they kept and the efforts they went to for drawing in customers. I listened to the way they spoke to people. Watched how they worked tirelessly behind the scenes when no one was looking.

"I think it's good to work. Keeps you busy . . . and honest." Brock looked my way with a nod. "People might not think acting is hard work, but it is. And our hours are grueling sometimes."

"If anyone understands grueling hours, I do. I've witnessed it firsthand for years. I wish you could've seen Uncle Laz when we first moved to the island back in the '80s."

"Oh?"

"Money was tight back then. But that didn't stop him from building his dream. He leased the space that would eventually become Parma John's, struggling every month to make the rent. I still remember the hours he worked slaving over that restaurant, getting every detail right. He did it all on a dime and turned it into a thriving business."

"Wow. I'd really like to see it someday."

"Sure." I nodded, then thought about what he'd said about my aunt. "I think it's funny that you mentioned Rosa working so hard—funny coincidental, not funny ha-ha. She's probably my best example of what it means to work hard. From the minute I get out of bed in the morning until I drop into bed at night, she's on her feet. She doesn't just love to cook, she *lives* to cook."

"That much is obvious. And she's definitely the best."

"Oh yes. And nothing from a box. No way. She'd have a fit if someone in the family showed up with a package of store-bought pasta. I'm pretty sure it would give her nightmares. She creates pretty much everything from scratch."

"Since you brought up Rosa's cooking, I should tell you something."

"Oh?" I responded to the sound of excitement in his voice. "What's up?"

"I didn't mention this last night, but I have a friend at the Food Network. She owned the catering company we used while filming *The Pirate's Lady* in Savannah years ago."

"Really? Wow. You've got friends in all sorts of places."

"Yes, I do." He flashed a grin. "And sometimes I call in favors. This particular chef happens to owe me one."

"Yeah? How come?"

"When I saw how good her cooking skills were, I made a couple of calls. Before she could say, 'Butter makes it better, y'all,' they were flying her to New York to audition for the Food Network. She started out as an unknown, but now she's got her own show. More than one, actually. Her recipe books are sold all over the world. Maybe you've heard of her." Brock whispered the name in my ear, and I almost choked on my gum.

"Y-you're kidding! She got her start because of you?"

"Mm-hmm." Brock leaned back, looking a little too content with himself. "She always said to call if I ever needed anything food related. And I thought maybe . . ."

"Well, I really don't know if that's ethical," I said. "See, Rosa is just one of many people being featured on this show. And it's just a onetime deal. When they're done, they're done."

"Not if I have my way." He gave me a pensive look. "That chicken parmesan was the best I've ever had. And I've had a lot of chicken, trust me." Brock laughed and rolled his eyes. "Chicken Kiev, chicken cacciatore, chicken cordon bleu, chicken à la king . . ." On and on he went, naming the various chicken dishes he'd had to endure through the years.

He lost me somewhere around chicken à la king. At that moment, something caught my eye. I glanced across the street to see Dakota, the neighbor kid, with binoculars in his hand. He appeared to be watching us.

"Yikes!" I jumped to my feet and grabbed Brock's hand, pulling him inside and closing the door behind us.

"What's happening?"

Peering out of the window, I groaned. "That's Dakota Burton from across the street. Great kid, but a little nosy. I'm pretty sure he had binoculars in his hand."

"Hmm. Guess we'll have to be more careful." He rested his hand on my shoulder—perhaps a bit longer than necessary. "Bella?"

"Y-yes?" I turned to face him, finding myself within inches of his broad shoulders.

"I've been thinking of asking you something but didn't know if it would be an imposition."

"W-what?" My response was a little shaky now that I could feel the warmth of his breath in my hair.

He looked into my eyes, then paused briefly, as if trying to think of something to say. "This is my first time to Galveston, and I've only seen a tiny portion of the island. I'm getting a little bored just sitting around, and I was wondering . . ."

"If I'd take you on a tour?"

"Yes." He gave me a boyish grin, and butterflies started fluttering in my stomach. "I saw all of the reports on the news after the hurricane hit," he said. "But I had no reference point because I've never been to any of those places."

"Do you think Rob would like to go with us?" I asked. I wasn't sure how I'd respond if he said no. I only knew I could not, under any circumstances, get in the car alone with Brock. It wouldn't be right, even if he wasn't so shockingly handsome and didn't have eyes the color of espresso.

"He's upstairs on his laptop checking emails. I'll go find him and ask."

Brock headed up the stairs. As I peered through the window, I caught another glimpse of Dakota, this time watching me from his front porch. I could imagine the wheels turning in the kid's head now. Hopefully his speculations wouldn't give us away. All the more reason to leave for a while.

But not without calling D.J. first. I knew he wasn't crazy about the idea of Brock and Rob staying here, after all. He'd said as much after the crowd thinned last night. The last thing I wanted to do was upset him, but what could I do, really?

I reached for my cell phone and punched in D.J.'s number, but he didn't answer. Nothing unusual there. Whenever he was on a construction job, calls were usually overlooked. I quickly sent him a text message. Gone with the guys on an island tour. That ought to do it. If he had any qualms about it, he'd write back.

Seconds later, Brock and Rob met me in the foyer.

"I guess we're taking your car, since Marian took mine back to town." Rob shrugged. "Is that okay?"

"Of course. I know where I'm going anyway."

I turned, coming eye to eye with Brock, who gave me a wink. He flashed a smile warm enough to melt a chocolate bar.

Hmm. Maybe I didn't know where I was going after all.

9

My Kind of Town

I led the way to my SUV with Brock and Rob on my heels. We went out the back door—the one in the kitchen—to avoid Dakota's snooping. I still shuddered when I thought of what he might be up to. This was, after all, the kid who'd threatened my family with a lawsuit and held my father's Hakeem Olajuwon autographed basketball hostage over a mix-up involving a lousy skateboard.

When we reached the car, Rob opened the back door and climbed in. Great. That left Brock in front with me. Why this worried me was a mystery. I had a fella of my own, and besides, I wasn't really attracted to the guy.

Okay, yes I was. No point in denying it. But I already had the world's greatest man. Being with Brock shouldn't be a big deal.

Deep breath, Bella. Deep breath.

I climbed in the car and buckled my seat belt. Then I heard

Precious yapping. With a sigh, I looked out of the car to see Aunt Rosa holding my ornery pup.

"Better take this thing with you." She passed her through the open window. "The little monster's not going to stop whining until you do. I've got my Savvy Seniors group at the church, and your mom's gone to town. Remember what happened the last time we left the dog alone in the house."

"Ugh." I remembered all right. She'd chewed the leg on Mama's antique rice bed. The repair had cost several hundred dollars.

As I held on to the squirming pup, I tried to figure out what to do next.

Brock looked at me with a shrug. "Want me to hold her?"

I'm sure that made perfect sense to him, but he didn't know Precious. She wouldn't stop whining until I took her back in my arms—not an easy task behind the wheel. Besides, she'd tried to bite his hand off last time he touched her.

"I . . ." Shaking my head, I tried to explain. "That won't work."

"Need me to drive then?"

"Oh, I don't know . . ."

He unbuckled his seat belt and came around to my side, opening my door.

I looked up at him through the open window, a little unnerved. "Are you sure?"

"Of course. I haven't driven in over a week, and I'm losing my touch."

"That doesn't sound hopeful." I scooted out of the car, pup in hand.

"Just don't get too heavy on the accelerator," Rob said. "Remember what happened that summer in Laguna?"

"Yep." Brock chuckled as he took the driver's seat.

I thought about their words as I made my way to the passenger side. Whatever had happened in Laguna could stay in Laguna. I didn't need to know. As long as we arrived home in one piece.

Brock barreled backwards out of the driveway. I held on to Precious, who growled at him under her breath. When we paused at the end of the driveway to wait on traffic, Brock looked my way. "Just one question. What are Savvy Seniors?"

I smiled at the funny look on his face. "It's a seniors group at St. Patrick's. In case you haven't figured it out yet, Rosa is Catholic."

"Yeah. I didn't know there were that many saints, but I think I've heard her calling on at least a dozen since I got here."

I laughed. "Yeah, that's Aunt Rosa. She and Uncle Laz attend St. Patrick's. The rest of us are Methodist, except D.J. and his family. They're Full Gospel."

"Full Gospel? As opposed to half-full?" Brock had a good laugh at that one. "Seriously," he said when the laughter stopped, "I don't have a clue what that means."

"Sure you do," Rob interjected from the backseat. "I took you to church with me as a kid. Don't you remember?"

"Ooohhh." Brock nodded. "Got it. Lots of 'amens' and even a few gymnastics, if memory serves me correctly. Never could figure out what they were all so excited about."

"Oh, that's easy. They're in love with Jesus." I closed my eyes after he backed out onto Broadway and barely missed an oncoming car.

"In love with Jesus." Brock shifted into drive, then looked at me like I'd lost my mind. "Not sure how that's possible. Last thing I heard, he wasn't around anymore. Right?"

"Oh, he's around. Trust me." I stopped right there, finding it a nice stopping point. Might give the boy something to chew on. In the meantime, we had an island to see.

Pointing to the left, I directed Brock south on Broadway, Galveston's main thoroughfare. I happened to glance across the street at the Burton place and saw Dakota on the roof. What would the kid be doing on the roof? For that matter, why wasn't he in school like the other kids? Something was definitely fishy here.

Hmm. Better not mention any of this to my guests. Didn't want to borrow trouble, as Aunt Rosa was prone to say.

As we headed down Broadway, I turned up my radio station. Though I'd never really listened to country music before meeting D.J.—the Christian station being my music of choice—I'd taken to occasionally listening to a local country station just for fun. Turned out country-western music had more themes than just the usual "Let's get drunk and cheat on each other." In fact, I'd discovered some heartrending songs filled with truth and emotion.

However, as the music began to play, I couldn't help but notice the look on Brock's face.

"What?" I asked. "Don't you like country music?"

He shook his head. "We don't get a lot of this out in L.A."

"Humph." I thought about it a moment before responding. "You don't know what you're missing!" I turned up the volume, singing along with a great Taylor Swift song.

Brock leaned back against his seat and rolled his eyes. "So, tell me about your island," he said, his voice rising above the radio.

"Oh, sure." I turned down the music, doing my best to focus. "Our street was hit pretty hard during the storm, but not as bad as the Strand."

"The Strand? What's that?"

"Oh, the best street in town, next to the seawall. Turn left at the next light and I'll show you."

He did as instructed. We passed downtown, finally reaching the quaint, historic cobblestone street I loved so much. How many hours had I spent here as a teen? Hundreds? Thousands?

"Oh, wow." Brock pulled the car off to the side of the road and took it in. "These old buildings are great. They remind me of the storefronts at Universal Studios, where we filmed *Once in Manhattan*. Very authentic."

I couldn't help but laugh. "That's because they're real. They've been here more than a century. They've taken a lot of damage, both in the storm of 1900 and from storms since, but they're a testament to the strength of the island, still standing strong." I pointed to the Confectionery, my favorite hangout next to Parma John's. "They've got the best taffy on the island, if you're interested in that sort of thing. And their ice cream is to die for."

"Want some?" Brock waggled his eyebrows, as if to taunt me.

"H-how?" I wasn't sure how he thought we could pull that off.

Before I could say anything else, I heard a grunt from the backseat. "I know, I know." Rob sighed and opened the back door. "What do you want?"

Brock laughed. He gestured to Rob, saying, "He's done this before."

"Clearly." I nodded. "But it doesn't look like he minds."

"I don't," Rob said. "But sometime today, okay? What do you guys want?"

"Rocky road, man. And some of that taffy."

"What flavor?" Rob leaned in my window and gave me an inquisitive look.

"Mmm. Cherry for me," I said.

Brock flashed a boyish smile and passed a fifty-dollar bill through my window.

While we waited for Rob to return, Brock quizzed me about all sorts of things—things that took me by surprise. Turning in his seat to face me, he asked, "How long have you worked at the wedding facility?"

"Oh, I've worked there for years helping my parents, but just took over managing the place early this summer."

"I saw one of your brochures. You do theme weddings."

"Right."

"That's a pretty creative occupation, Bella." He gave me an admiring look. "And being in the wedding business . . ." He let out an admiring whistle. "I think that's pretty cool."

"You do?"

"Sure. You make people's dreams come true."

I felt my cheeks flush and tilted my head down to scratch Precious behind the ears, hoping Brock wouldn't see my embarrassment. There was something about talking weddings with this guy that got me all flustered. Especially the part where he made me feel so good about what I did for others. It was fun making other people's dreams come true.

"I just like to think outside the box," I said. "And apparently so do a lot of brides and grooms. You can't believe how many calls I've had from people since we announced the theme weddings."

"Oh?"

"Yes. We had a Boot-Scootin' hoedown a few months ago. Now, of course, we're having the medieval wedding. I've had several calls from brides interested in themed weddings, so it looks like we're off to a great start."

"I think—if I ever found the perfect woman, I mean—that I'd like to have a pirate-themed wedding. Could you pull off one of those?" Brock gave me an inquisitive look.

"Hmm." I leaned back against my seat, thinking about the possibilities. "Would it require building a ship?"

"Well, of course."

"Ah. I see." After a pause, I added, "And would all of the guests have to fit on the ship too, or would that spot serve as a stage for the wedding party?"

"Hmm. Just a stage. The bride and groom should have a special spot above the crowd, don't you think?" He gave me a penetrating look, and I shifted my attention to the dog once again, my heart now thumping wildly. Brock could speak a million words with those eyes of his.

"Right, right."

"I think it's doable." Brock began to fill my head with possibilities, laughter lacing his words. He explained everything—right down to the costumes everyone would wear and the lines the preacher would speak. "Arrr! By the power vested in me, I now pronounce ye mate and matey!"

He went on in pirate-speak for a couple of minutes, and I finally joined in. Couldn't help myself, really. There was something pretty mesmerizing about Brock Benson once he got rolling.

By the time we finished, I'd pretty much decided he was right. I could pull off a pirate-themed wedding. With his help, anyway.

I paused from our conversation for a moment, glancing out the window. In all of our chattering, I'd forgotten that I was supposed to be protecting Brock's identity. With a sweep of my eyes, I did my best to assess our surroundings. What we didn't need was anyone hiding behind a parking meter with a camera in hand.

"Are you nervous?' Brock asked with a smile.

"A little."

"I think we're okay. You've got tinted windows. But there are quite a few people out. More than I expected."

"Well, it's only late September," I said. "The kids have been back in school a few weeks, but we still get quite a few tourists, as long as it's still warm."

"You like it here?" he asked.

"Of course! What's not to like? Look around you. This area is like something from a painting. And the houses on Broadway are amazing. They're some of the oldest ginger-bread Victorians in the state."

Brock laughed. "I guess you do like it here." He pointed to a couple of women passing by. "It doesn't bother you, having so many tourists around? I'd think that would get annoying."

"On the contrary. They're the bread and butter of the island. We *want* them to come. We *need* them to come." I sighed.

"What? Are you frustrated with all my questions?"

"No, it's not that. It's just that getting people to the island is so important. That's one reason I changed the layout of the wedding facility, to draw people from the mainland. Not just for our family's sake but for the island's sake too."

"What do you mean?"

"The more weddings we facilitate, the more the hotels and restaurants benefit. So I figure I'm really helping lots of people when I sign a wedding. Mama feels the same way about the opera house. She's a sponsor and a volunteer. She loves it, but it's not just about that. She wants to do anything she can to draw a crowd so that the island will keep going strong."

"You Rossis are do-gooders, that's for sure." He leaned

back against his seat and crossed his arms at his chest, giving me a look I'd never seen from him before, one I couldn't really interpret. "Why do you care so much about other people, anyway? Just build your business for yourself. Your family. Let your mom enjoy the opera for herself."

Shaking my head, I responded, "It's not in us to be like that. And we're not hurting for money. It's not about that. We could shut down the wedding facility today and be fine. I keep the wedding facility going for the same reason Uncle Laz keeps Parma John's open."

"Why's that?"

"We love people. We love the island. And—especially after the hurricane—we've got to do what we can to help rebuild. That's why I'm working double time to prove myself with the wedding facility, because it means so much to our family to make a contribution to the island. Like I said, it's not about us."

Brock laughed. "I'm trying to envision someone where I come from using those words." He closed his eyes for a moment, then shook his head. "Nope. Can't imagine anyone saying that."

A rap on Brock's window jarred us back to attention. I looked up, expecting to see Rob, but was stunned to find a police officer standing there with a scowl on his face.

Yikes. "Now what?" I whispered.

Brock shrugged. "Now I roll down the window." He did just that, flashing a winning smile at the elderly officer. "Good afternoon, sir."

"Mm-hmm." The officer gave a curt nod, then looked over at me. Instantly, Precious began to growl. She tried to lunge out of my arms, but I held on tight, praying all the while. The creases between the fellow's eyes deepened as his gaze shifted back to Brock.

"Have we done something wrong, Officer?" Brock asked.

"You're parked at a meter but haven't put any money in it."

Brock glanced at the meter to our right. "Oh, you're so right. We were waiting here on a friend and got carried away. We'll take care of it right now." He pulled out his wallet, coming up with another fifty-dollar bill.

"The machines take quarters, son." The officer scrutinized Brock, a hint of recognition in his eyes. "You're not from the island, are you?"

"No, sir. You're right about that. This is my first time to visit your beautiful island, and I'm overwhelmed at everything my tour guide is showing me. I'm particularly drawn in by the buildings on this street. Remarkable history, from what I understand."

"Mm-hmm. You got any quarters, son?"

"I . . ." Brock shook his head. "I don't, Officer."

"Oh, I might." I scrambled around in my purse, coming up with a couple of pennies and a ten-dollar bill.

"What are we looking for?" Rob's voice rang out. I looked through Brock's open window to see him standing next to the officer.

"Oh, we didn't put a quarter in the meter," I said.

"No problem. I've got plenty of change." He turned to the policeman with a smile. "Just spent a fortune at the Confectionery. Great place."

"Mm-hmm." The officer glanced at Rob for a second, then turned back to Brock. "Where are you from, anyway?"

"Oh . . . well, my family's originally from Jersey."

"No way!" I couldn't help but interject. "Why didn't you mention that when I told you we were from Atlantic City?"

Brock shrugged. "Didn't think about it."

We dove into a discussion about his long history of visiting the boardwalk when the officer cleared his throat. "Is anyone going to put a quarter in that meter?"

"Done." Rob pointed to the machine, which he'd apparently loaded with change while we were gabbing.

"Thank you for visiting sunny Galveston Isle." The officer tipped his hat and took a few steps away. He turned back to look at Brock one last time, shaking his head. "New to the island, huh? Could've sworn I'd seen you before."

Rob climbed into the backseat, and we all erupted in laughter as soon as the officer turned to leave.

"I get that all the time," Brock said, looking my way. He downed a small container of rocky road ice cream, then gazed at me with a smile. "Now where?"

"I guess we could drive past Uncle Laz's pizzeria. At least you'd have a visual for what we're always talking about."

"I'd like that."

I pointed him in the direction of Parma John's with an idea whirling around in my brain.

10

Blue Skies

As we pulled up to Parma John's, I tucked Precious into my oversized handbag and worked up the courage to ask Brock for a huge favor. Turning to him, I said, "Brock, I, um . . . I need to ask you something."

"What's that?"

"My best friend, Jenna. She would flip if she knew you were here. I've been dying to tell her. It's killing me not to. If you knew anything about girls, you'd know what I mean. I've been trying to hold this secret inside, and I know she'd keep it to herself . . . if you don't mind."

He shrugged. "I guess I don't mind. But remember what we talked about earlier at your house. The fewer people who know, the better. You're sure she won't say anything to anyone?"

"I'm sure. We can trust her." I hoped.

"Well then, why don't I just go in there with you?" Brock unbuckled his seat belt and reached for the door.

"Not a good idea, Brock," Rob said. "I've been in there before, and it's always a mob scene."

"I wouldn't suggest it either," I said, "unless you want to be seen by fifty or sixty teens and twentysomethings. Parma John's is the island's biggest hangout. And it's lunchtime, so . . ."

"Say no more." He leaned back in his seat and waited. I sprinted to the door, found Jenna inside, and pulled her by the hand out to the curb. She took one look through the open window at Brock and buckled at the knees, letting out a squeal that could've raised the dead.

Maybe I should've given her some warning.

"You . . . you . . . you . . ." She shook her head, and tears sprang to her eyes. "Oh, I look awful!" She pulled off her apron and ran her fingers through her mop of red hair. "Isn't that just the way life is? You get your once-in-a-lifetime opportunity to meet someone famous, and it's on the one day you didn't wash your hair."

"I'm Brock Benson." He extended his hand and she grabbed it, babbling incoherently.

I looked his way and shrugged, then mouthed the word, "Sorry."

"Nah. I get this a lot. But, um . . . I could use my hand back."

"Of course!" Jenna released it, then turned my way and punched me in the arm.

"Ouch!" I rubbed my aching arm and glared at her.

"Bella, you should've told me."

"We're sworn to secrecy. It's kind of complicated."

"But, he's Brock Benson. He's a famous movie star." Interesting how she continued to talk about him in the third person, as if he weren't seated right in front of her. Brock seemed to find some humor in this. Leaning back against the seat, he watched her performance. All the boy needed was popcorn and a soda, and the afternoon would be complete.

Jenna reached to grab my arm and asked, "What's he doing here, anyway?"

Okay, so we were still talking in the third person. I'd have to break her of that.

Rob piped up from the backseat. "Brock is the best man at my wedding next week."

Jenna leaned in the car and said, "Oh, hey, Rob." Then her eyes darted back to Brock, who couldn't seem to stop smiling.

To be honest, I was thrilled at her response, because I'd secretly wondered if Sophia or Bubba might've already told her. Looked like no one had let the cat out of the bag, and that was a very good thing.

"What are y'all doing?" Jenna asked. "Just driving around?"

"Brock wanted to see the island. He's never been here before, so I offered to give him the grand tour—east to west."

Jenna's eyes widened. "Let me ask Laz if I can have an hour off. I want to go too."

She sprinted back inside, then came back seconds later and climbed into the backseat. I flashed an apology to Brock with my eyes, but he just smiled. Obviously my best friend's zeal didn't faze him.

"I hope I don't get carsick back here," Jenna said with an overdramatic sigh as she closed the back door.

"Huh?" I looked at her, puzzled.

She gave me a knowing look. "You know how I am, Bella. Whenever I ride in the backseat, I get a little queasy."

Sure you do. I could see what she was up to. No doubt

about it, she wanted to switch places. No problem. I'd let the girl have her moment. Then she could say for the rest of her life that she'd ridden in the front seat of a car with Brock Benson.

"C'mon, Jenna. Get in front." I opened the door and stepped outside. Sitting in the back would likely calm Precious down, anyway. She was still acting a little too keyed up. And it was high time I pulled my thoughts away from Brock Benson. That way the butterflies in my stomach could finally take a siesta.

Since we were on the east end of the island, I decided our first stop should be at Stuart Beach. I had Brock pull the car into the parking lot and paused a moment. Though the height of the season had passed, there were still quite a few colorful umbrellas dotting the sand. For a moment I was tempted to get out of the car and dip my toes in the water. Strange how I could live this close to the Gulf of Mexico and never go in it. Life moved too fast these days.

"It's not quite the Pacific," Brock observed with a hint of laughter in his voice.

"Yeah, I know." I'd seen the Pacific. In fact, Pop had taken us to Laguna Beach a couple of years ago for a family vacation, renting a house for several weeks. The brown waters of the gulf couldn't compare. Neither could the sand, for that matter. In Galveston, we didn't have that brilliant contrast of blue against white, and we certainly didn't have any rocky cliffs. Everything here had more of a brown-against-tan hue.

Still, I found it beautiful. There was nothing nicer than the sound of the waves lapping the shore to remind you that someone rather magnificent had created all of this. And watching the steady flow of the water—back and forth, back and forth—created the most beautiful picture in my mind of God's consistency with me. I'd mess up . . . he'd pull me back. I'd mess up again . . . he'd pull me back again.

Brock dove into a story about a trip he'd taken to the Mediterranean last summer, which led to a story from me about my parents' desire to return to Italy to visit their siblings.

"Mama and Rosa have twin sisters between them," I said. "Bianca and Bertina. They live in Napoli. And Pop and Laz have a brother, Emilio, who lives there too."

"I've been to Naples," Brock said with a nod. "Filmed a few scenes there. Beautiful place. I hope to go back someday."

"Oh, me too." I sighed, thinking about it. "I can't even imagine what it would be like to vacation in Italy. It's been so long since I've been there." Looking at the brown waters of the gulf, I shrugged. "Not exactly the same, I guess. But there's still something about Galveston that does my heart good. I love it here."

"Oh, me too." Jenna dove into a lengthy story about the summers we'd spent on this beach as teenagers and all of the shenanigans we'd pulled, but my thoughts had shifted back to something Brock had said earlier about living for yourself instead of others. That comment still bothered me, in part because it showed just how different we really were. Several things set Brock Benson apart from the Rossis, of course, but perhaps this was the greatest one of all. In many ways, it was a gulf wider than the one I was staring at now.

On and on Jenna went, talking about our teen years. Catching her between sentences, I turned to Brock and asked, "Ready to move on?"

"Mm-hmm."

He pulled the car back out onto the seawall, and we continued west. We spent the next hour driving the island from end to end. I could see the emotion on Brock's face as we paused at the places hit hardest by the storm.

"Stop right here." I pointed to a spot on the side of the seawall. As the car came to a stop, I sighed. "The Balinese used to be right there."

"The Balinese?" His eyes lit up. "Didn't Sinatra sing there?"

"Yes. And a host of other famous people. The place was renowned. And not just for its music. Now it's gone forever."

"Sad how things can seem so perfect one minute and completely devastated the next." Brock's voice hinted of something deeper, but I didn't ask.

I couldn't get past the feeling that he had been through some sort of personal trauma in his life. An experience with a woman, perhaps? I'd have to check the Internet to find out who he'd dated to get that answer.

By the time we dropped Jenna off back at Parma John's, I was ready for some food. Apparently so were the guys.

"What do you think Rosa's making for lunch?" Brock pointed the car toward home.

"Oh, I heard her say something about meatball sandwiches."

"Mmm." Brock grinned. "I knew I'd landed in the right house."

As I gazed at the reflection of his eyes in the rearview mirror—eyes that shimmered with mirth and mischief—I had to say . . . I wasn't so sure he'd landed in the right house. Having Brock Benson so close was really doing a number on me. How could I possibly pull off a medieval wedding and guard him from the paparazzi when I was so easily swayed by those cappuccino eyes?

11

I've Got the World on a String

On Saturday afternoon, D.J., Sophia, Brock, and I settled down on the sofas in the living room to rest. And talk. After all the work I'd done preparing for the wedding, I was ready to relax.

Sophia, who had spent every waking moment of the past three days drooling over Brock, couldn't wait for another opportunity to do more of the same. Ogling him had become a full-time job. Well, that, and perfecting her appearance. I'd never seen the girl take so much care with how she looked, and today she did not disappoint. Talk about a classic Italian beauty! She had fixed her hair in that style I loved so much—the one where she pulled back a bit of it off her face and let the rest flow freely down her back. I didn't know anyone who had hair as pretty as my sister. And I could rarely recall ever seeing even one strand out of place. No, she'd definitely inherited my mother's penchant for perfection, especially when it came to looks.

I, on the other hand, was more free-spirited. Sure, I took care with my appearance. It would be a rare day for me to go out to the grocery store or florist's shop without a touch of makeup. And I always took care to make sure my long curls were under control. But I didn't slave over my appearance like Mama and Sophia did. It wasn't that I didn't care. I just didn't have as much to work with.

And now, completely done up, Sophia sat next to Brock on one sofa, glued to his every word. D.J. and I sat across from them on the other one, hands clasped.

For whatever reason, holding hands with D.J. in front of Brock was a little unnerving. Might have had something to do with the fact that Brock kept wiggling his eyebrows, as if to say, "This one's a keeper, Bella!" Or was he saying, "Choose me instead"? Sometimes I couldn't tell. He flirted endlessly with Sophia, but I'd caught him schmoozing me a couple of times too, especially yesterday afternoon in the car.

D.J., on the other hand, seemed a little out of sorts. Though he hadn't said much about Brock, I sensed his discomfort with the situation. And who could blame him? Still, there was little I could do . . . at least at this point.

We'd just settled in for a long chat—coffee cups in hand and some of Rosa's homemade cookies on a tray in front of us—when the doorbell rang.

Sophia quirked a perfectly sculpted brow. "Do you think Rob and Marian are back from their date to Moody Gardens this quickly?" She rose and went to the door. Seconds later, the house came alive with noise.

"Hello, Sophia!" a woman's voice called out. "Why, if you don't look pretty as a picture! Now, where is that Bella? We need a word with her."

I looked at D.J., shocked. "Did you invite Sister Twila?"

91

He shook his head, a stunned look on his face. "No way. I mean, I know some of the folks from my church are coming down to the island tonight to see Bubba perform, but it's only 3:00. And I've never told her anything about where you live, so . . ."

Now I heard other voices. Of course, I recognized every one. Sister Twila, Sister Jolene, and Sister Bonnie Sue—three very boisterous ladies from D.J.'s church in Splendora, who happened to be as full figured as the church was Full Gospel. They weren't really sisters, of course. Nor were they nuns. No, at D.J.'s home church, every member was referred to as "brother" or "sister." And these three sisters were the cream of the crop. Their mission? To spread both the love of Jesus and Sister Twila's original beauty secrets. They'd already gotten to my mama, who now used hemorrhoid cream to rid herself of wrinkles around the eyes. Still, I couldn't figure out what the God-loving self-proclaimed beauticians were doing here.

Brock rose from the sofa, grabbed a couple of cookies, and rushed to the door. Unfortunately, he didn't make it in time. Sister Jolene met him coming and going. "Oh, so sorry." She stepped back, her cheeks turning pink. "Oh my. You're . . . you're . . ."

Brock turned on his heels and ran. As I peered into the foyer, I caught a glimpse of him loping up the stairs.

Jolene looked at me, her mouth hanging open. "Bella, was that really . . . ?"

"Really who, Jolene?" Twila stepped into the room with Bonnie Sue on her heels. The sisters were dressed to kill today. In fact, they must've spent hours applying the makeup alone. I'd never seen so much blue eye shadow in my life. And the dresses! I didn't know sequins came in that size, but the room was suddenly filled with glittering, sparkling, plus-sized females who babbled nonsensically.

Well, all but Jolene. She hadn't said a word since Brock's disappearing act. Instead, she continued to stare, mouth wide open. Twila reached over and closed it for her. "We've talked about this before, honey. An open mind and an open mouth are not one and the same. Now, close that garage door before a car drives in."

D.J. lost it and started laughing. I'd never seen him so out of control. Trying to maintain a sense of decorum, I ushered the women into the room. They spent a few minutes covering my cheeks with kisses. As I gestured for them to be seated, they crowded onto one sofa, which creaked its displeasure under their weight. They didn't seem to notice. Or maybe they simply didn't mind. They were, after all, quite proud of their physiques.

Jolene continued staring out into the foyer. "I . . . I was sure I saw . . ." She looked at me for help.

I swallowed hard and said, "Vinny. Vinny DiMarco. Great guy. He's here for a visit from out of state. But I think he's tired, so we'll let him nap."

"Oh." Jolene's brow wrinkled, and she shrugged. "I really need to get my eyes checked. This astigmatism is causing me to see things."

"Honey, I've been telling you that for months." Bonnie Sue waved her hand. "You've got to see my optometrist, Dr. McYummy."

"All in favor of Jolene getting some glasses?" Twila asked, raising her hand. We all reluctantly put up our hands, and she said, "The ayes have it!" Turning to Jolene, she giggled. "Get it? The *eyes* have it."

"Got it. Got it." Jolene shrugged but continued to stare in the direction of the foyer.

Determined to keep this ship sailing in the right direction, I smiled and offered an opening line. "To what do we owe this honor, ladies?"

"Well, we were coming to Bubba's debut tonight anyway," Twila said. "And I remembered you said your family's place was next door to the wedding facility." She nodded, as if that answered my question.

"So we looked you up on Mapquest," Bonnie Sue threw in. "And voilà! Here we are."

"Dressed for the opera already!" I added.

"Heavens, yes. We didn't know what the day would hold and wanted to be ready," Jolene said. She leaned forward to whisper, "Besides, you never know when you might meet up with a handsome man, and I for one want to be ready to sweep him off his feet." She gave me a wink.

I couldn't help but think she certainly had the potential to sweep a man off his feet, but not necessarily in the way she implied. But that still didn't answer the question about why they'd come for a visit.

"Bella, no point in beating around the bush." Twila put her hands on her knees and looked me straight in the eye. "We're leaving on a cruise tomorrow morning and want to know if we can leave my car here for the seven days we're out to sea."

"Oh?" I shrugged, unsure of how to respond. The Rossis already had a plethora of vehicles lining the driveway. What would we do with another?

"If we leave it in the parking lot at the pier, it's going to cost us ten dollars a day," she said. "Ten dollars a day!" Twila fanned herself, as if she found this the most unthinkable thing ever.

Jolene giggled. "We would much rather spend that money

on excursions while we're in Cozumel. We plan to go snorkeling."

Now *that* created quite an image.

"You don't mind, do you honey?" Twila asked, batting her eyelashes. "Surely you could drive us to the pier tomorrow. Wouldn't take more than a minute."

"I told them you wouldn't mind," Bonnie Sue added. "Because you're the sweetest little thing on Planet Earth, Bella."

Now what, Lord?

I did my best to put together a plan. "Well, we don't have space in the driveway at our house. But I can park it in front of the wedding facility, I guess. If you leave me the keys." *Because I'm going to hide it from the masses on the day of the wedding, that's for sure.*

Twila reached into her purse and came up with a set of rhinestone-studded keys, which she jangled in front of me. "I'll pass these off to you or your mama after the opera tonight." She tucked the keys back into her tiny handbag and leaned back against the sofa. "That Pinto of mine is going to think she's died and gone to heaven down here so near the gulf."

"P-pinto?" Sophia reached for a magazine from the coffee table and began to fan herself.

"Sure, honey. Best car ever made. I've driven Gertrude since 1983. I'll bet you've never seen a car with two hundred eighty thousand miles on it before." She gave me a wink.

"Twila really gets around." Jolene giggled, then her cheeks flushed pink as Twila slugged her in the arm.

"That joke was funny in the nineties, Jolene, but it passed its expiration date ten years ago."

"So, tell us more about your cruise," D.J. said. "I've never been on one."

"Oh, honey! You've never been on a cruise?" Twila looked stunned when D.J. shook his head. She turned to Sophia.

"I think I would go stir-crazy on a cruise ship," my sister said with a shrug.

"Heavens, no!" Jolene countered. "Why, think of all the handsome men you could meet hanging out at the pool or at the midnight chocolate buffet."

Sophia perked up at the word *chocolate*.

Twila looked my way. "What about you, Bella?"

"No." I shook my head. "I know it's strange, since I live so close to the pier and all, but I've never been."

"You simply *have* to go!" Jolene's eyes lit up. "Cruises are absolutely glorious. It's very freeing being out there on the open seas."

"This is our fifth," Twila said. "And it won't be our last. Well, unless Jesus comes back or one of us crosses over the Jordan to the Promised Land. But I think I've got a few more years left in me. What do you think, girls?"

"Oh, I plan to be around awhile," Bonnie Sue said, checking her hair in her tiny compact mirror. "I promised myself I wouldn't die till I found Mr. Right."

"So you plan to find him and *then* die?" Jolene slapped her knee. "Poor guy!"

"Or poor Bonnie Sue," Twila said with a giggle.

Bonnie Sue sighed. "There's no explaining anything to you ladies. I'm just saying that I don't plan to die anytime soon, that's all."

I wasn't sure what all of this talk of dying had to do with cruising, but they eventually got back around to telling us all about the adventures they planned to share over the next several days.

"There's an ice-skating rink on our ship," Bonnie Sue said.

"Ice-skating! Can you imagine? They perform the most wonderful ice shows. I once saw a man do a triple lutz."

"No kidding." I did my best to get involved but didn't know how long I could take this.

"And not just ice shows," Twila threw in. "There's the most marvelous theater on board the ship, and they put on real Broadway-type productions. Great song-and-dance numbers."

"Remember that fifties extravaganza they did last year?" Jolene giggled. "I knew every word to every song." She lit into a chorus of "At the Hop," and before long they were all singing. I had to admit, they weren't bad. Still, it didn't make me want to go on a cruise.

Twila sighed as she looked my way. "You've just got to go on a cruise, Bella." Her eyes lit up. "Oh, I have the most wonderful idea!"

I was terrified to ask what it was.

"Next year you can go with us!" She let out a squeal, and all of the ladies followed suit.

"Oh, that's the perfect plan!" Jolene said. "Twila and I can share one cabin, and you can bunk with Bonnie Sue."

"Just bring your earplugs," Bonnie Sue said with a wink, "because I snore. Or so I've been told."

"I used to snore, but now I use one of those CPAP machines," Twila said with a nod. "It's been a real lifesaver."

"And the mask is really chic," Jolene added.

I tried to envision what it might be like to travel the high seas with the Splendora trio, but couldn't. Besides, I'd never done very well on boats.

"Well, think on that," Twila said, standing. "We want you to come with, but you may have other plans." She gave D.J. a wink.

"Other plans?" I looked at her, curiosity setting in.

"You know . . ." Twila pointed to her ring finger and grinned in D.J.'s direction. "Other plans." She began to hum "Here Comes the Bride," and I almost fell off the sofa.

"Why don't Sophia and I show you the house?" I stood and gestured for them to join me.

"Sure." Twila nodded. "We've got some time to kill before we check in at the Tremont. We'd love to take a tour of your house, Bella. We don't see a lot of these old Victorians up Splendora-way."

"Oh, okay." My thoughts raced as I tried to imagine where Brock had gone. Likely up to his room. Easy enough. I'd just avoid that one on the tour. Then again, there was Mama to contend with. She was up in her bathroom, putting on her makeup. She'd been a nervous wreck all morning. How would she take to having our Splendora friends look over her house on such a hectic day?

Twila harrumphed as she hefted herself from the sofa. Then she extended a hand to help Bonnie Sue, whose joints cracked and popped as she stood. Jolene was the last to rise, her beehive hairdo waggling back and forth as she struggled to balance on her sparkling, high-heeled shoes.

"I guess we're ready." I looked to D.J. for moral support, and he rolled his eyes in playful fashion. Great.

We made the rounds from room to room, starting with the downstairs. Just as I led the women into the dining room, I thought I caught a glimpse of Brock shooting across the hall into the kitchen. Yikes. Maybe I could avoid that room.

No such luck. Bonnie Sue claimed she "must see that kitchen or die trying," so I took a few tentative steps into the room. As was often the case, I found Rosa working diligently. In the background, the tiny television set was playing a show from the Food Network. This time it was *The Barefoot*

Contessa, one of Rosa's favorites. The woman on the screen was making some sort of potato dish, which she served to her husband and a couple of his friends.

My aunt looked up as we entered the room, brushed her hands on her flour-covered apron, and broke into a smile as she saw the three ladies.

"Oh, three of my favorite people in the world!" She clasped her hands together. "I'm so happy you've come! It's been ages since that wonderful Fourth of July picnic. Can you stay for dinner?"

My mind began to reel as panic set in. How in the world could I keep Brock hidden from the trio if they stayed for dinner? I ushered up a silent prayer, begging the Lord for mercy.

"Well, I don't know." Jolene looked at Bonnie Sue, who looked at Twila. "We're going to the opera at seven, you know."

"Oh, we all are." Rosa practically beamed. "That's why we're having an early dinner. I'm making my homemade ravioli with gravy."

"Gravy?" Bonnie Sue's nose wrinkled. "On pasta?"

"Red sauce," I explained. "We always call it gravy."

I got hungry just thinking of it. Ravioli day was always my favorite. From the time I was in elementary school, I'd loved watching Aunt Rosa roll out the dough and stuff it. In fact, I'd helped on many occasions. She just had a way with pasta, though. When no one else could get it right, Rosa could.

And talk about the perfect gravy—Rosa's red sauce was out of this world! Of course, she started with tomatoes from Laz's garden out back, so that gave her an added advantage. And not just any tomatoes, of course—only Romas. A gravy-making day was really something to behold. In fact, it could take the major portion of a day and leave the kitchen a bit of a mess. Oh, but it was worth it! The first time you ladled a spoonful of that tasty tomato-y stuff into your mouth, you thought you'd died and gone to heaven.

"My ravioli is the best, if I do say so myself." Rosa nodded, settling the deal.

"Humph." Laz chose that moment to enter the room. He opened the fridge, grabbed a soda, then looked at the three women with a scrutinizing eye. "What have we here?"

"We're going to the opera, Lazarro. Are you coming too?" Jolene took a few steps in his direction, her eyes firmly locked on his. Suddenly all of this made sense. They'd come not just because of the car but because one of them had her eye on my uncle.

Rosa's eyes darted back and forth between Jolene and Laz, her jaw tightening.

Aha. So I was right.

Rosa began to mutter something about needing to get the Crisco out of the pantry for her piecrust, and Twila piped up, "Oh, have you tried Crisco to remove your makeup? The *Splendora Daily* did a write-up on my beauty secrets, and Crisco is number one on my list. It works wonders."

Laz grunted. "Rosa? Makeup?"

At this point, Rosa's anger apparently got the better of her. She went to the pantry door and yanked it open. This simple act was followed by a bloodcurdling scream that sent the hairs on the back of my neck standing on end.

Unfortunately, Rosa didn't come out with Crisco.

She came out with Brock Benson.

12

The Way You Look Tonight

As I laid eyes on Brock, unexpected laughter almost got the better of me. In the length of time we'd been visiting with the ladies, he'd apparently gotten into my brother's dresser and pulled out a worn plaid shirt and some jeans that were about three inches too short. He'd donned Armando's old glasses too, the ones with the broken frames that had been taped together. And his hair . . . what had the boy done to his hair? Instead of the usual well-kept 'do, he'd lopped it to one side, giving himself a strange, geeky look. Of course, the hair looked better than the tube socks. They really took the cake. The guy looked like an Italian Steve Urkel. Only . . . worse.

Rosa inched her way out of the pantry, hands over her mouth. I could almost read her thoughts. She knew better than to give him away, of course, but he'd clearly scared the daylights out of her. I had a feeling she would get him back later.

Can anyone spell "food poisoning"?

Sophia appeared in the doorway and clamped a hand over her mouth as she saw Brock. Before she could open her mouth and say something we'd all regret, I made quick introductions. Steadying my voice, I said, "Ladies, you heard me mention our good friend Vinny DiMarco. Vinny, meet Jolene, Twila, and Bonnie Sue, our friends from Splendora. They're here to see Bubba in *The Marriage of Figaro*."

Thank goodness Brock's acting skills were better than mine. He grabbed Twila's hand and kissed it.

Out of the corner of my eye, I saw D.J. roll his eyes.

Brock seemed not to notice. He kept his gaze on the trio. Giving a slight bow, he said, "Ladies, I'm delighted."

"Wish I could say the same," Twila responded, looking a little bug-eyed. "You scared me to death."

"So very sorry. I was looking for a . . ."

"Oh, that Vinny." Rosa waved her hand. "He just snacks all day long. I can't tell you how many times I've found him defrosting the fridge, looking for a between-meal treat. He just eats me out of house and home." She turned to him, giving him the evil eye. "But this time you've almost gone too far, boy. You could've given an old woman a heart attack hiding in the pantry like that. I never even saw you come in the room. You're quite a sneak."

"Yes, *Vinny*." D.J. pursed his lips and crossed his arms at his chest. "You really need to watch what you're doing."

Okay then. Things were going well.

"My apologies." Brock offered up a rehearsed pout.

Twila shook her head, looking him up and down. "I find it hard to believe this kid eats all day long when he hasn't got an ounce of fat on him. Doesn't seem possible. Where does he put it all?"

"Must have a hollow leg," Bonnie Sue observed.

"How's he ever gonna catch a girl if he's skinny as a rail?" Jolene asked with a worried look crossing her face. "We've got to fatten him up."

I saw the look of concern in Brock's eyes and noticed him eyeing the door. Probably looking for an escape route.

"I don't think he's too thin," Sophia said. "He's just right."

"Humph. Well, it's not just his *size*." Twila cocked her head as she continued to look him over. "It's the clothing. Surely you Rossis can help him in that department."

A giggle worked its way out of me, and I clamped a hand over my mouth.

"What, Bella?" Twila turned my way. "You think he's hopeless? I'll have you know my beauty secrets could turn this boy around in no time. We'll have him looking—and dressing—like a Hollywood hottie before you know it. All it takes is a little work."

Behind the glasses, Brock's eyes sparkled. "You think so? You *really* think so?" He took Twila by the hand again. "I'm willing to do the work. I promise I am. If I could just win the heart of a girl . . ." He looked my way and sighed. "I'd be the happiest guy on the planet."

"Well, you can't have this one," Jolene said with a brusque nod. "She's already spoken for."

"Yes, she is." D.J. slipped a protective arm over my shoulder and drew me close. His gesture spoke a thousand words.

I could see the momentary flicker of something odd in Brock's expression. Hmm. Perhaps he was just acting, but I had to give him a trophy for this one. For a second there, I thought I saw hope in his eyes—hope that he would somehow win my heart.

Not that *that* was possible. No, my heart was already given to D.J., who now held me so tightly I could scarcely breathe. Yep. This was going well.

"How are you going to help him?" Bonnie Sue asked. "We need a jumping-off place, don't you think?"

"Hmm." Twila stood back and crossed her arms at her chest. "I'm not sure yet, but I'll think of something. How long are you staying in Texas, Vinny?"

"Oh, another week or so."

"It's a shame we'll be out to sea for much of that time. You really need a lot of work."

"Do I?" He forced another pout.

"Yes." Twila snapped her fingers, then looked at me. "I know! Tonight after the opera I'll go back to my hotel room and put together a list of things you can be working on while we're gone. Then you can surprise us when we get back." She grinned. "Bella, you can do it." She turned to Sophia. "Both of you girls work together. You can help this poor boy out. Turn this ugly duckling into a swan in no time at all."

"It'll be just like *My Fair Lady*," Jolene added. "Only not."

Brock turned to me with a far-too-serious look on his face. "I will be your doting pupil, I promise."

I'll bet you will.

He turned Sophia's way and offered a smile. Her cheeks flamed pink as she responded, "It will be my pleasure."

For the sake of the women, I gave a hearty response. "I'll give it my best shot."

Brock schlepped off into the other room, grabbing an apple along the way. As he left the room, he turned back to holler, "Thanks, ladies. I owe you!"

Jolene began to cluck her tongue in motherly fashion.

"Poor guy. I can't believe he's gone this long in such bad shape." She turned to me with a broad smile. "But I know you, Bella. You've put a new sparkle in D.J.'s eye. Surely you can put a sparkle in Vinny's. Well, in his wardrobe, at the very least." She erupted in laughter and I joined in. What else could I do, after all? If I couldn't beat 'em, I might as well join 'em.

"I've learned that every frog is really a prince," Twila said with a pensive look on her face. "All it takes is a Texas spit shine to bring it out."

"Not sure I'd agree with that," Bonnie Sue said, wrinkling her nose. "Remember Jim Bob Hooligan from Madisonville? That man was a frog through and through."

Twila shook her head. "Au contraire. In order for a frog to see himself as a prince, he's got to be convinced. Problem with Jim Bob was, he never found the right woman to convince him."

Bonnie Sue muttered something about how there weren't enough fickle women in the state of Texas to do the trick, but Twila didn't seem to hear. No, she was hard at work putting together a list of things I needed to do to whip Brock—er, Vinny—into shape while she was on her cruise.

Just what I needed. Another assignment.

13

From Both Sides, Now

By late Saturday afternoon, the entire Rossi household was in a frantic state. Mama was worried about Bubba, of course. Pop was worried about Mama, who hadn't slept in days and hadn't eaten a decent meal. I was fretting over the whole Twila, Jolene, Bonnie Sue fiasco. And Brock . . . well, Brock seemed to find the entire situation hilarious. The more tickled he got, the more attractive my sister found him, despite his change in wardrobe. And the more attractive she found him, the more my brother Joey ribbed her. Somewhere in the midst of all this, D.J. scooted off to Landry's to have dinner with his family, then on home to dress for the opera.

With all of the chaos in the house, Guido took to singing. Not "Amazing Grace," but that age-old classic and everyone's favorite—"Ninety-Nine Bottles of Beer on the Wall." By the time Rob and Marian arrived home from Moody Gardens at 4:30, Guido was down to thirty-seven bottles of beer and I thought I might snap like a twig. Unfortunately, I didn't have the time or the patience for a nervous breakdown today. I had places to go, people to see. After dinner, of course.

Just a few minutes before we were set to eat, my cell phone rang. I looked at it, stunned to see my ex-boyfriend's number.

I answered with a tentative "Hello? Tony?"

His voice sounded strained. "Bella, have you, um, have you seen Sophia?" The anxiety in his voice confirmed what I'd come to suspect—he had a thing for my sister. And he must wonder what she'd been up to lately. Since Brock's arrival, she had pretty much shut herself off from the world.

"I wanted to sit with her at the opera tonight," he said. "Do you think she'll sit with me?"

"Oh, I don't know." I paused, then said, "Have you tried her cell phone?"

"Yeah. She's not answering."

"Well, I know she's been really busy lately."

Tony sighed. "Helping Laz at the restaurant?"

"Oh, sometimes." *But that's not why she's busy right now. She's busy ogling Brock Benson.* "She's been spending time at home with the family. You know, Rosa's got that big thing coming up with the Food Network."

"Right." Another sigh from Tony let me know he had truly been missing my sister.

"I'll tell her you've been trying to reach her. I think she's just distracted right now. But don't give up the ship, okay?"

"I won't." After a moment's silence, he whispered, "And thanks, Bella. I know this has to be weird . . . me liking your sister."

"I'll admit, it's taken some getting used to, Tony. But I hope things work out between you and Sophia. I really do."

"Thanks. And I really meant what I said earlier. I want to see her at the opera tonight. Does she . . . well, do you know if she already has a date?"

"Not that I know of." *And this will be the perfect thing to take her mind off Brock Benson.* "Call her one more time, Tony. I think she'll sit with you. And even if you can't reach her, just come and sit with us, like you normally do. You know Mama included you when she got the tickets, same as always." In fact, at the time Mama got the tickets, Tony and I had still been dating. Amazing how much had changed in such a short period of time.

"Perfect." He paused, then added, "And thanks, Bella. I don't know what I'd do without you."

Strange words, coming from my ex.

We ended the call, and I thought about all of the changes in my life over the past few months. Had I really known D.J. for only one summer? Crazy!

At 5:00 I met the others in the dining room. Mama had already gone on to the theater—no big surprise there—and Pop was dressed for the opera. It had been some time since I'd seen him this done up. I gave him a kiss on the cheek and whispered, "You're the handsomest man at the table," to which he responded, "I'm the *only* man at the table."

"Ah. Right." Joey hadn't come downstairs yet, and Brock and Rob were in the kitchen, likely putting Crisco in someone's hair. Or under their eyes.

Soon we were all in place, and Pop prayed—not just for the meal but also for tonight's performance. He added an extra prayer that Mama would live to tell about all of this. Then we dove into the meal Rosa had prepared.

The sisters sang my aunt's praises as they tunneled through plate after plate of ravioli. Marian and Rob watched this whole thing in silence. No doubt they wondered if they'd come back to the same house they'd left hours earlier, especially with Brock in such interesting attire.

Pop scraped the cheese off his food and groaned. "Rosa . . ."

"What, Cosmo? What have I done this time?"

"It's the cheese. Don't you remember? I'm lactose intolerant."

She muttered something under her breath, which he asked her to repeat.

"You're intolerant, all right," she sputtered. "But it doesn't have anything to do with cheese."

I thought his temper might flare, but instead Pop just laughed. Before long we were all laughing. Oh, if only all of life's problems could end with such ease!

Thankfully, our guests didn't seem at all put off by Pop's aversion to cheese or Rosa's slight temper problems. Twila in particular seemed to enjoy our family. "I am just so excited about Bubba's performance at the opera," she said, dabbing at her lips with a napkin. "He's going to put Splendora on the map."

"Oh yes. Half the town is here!" Bonnie Sue said. "Including Harry Pitts, the editor of the *Splendora Daily*. This is big time."

"Harry Pitts, eh?" Brock quirked a brow. "Sounds like we've hit the big time." He took a bite of ravioli and leaned back in his chair. "Sorry I'm going to miss it."

"Miss it?" Jolene looked horrified. "What do you mean? You're not going?"

"None of us are." Brock pointed to Rob and Marian. "We've got other plans."

"Well, pooh on that!" Twila pointed her fork at him, probably not realizing that a piece of ravioli dangled precariously from the end. "How in the world do you expect to morph into a prince if you're satisfied to hang out at the pond with the frogs?"

Rob turned to her with a stunned look on his face. "A-are you calling me a frog?"

Twila paled as she pressed the ravioli into her mouth. After swallowing, she answered his question. "I'm not calling you a frog, young man. I'm just saying Vinny needs to get out more, and what better place than the opera? He needs culture. Refinement."

"Yeah." Brock nodded, a twinkle in his eye. "I need refinement."

"We've got extra tickets," Pop threw in. "So you're welcome to join us."

Brock turned to my sister. "What do you think, Sophia? Want to take an unrefined guy like me to the opera?"

You could've heard a pin drop in the room. Every head turned Sophia's way. If she responded with a yes, the whole of Galveston was likely to figure out our secret. On the other hand, if she turned him down for this date, she'd regret it for the rest of her life, knowing Sophia. I mean, who got asked out by Hollywood's leading man?

I closed my eyes, ushering up several prayers. *Lord, give her wisdom. Lord, give her wisdom.*

"I . . ." She hesitated and then choked out, "I would be honored."

"Oh, but what will he wear?" Twila pursed her lips and shook her head. "This is a real dilemma."

"Don't worry about that." My pop waved a hand. "We got enough suits and tuxedos around here to clothe an entire wedding party. We'll figure it out."

"Wonderful!" Twila clapped her hands together and smiled. "Oh, what a night this is going to be!"

Yes. What a night this was going to be.

I glared at Brock, hoping he would realize just what a pickle this put me in.

110

We finished the meal by 5:45, and everyone flew into action. Marian headed back to the mainland, and Rob informed us he planned to spend the evening catching up on last-minute details related to the honeymoon. Twila, Bonnie Sue, and Jolene left to meet up with Earline and others from Splendora. Sophia and I raced up the stairs to dress for the opera. Brock followed along on Pop's heels, nodding as my father chatted about the various suits and ties he owned.

Man. Were we ever in for a crazy evening. How would I survive the chaos?

I slipped into my room and pulled my favorite green dress from the closet. D.J. always said it looked great against my olive skin, and it was just fancy enough for the opera house. Then I touched up my makeup and pulled my curls into an updo. I could hardly wait to see D.J.'s face when he got a look at me.

I was nearly ready to roll when I heard a rap on the door. Sophia popped her head in. "You ready?"

"Mm-hmm." I looked at her, taking in the beautiful black and silver dress. Man. Did she look amazing, or what? "What in the world are we going to do about Brock, though? Everyone in town is going to know who he is."

"I know." She groaned. "And I'm so sorry for saying I'd go with him. I just didn't know how to say no. Can you imagine looking into those eyes and turning him down?"

Hmm. What to say, what to say . . .

"It's not your fault, Sophia. He set you up. Though why he set you up, I'm not sure. Surely he knows the risks involved." I released a sigh, feeling the weight lift a little. "It's on his head now. We're not to blame."

"What do you suppose he's going to wear?" Sophia chuckled. "And what's he going to do with his hair? Do you think he'll wear it like that in public?"

"I haven't got a clue. But it sure helps hide his identity, so I hope so."

We got our answer a few minutes later, though I had to hold my hand over my mouth to keep from laughing. Loaded with an overabundance of gel, Brock's hair looked even geekier than before, but that wasn't really what jumped out at me. Pop must've rummaged in the very back of his closet to come up with the outfit Brock had donned—a tuxedo that looked like it had passed its expiration date in the '70s, complete with a black-on-white ruffled shirt poking out underneath.

The white polyester jacket with single-button closure was accented with a black velvet lapel. Very . . . unique. And dated. Brock turned around to show off the rear vent. Flapping it, he said, "Think I'll get any hot dates in this getup?"

Responding was completely out of the question, since I couldn't have squeezed any words past the laughter that had bubbled up in my throat.

"Where in the world did you get that?" Sophia asked, looking stunned.

Pop grinned. "I'm surprised you don't recognize it from the photos hanging on the wall downstairs. I wore this the day your mother and I got married. Doesn't fit me now." He rubbed his midsection. "But it fits Vinny here like a glove."

"Unless you count the legs." I looked at the black slacks, which were about an inch too short. Maybe two inches. Brock's white socks stuck out like a sore thumb, and the shoes . . . well, there wasn't really any way to do the shoes justice. They must've come from the '70s too.

Brock slipped Armando's taped-up glasses back on, completing his look. "Think anyone will recognize me?"

"Not a chance in the world," I said. "I hardly recognize you myself."

"Perfect."

Minutes later, Rosa appeared in the foyer, dressed in the most beautiful black chiffon dress I'd ever seen. "Rosa!" Sophia and I spoke in unison. "Where did you get that dress?"

"Oh, I bought it a couple of weeks ago at a shop on the mainland." She peered in the mirror, touched up her lipstick, and looked back at us. "Do you like it?"

"Like it?" Sophia asked, her mouth now hanging open. "Are you kidding? It's to die for!"

"Really?" Rosa beamed. "You think so?" She fidgeted with her bun, which she'd fashioned in a looser, more flowing style.

"What's to die for?" Laz entered the room wearing his black suit, the same one I'd seen him wear dozens of times to church. He took one look at Rosa and the shock registered on his face. He managed one word—"Oh." Not much, but it spoke volumes. I'd never seen that look in his eyes before.

Apparently, neither had Rosa. Her lips almost betrayed her as they curled up in a smile. Quickly she turned back to the mirror for a final glance, then tucked the lipstick into her tiny purse.

"Everyone ready?" Pop asked. "Let's go see Bubba in his debut."

For a second there, I felt like Dorothy taking her first step on the yellow-brick road. I certainly had the right traveling companions. As we headed out the door, I found myself singing, "We're off to see the wizard."

What a night this was turning out to be!

14

Strangers in the Night

We arrived at the opera house at 6:30, exactly thirty minutes before the performance was set to begin. Being a patron, Mama had several seats front and center. Not that we would see her anytime soon. No, with such a crowd about, it would take awhile to get inside the theater.

Thankfully, no one in the crowded lobby looked twice at Brock, except one man who pointed and said, "I wore a tux just like that to my high school prom back in '74." We all got a good laugh out of that. Well, all but D.J., who appeared at my side and slipped an arm around my waist. He gave me a gentle kiss on the cheek, then let out a little whistle.

"Bella, you look like a million bucks."

"Really?" I did a slow turn to show off the dress, and he nodded. "Make that two million."

D.J. turned to face Brock with a hint of a frown forming. To put his mind at ease—D.J.'s, not Brock's—I returned his kiss and nestled against him. For a moment, anyway. The crowd very nearly swallowed us alive, and now several people were staring at Brock.

I took D.J.'s hand, and we made our way through the throng of people with Brock following closely behind. I prayed no one would see through his disguise. I was doing pretty well too, until I ran headlong into my mom's newest—and best—friend, Phoebe Burton. Dakota's mom. She stopped when she saw me, of course, and gushed over what a fine job Bubba had done in rehearsals.

"Your mother really hit this nail on the head, Bella," Phoebe said. "Bubba is the cat's meow. I think you're going to be so surprised at what a great job he does in tonight's performance. Everyone is!"

D.J. grinned from ear to ear. "Thanks, Mrs. Burton. I know my brother's really looking forward to this."

"Oh, none of this Mrs. Burton stuff!" She laughed. "Call me Phoebe."

D.J. nodded and said, "Phoebe."

She turned back to me. "I'm so happy she introduced me to all of her friends here at the opera house. I've had the time of my life." Tears filled her eyes, and she squeezed my hand. "Your family has been so wonderful to us, welcoming us to the island. I can't believe we've been here such a short time. Feels like forever."

Yes. And it felt like forever standing in the crowded foyer with her. I just wanted to get to my seat, to hide Brock from the masses.

Just when I thought we were in the clear, Phoebe turned his way. She offered a confused smile. "Who have we here?"

"Oh, this is our guest, Vinny DiMarco," D.J. said. "He's in town for a few days, and we thought he might enjoy tonight's performance. He doesn't get to Galveston much."

"In fact, this is my first trip," Brock said, extending his hand in Phoebe's direction.

Phoebe nodded as she shook it. "Young man, you're in for a real treat. You couldn't have come at a better time. Now, I don't know where you come from . . . whether you get to the opera much . . . but I'm telling you this is going to be a performance you'll be talking about for decades."

No doubt.

We were just about to say our good-byes when Dakota came running up with a camera in his hand. He took one look at Vinny and started snapping pictures right and left.

"Dakota!" His mother reached to stop him, a stunned look on her face. "What do you think you're doing?"

The kid gave me a knowing look, then turned back to her as he spouted, "Making memories."

"Well, make them someplace else, honey. You're making Mama nervous."

She turned to greet another friend, and Dakota looked my way, his eyes squinted. Then he turned to Brock, making the "L" sign and whispering, "Loser!" before disappearing into the crowd.

I turned to Brock, stunned. "W-what was that about?"

"Oh, I have my suspicions," he said. "That's the same kid who was on the roof yesterday, right?"

"Y-you saw that?"

"Of course." He laughed. "Bella, remember, this is my life. It's what I do. I see people behind bushes, in trees, on top of buildings. They're everywhere."

"So, you're not worried about him?"

"Nah. He's just a harmless kid. I've got a feeling about this one. We'll win him over."

"Okay, but I would still feel better if we went inside and sat down. Not so many gawking people that way."

We took a few steps but didn't make it very far. Earline Neeley came buzzing through the crowd with her husband, Dwayne Sr., at her side. Dwayne looked pretty snazzy with his suit and tie and his perfectly sculpted hair, which I'd only recently discovered was a toupee. But Earline . . . wowza! I hardly recognized her in the fabulous gown and upswept hair.

D.J. whistled as he saw his mother. He gave her a kiss on the cheek. "Good thing you've already got a date, or every guy in this place would be wanting to sit next to you."

She hit him with her little sequined purse. "Aw, quit it, D.J. That's too much."

"No, you're too much." He gave her another kiss on the cheek.

"He's right!" I gestured for her to turn around. "You look like something out of the movies!"

"Your mama is a wonder!" she said. "She picked out my dress and made me get my nails done." Earline extended her hands, and I saw the lovely French manicure.

"Beautiful!"

Leaning in, Earline whispered, "You'll never guess who did my makeup."

"Who?"

"Twila. Turns out she really is a wonder with a mascara wand and lipstick!"

"Oh, you don't have to tell me twice." I nodded. "Twila's got the best beauty secrets around. She's got Mama using kitty litter as a facial scrub. And don't get me started on the udder cream."

"Oh, I know all about it." Earline held out her hands for my examination. "It's made my hands silky smooth."

"Did she make you put potato slices under your eyes so you would look more refreshed?" I asked.

Earline nodded and said, "Who knew?" in response. We had a good laugh at that.

Brock remained silent throughout this exchange, but I could see the anxiety in his eyes. He excused himself, turned, and headed toward the interior of the theater. I started to follow him but then caught a glimpse of Jenna, who looked heavenly in her sky blue gown. She approached and did a little twirl, and I let out a whistle. "Girl, you look fabulous."

"Well, this is my honey's debut!" she said with a giggle. "I have to look good."

"How's he doing?" I asked.

"He's wound up tighter than a clock, but I don't blame him. I'm a nervous wreck too. Can you imagine Bubba singing at the opera?" She giggled and I joined her.

"No, I can't, to be honest. Though I overheard a number he and Mama were working on, and he sounded pretty good."

"Oh, I'm sure he's going to be wonderful." She leaned in and whispered, "I'm just wondering what he's going to look like in tights!" We erupted in laughter.

As we reached our seats, we ran smack-dab into Sister Twila. She took one look at me in my green gown and began to sing my praises. Then she looked at Brock. The poor woman closed her eyes and shook her head, then opened her eyes, perhaps hoping for a different outcome. She reached out and touched his arm, muttering, "You poor dear. This really *is* going to take some work, isn't it?" Then she looked at me. "You're the right girl for the job, hon. Just keep working on him."

"I'll give it my best shot," I promised her.

She headed off to join the other women. I wanted to take a seat but found myself struggling to figure out where. With the entire Splendora clan to accommodate, I needed to think fast on my feet. Shuffling down the row, I took the seat in the middle of the row, saving a spot to my left for D.J., who had headed backstage to say hello to Bubba. The others would just have to figure out where to sit on their own.

The orchestra tuned up, and I squirmed, trying to rid myself of the anxieties that now gripped me. So many things just felt . . . off.

Brock settled into the seat on my right, with Sophia on his right. I didn't figure he'd be much of a distraction, since my sister kept him occupied with her stimulating conversations about the color of her nail polish and so on. Still, I felt a little uncomfortable with the Hollywood actor seated this close.

I peered at him over my program, smiling as he caught me in the act. *He's just a guy, Bella, like any other guy.* Shifting my gaze downward, I pretended to read the bios on the performers. When I saw Bubba's picture, my heart swelled with joy. Man, did that head shot look good. Talk about a radical transformation!

A familiar voice rang out. I looked up to see Tony standing at the end of our row. The moment I laid eyes on him, I realized I'd forgotten to tell Sophia he was coming. Having him here without Brock in the mix was one thing, but now . . . Yikes! What had I done?

He looked at the empty seat on Sophia's right and gestured to it.

She stared at him, looking like she'd been caught with her hand in the cookie jar, then rose and scooted down the aisle in his direction, dragging me behind her. I had a feeling I'd hear about this later. When we reached Tony, his face lit with joy. Sophia, on the other hand, didn't look so happy. "Tony, what are you doing here?"

"Well, I . . . I'm joining your family at the opera. I hope that's okay."

She sighed. Loudly. "I guess. But there's one little problem . . ." She gestured to Brock, who seemed oblivious to our conversation. He sat with the program open, reading with a crooked smile on his face.

"You have a date with someone else?" Tony asked, the pain in his eyes evident for all to see.

"We have a family friend in town." Sophia gave Brock another nod. Lowering her voice, she said, "And, um, I'm trying to be nice to him."

"Oh . . ." Tony winked at her and lowered his voice too. "I get it. A mercy date."

I had to laugh at that one. If he had any idea!

"I guess you could call it that," Sophia whispered. "But it's going to be a little awkward if you—"

"Oh, that's okay. I'll just sit in the seat on the other side of you." He led the way down the row to the seat on the other side of Sophia, and she followed along behind him, then dropped into the chair between the two guys. I could almost read her mind. She was the cream in the middle of an Oreo cookie. But nothing about this felt comfortable—I could see it in her pained expression.

Well, in some ways it served her right. She'd been avoiding Tony for days, ever since Brock Benson waltzed into the house. Maybe this would be a wake-up call for her.

I made my way back down the row, deciding introductions were in order, and the sooner the better. "Vinny, meet Tony. Tony, meet Vinny."

"Hey, Tony." Brock stuck out his hand for a shake.

Tony stared at him with the most perplexed look on his face. I could only imagine what he must be thinking. Surely the whole mercy date explanation made sense, now that he saw geeky Vinny DiMarco up close.

Or not.

As Tony leaned back in his chair, I still sensed something rather territorial in his expression. Clearly he didn't want Vinny here one way or the other.

The music began, and my heart raced to my throat. Though I felt a little childish admitting it, there was something about performances—plays, operas, and even some movies—that held me spellbound. Would *The Marriage of Figaro* be the same?

D.J. made his way down the row, stepping on more than a few toes with those boots of his. He made apologies all the way. Settling into the seat on my left, he reached for my hand and gave it a squeeze.

"How's Bubba doing?" I asked.

"You don't want to know." D.J. chuckled. "Let's just say the tights are an issue and leave it at that."

I giggled, trying to picture Bubba's angst.

Just then Brock leaned over and whispered in my ear from the other side. "Have you seen this opera before?"

"No," I whispered back.

"It was written as a political piece—a satire."

"Oh, wow. I had no idea."

"Yes. And it's one of only three collaborations between Mozart and a man named da Ponte. Written in Italian, of course."

"Of course."

"The language of love." Brock winked, and my heart fluttered.

D.J. cleared his throat. Loudly. I pulled away from Brock and leaned a bit to the left to put some space between us.

Thankfully, at that moment Sophia looked over at Brock, and he turned to her. I whispered a quick "Thank you, Lord," then focused on the stage.

Bubba came out in full regalia as Figaro. I had to admit, he looked completely authentic. I never would've guessed him to be a country boy from Splendora. No, this polished opera singer was the real deal, from the top of his head to the bottom of his well-clad toes. And there was something about his presence. He literally commanded the stage. Who would have known?

As I checked out his costume, I realized just how much it resembled the ones I'd be seeing next weekend at Rob and Marian's wedding. How interesting that my life had taken on a Renaissance theme. I closed my eyes to see if the performance would be any less thrilling that way. Ironically, Bubba sounded even better, if that were possible.

Man! Can that boy sing or what!

I wondered what D.J. thought of his brother right about now. One glance answered my question. But was he grinning because his baby brother was wearing tights, or had he somehow looked beyond the costume to see the talent? He looked at me and mouthed, "Wow," and I nodded.

Yep. The boy was proud of his little brother. No doubt about that. I was proud too—of both Bubba and my mother, who'd suggested he audition for the role. How could she have known he would turn out to be this good? I glanced down the row at her and could see the tears in her eyes as the music swelled. Pop, on the other hand, looked like he'd rather be just about anyplace else.

I closed my eyes, letting the music take me to a far-off place in my imagination. Something about the lyrical Italian words made me feel as if I'd actually been whisked off to Europe. Perhaps one day I would be.

"This story takes place in a single day," Brock explained with a hoarse whisper. "And it's all about . . . well, infidelity."

D.J. cleared his throat again and shifted in his seat.

"O-oh?" For whatever reason, my heart skipped a beat at the word *infidelity*. "Really?"

"Mm-hmm." He pointed to the stage. "See that guy right there? He's Count Almaviva. He's married to Rosina, the countess." Brock pointed to a beautiful woman in a dark red dress.

"Oh, wow. She's gorgeous."

"Yes, but the count is . . . he's infatuated with another woman—Susanna."

"Yikes."

"Right." Brock gave me a knowing look. "But Susanna's in love with the man of her dreams, Figaro."

"Bubba."

"Yes." Brock smiled. "Bubba. But the plot thickens. See that guy right there?" He pointed to a male singer wearing black. "That's Cherubino. He's got his eye on the countess."

"Whoa. This story is all twisted up."

"Yeah. Keep an eye on Cherubino. And watch Figaro and Susanna too. Their sole purpose is to expose the count's infidelity and make a public spectacle of him."

"Serves him right." I paused for a moment, then looked at Brock. "How do you know all of this, anyway?"

He held up his program. "Read the synopsis."

"Ah." I let it go at that, but I had a feeling there was more to this story than meets the eye. Kind of like Brock. There was certainly more to him than meets the eye. He might come across as a self-absorbed Hollywood hunk-a-man, but I'd already figured out there was much more to him.

D.J. looked my way with confusion registering in his eyes. Ouch. I'd hurt his feelings by talking to Brock. But what could I do about it? I didn't want to be rude, after all. Right? On the other hand, maybe he felt left out. I leaned his way, grasped his hand, and gave it a squeeze, which he returned.

I watched the rest of the show in rapt awe. Mama had hit the nail on the head where Bubba was concerned. The boy could've taken home an award for his performance. And the folks in the wardrobe department were probably celebrating the fact that he'd put on every outfit.

After he sang his last song, the audience erupted in applause, and I joined them, clapping until my palms smarted. What a transformation a costume could make.

I glanced at Brock, unable to hide the smile. Yes, what a difference a costume could make.

15

Just One of Those Things

On Sunday morning I drove the Splendora trio to the pier, then met my family at church. Brock and Rob stayed home, but the rest of us enjoyed a break from the craziness of the week. The reception from our friends at church didn't surprise me. Mama was congratulated on every side by people who had seen last night's production. She took it all in stride, but I could see the appreciation in her eyes.

D.J. joined us as the service began, settling into the spot next to me in the pew. I loved going to church with him more than almost anything else, in part because he sang with such abandon. And he truly loved the people. That much was evident in all he said and did.

Still, I had to wonder how he felt about the Methodist church after growing up in a Full Gospel congregation. Did he find us tame in comparison? If so, he hadn't said. I somehow imagined D.J. Neeley would be at home in any church, as long as the Lord met him there. And as long as I was sitting at his side.

Our pastor chose a topic that seemed to correspond with what the Lord had been showing me of late. It was all about old things becoming new. I opened my Bible to 2 Corinthians and read along as he quoted the text for the message: "Therefore, if any man be in Christ, he is a new creature: old things are passed away; behold, all things are become new."

Hmm. For whatever reason, that verse made me think of Brock Benson. He was a great guy, clearly. But I had the strongest feeling God had led him here to Galveston Island for more than just a wedding. He was at a fork in the road. I could sense it. And God wanted to do something fresh and new in his life. I spent the next few minutes praying for him, then focused on the message.

After church, I found Brock in the kitchen, looking at Guido's cage. "What's with the white cloth over the cage?" Brock asked. "Is he being punished?"

I laughed, then did my best to explain. "Not exactly. That's a prayer cloth."

"Prayer cloth?"

"Yeah." No doubt he'd find this interesting. "See, Rosa has a theory that whenever Guido's under the covering of her prayer cloth, he's one bird—calm, cool, and collected. Then, when the cover is removed, he's another."

Brock quirked a brow. "I think I'd just leave him under there 24-7."

"Right." I sighed. "But then there's Laz. He's nuts about Guido. Probably because Guido actually belongs to his old friend Sal, who lives up north. Sal had a stroke a few months ago and is in rehab, so Laz is watching over Guido for him."

"Oh, man. Now I feel sorry for the poor little guy." Brock lifted the edge of the prayer cloth, and Guido hollered, "Wise guy!" Dropping the cloth, Brock said, "But not that sorry."

He went off to find Rosa, and I headed upstairs to my parents' room. I rapped on their door, surprised to find Mama taking a nap. "Oh, sorry." I shrugged. "I need the keys to Twila's car. I can't leave it at the wedding facility all week. Bad for business."

"Where are you going to park it?" Mama's pursed lips let me know that parking it in the driveway was out of the question.

"Oh, not to worry. D.J. said he'd drive it over to his condo. I don't know why we didn't think of that sooner."

"Great idea. To be honest, I'm a little relieved that the people from the Food Network won't see it. The kind of car in a person's driveway makes a vivid first impression. Not that I'm out to impress anyone, but a 1983 Pinto, well . . ."

"Say no more. I've got this under control. Just need to get the keys from you."

"From me?" Her brow wrinkled. "What makes you think I have the keys to Twila's car?"

"She told me yesterday that she would leave them with you." I paused, deep in thought. "Or maybe she said Rosa. Let me check."

I practically sprinted to the kitchen, anxious to get this over and done with. I found Rosa hard at work counting out the pans for Marian's wedding cakes. In the midst of all the chaos, I'd forgotten she'd agreed to make the cakes for the big day.

I glanced over at the small television, Rosa's constant companion while she cooked, to see Giada De Laurentiis on the Food Network. "Oh, it's *Everyday Italian*, your favorite show!"

Swinging on a Star

"*Every* show on the Food Network is my favorite." She giggled. "Last night I watched *Ace of Cakes* to get in the mood for baking. And then I watched a great cake-decorating competition. Cute show. Oh, but speaking of the Food Network . . ." She dove into a long-winded story about Iron Chef Bobby Flay. Turned out she'd started to suspect this whole Food Network gig was really just a ruse. Maybe Bobby was coming to the house to challenge her to a throw down. Now *that* would really be something!

We got so caught up in our conversation about food that I almost forgot the reason I'd come to talk to Rosa in the first place. "Rosa, do you have the keys to Twila's Pinto?"

"Keys? Hmm?"

"To the Pinto."

"Bella, I haven't driven since the '70s. You know that." She went back to work, muttering under her breath about not having enough pans.

"Yes, but I thought Twila said she would leave her keys with you so we could move her car before the wedding."

"Ask your mother."

"I did. She doesn't have them."

Rosa shook her head. "Me either. And I'm a little distracted right now, Bella. Once I finish up here, I have to figure out how to memorize those lines they've given me to say next Friday."

"Lines?" I smiled. "I have the perfect idea. Get Brock to help you. He loves running lines with people. Told me so himself."

Rosa looked over at me, relief in her expression. "Oh, Bella! That's a wonderful idea. I can't believe I didn't think of it myself."

"Well, you've got a few other things on your mind." I

walked over and gave her a kiss on the cheek. "I know I've already told you this, but it's worth repeating. I'm so thrilled for you, Rosa. You're the best cook I've ever known. If anyone deserves a spot on national television for their cooking, you do."

"Humph." Laz walked through the room, reached over to snatch a piece of chicken, then kept walking.

Rosa sighed as he disappeared from view. "What am I going to do with that man, Bella? He drives me out of my ever-loving mind."

"Yep. I know." I started to say, "Marry him," but thought that might stir up trouble. Instead, I whispered, "You know, I think he's a little jealous."

"Jealous?"

"Yes." I leaned in close, hoping Laz was out of earshot. "He makes a pretty mean pizza. Think about it. He owns his own restaurant. But no one much talks about his cooking skills. I think this whole Food Network thing has him a little, well, envious of you."

"Oh." She paused from her labors and shook her head. "I don't know why it didn't occur to me, but I'm sure you're right. Maybe I need to ask him to cook a couple of nights this week. Might give me a chance to rest, anyway. I'm pretty worn out. Been on my feet for, well, sixty-five years." She winked and I laughed. Truly, she had worked in a kitchen most of her life. All the more reason she deserved a spot on national television.

As I left the kitchen, I passed Laz in the hallway with Guido on his shoulder. The bird was quoting John 3:16. Not bad, I had to admit. My uncle had been working on the parrot for several months, and all with only one thought in mind— sending him back to his original owner with the salvation message in his beak.

"How do you think Sal will feel when he finds out his bird has come to know the Lord during his stay in Texas?" I asked with a grin.

"Don't know. But I have to reach Sal with the gospel somehow. After all of those years he spent in the mob . . ." Laz dove into a story about the old days, but my cell phone rang, interrupting him. I smiled when I saw D.J.'s number.

"Hey, you."

"Hey, yourself," he said. "Did you find Twila's keys? Are we moving her car to my place?"

"It's the strangest thing. I can't find her keys anywhere."

"No problem," he said, putting my mind at ease. "Bubba's got the wrecker parked at my condo. He can come over to your house with me after his matinee, and we'll load up the car and take it to my place."

"It won't damage the car?" I asked, trying to envision the look on Twila's face if we dented her little baby.

D.J. laughed. "Not at all, Bella. Don't worry. We've got this under control."

"Of course you do." He always had everything under control. Why did I doubt him?

Awhile later, the guys pulled the family wrecker into the drive at the wedding facility.

"I've seen this car in the parking lot at church every Sunday up Splendora-way," Bubba said, "but I've never had the courage to ask Sister Twila why she chose the color pink."

I pointed to the faded Mary Kay sticker on the back. "I have a feeling she won this car in the '80s for selling makeup."

"No joke?" He pulled off his baseball cap and scratched his head. "I'm surprised it's still running."

"And her makeup is still going strong too." D.J. winked

and we all laughed. He turned to face the car, suddenly all business. "Let's get this show on the road."

"Oh, speaking of shows . . ." I looked at Bubba with a smile. "I know I told you this last night, but it bears repeating. You were absolutely amazing in that production. I was blown away, to be quite honest."

"Shoot." His gaze shifted to the ground. "I still can't believe it's really happening. My life has sure gone a different direction since I met all of you folks."

"So has mine." D.J. slipped his arm around my shoulder. "It's a little crazier, but I wouldn't change a thing."

Just then, Brock came walking across the front lawn of the wedding facility, dressed in his Urkel-like getup. Bubba burst out laughing at the sight of him. "What happened to you? Your pants shrink in the dryer? And what's up with the glasses? You having trouble seeing or something?"

Brock sighed. "Hey, it's just a part I'm playing. That's what I do. I'm an actor." His gaze narrowed, and he looked at Bubba with intensity. "That's what I wanted to talk to you about. I saw the show last night."

"You did?"

"Mm-hmm." Brock nodded. "And I have to say, that was the best version of *Figaro* I've seen . . . and I've seen it three times. You were very good. Impeccable."

"Well, shoot. Impeccable? What does that mean?"

"It means without flaw."

"Oh no!" Bubba put his hands up. "I'm plenty flawed, trust me. But I appreciate your kind words. They mean a lot to me."

Brock gave him a business card, which Bubba read with interest. "What's this about?"

"My agent, Arlen Collins. One of the best in the business.

I've already called him and told him all about you. There's a new movie being cast next month in Los Angeles, and they need a singer. I think you'd be perfect."

"W-what?" Bubba pressed the card back into Brock's hand. "No way. I'm not leaving Texas. And I don't sing." His cheeks turned red. "I mean, I guess I do sing, but not for a living." He shook his head and stammered, "Well, technically I guess I am getting paid for it now, but that doesn't make me a professional."

"If you're getting paid for it, that makes you a professional." Brock nodded. "And besides, Arlen is going to be looking for someone new, someone fresh. Best of all, this is a country-western movie, so all of the music would be right up your alley."

"Man, I don't know what to say."

"Just say you'll call Arlen. He's been a real door opener for me."

"Shoot." Bubba repeated his favorite word, then pulled off his cap and ran his fingers through his hair. "I've already got the best door opener of all. Don't know why I need an agent." When Brock quirked a brow, Bubba added, "Got the Lord on my side. He opens the doors that need opening."

Brock sighed. "You people and God. If I didn't know any better, I'd think he lives in Texas."

"He does," I said with a grin. "Among other places."

"Mm-hmm." Brock walked back toward the house, muttering all the way. He turned for a moment and called out, "Think about what I've said!"

Sighing, I turned back to the Neeley brothers. "What are we going to do with him?"

"What do you mean?" D.J. gave me a funny look.

"I mean, God apparently sent him here for a reason. We've

only got a few more days before the wedding, and he's going to be gone on a boating trip for most of those. I just feel this . . . pressure to let him know that God loves him."

"Bella." D.J. drew in a breath as he shook his head. "You're a wonderful, godly girl. Anyone who spends any time at all with you can see the love of Jesus in everything you do. Just be yourself. It's pretty obvious Brock knows where you stand. Where we *all* stand, for that matter. The seeds have been planted. We have to trust God to do the real work."

"Right."

D.J.'s words made sense, of course. But what if Brock went back to Hollywood in the same spiritual condition he'd arrived in? A wave of sadness washed over me as I contemplated that possibility.

"Hey, are we going to move that Pinto or what?" Bubba yawned. "I'm beat. Can't wait to fall into my bed and sleep straight through till tomorrow."

"Sure. Let's get 'er moved." D.J. led the way to the car and used some sort of a long, skinny tool to try to get the door unlocked. For whatever reason, it wouldn't budge. It did, however, set off the most annoying alarm I'd ever heard in my life.

"W-what is that?" Kind of sounded like the car was shouting something. I unplugged my ears and distinctively heard, "Back away from the car! The eyes of the Lord are upon you, and he knows where you live!"

"Did that car really say what I thought it said?" D.J. shook his head, looking like he didn't quite believe it.

As if to answer his question, the car blurted out the same words again. This time I realized I was hearing Twila's voice. *How did she do that?*

"That car just said it knows where I live." Bubba made a

funny face. "It's smarter than I am. I don't even know where I live these days—Splendora or Galveston. It's a toss-up." He laughed. "But one thing's for sure, I feel the wrath of the Lord when I touch this car, and that's not a good thing. Twila can be pretty intimidating, even coated in pink paint."

"I don't care if she shouts at the top of her lungs. We've got to get this car moved," I said. "The ladies aren't coming back till next Sunday, and we can move it back before they get here. She'll never know."

Bubba groaned. "Okay, if you say so. But I'm holding you responsible."

"I'll sign on the dotted line, taking full responsibility. The Pinto's gotta go."

Minutes later, the poor old girl was on the wrecker, ready to be hauled to her new home at D.J.'s condominium. I smiled as I saw her disappear down Broadway. No, Sister Twila might not be happy about this, but what other choice did I have? I couldn't help the fact that she'd forgotten to leave her keys. Or that one of us had lost them. I still hadn't figured out which one was more accurate.

Then again, who had time to think? I still had a wedding facility to organize, a program to print, and a castle to build. Better get to it!

16

The Tender Trap

On Monday, with Bubba's debut behind us and the trio of sisters out to sea, I could finally focus on the wedding. I spent the morning working on last-minute details, everything from the program to the centerpieces to a variety of decor items I'd rented. I didn't want to leave one thing undone.

As I walked into the yard behind the wedding facility, I looked at the cloudless sky and thanked God for small favors. With so much to do this week, we'd need continued good weather. I stood in silence for a moment, staring at the spot where the castle would be built. If I closed my eyes, I could envision it all. The musicians playing that melodic classical music. The smell of food straight off the grill. Those gorgeous Renaissance costumes. Everything.

I paused to pray everything would go well—not for my sake but for the sake of the beautiful bride. Then, glancing at my watch, I gasped. No standing around daydreaming—not with so much to do! Determined to stay on top of things, I headed off to the costume shop to pick up the guys' outfits for the big night.

Arriving home, I found Rob and Brock on the driveway in front of the basketball hoop. Rob held a ball in his hands. He looked at Brock—who was still dressed in his Urkel-esque attire—with a grin. "You game?"

Brock shrugged. "Sure. It's been years, but I guess I'm up to it."

"Years?" I asked. My brothers couldn't go two days without a basketball in their hands, and he'd gone years?

"Might sound strange, but I don't get out much," Brock said. "When I'm filming a movie, it's a fourteen-hour day usually. I get up, get ready, film, and then get ready for the next day."

"So . . ." Rob tossed the basketball his way. "Let's see if you've lost your touch. As I recall, you used to be quite a player."

Brock hesitantly dribbled the ball, then lifted off to send it flying. It hit the rim and toppled off, eventually bouncing against the driveway.

Rob snagged it and shrugged. "No problem. It's like riding a bike. It'll come back to you . . . with practice." He tossed the ball Brock's way, and this time he aimed and hit dead-on.

"There you go." Rob nodded. "You just needed to start over. Take a second shot."

Whoa. Exactly what the Lord had been speaking to my heart regarding Brock Benson. He needed to start over. Take a second shot.

Minutes later, the guys were really going strong. I watched them, mesmerized. What was it about guys, anyway? Why was everything a competition with them?

After about ten minutes of letting them burn off some

steam, I sent Rob and Brock to their rooms with costumes in hand and instructions to try them on. Rob appeared minutes later, still a little sweaty from playing basketball but looking quite dashing in his doublet and breeches. The jacket was designed in royal colors—rich purples and blues. I'd never seen such exquisite brocade.

He'd chosen black breeches, the perfect complement. And the boots! I hadn't expected them to make such a difference, but they really topped off the ensemble. Of course, the velvet Venetian hat wasn't too shabby either. No, he looked like he'd come straight from the castle, for sure. I could only imagine the look on Marian's face when she laid eyes on him for the first time.

I reached to straighten the twisted collar on his cream-colored shirt, then stepped back for a final look. "You're going to be the king of the castle Saturday night, Rob."

"Thanks."

Then I caught a glimpse of Brock in his medieval attire. Nothing could have prepared me for the sight of him in that dark blue tapestry doublet.

"Can you help me with this, Bella?" He pointed to the laces, and I drew near to fasten them. *Be still my heart!* Once I got everything in place, I reached to fuss with the ruffled sleeve of his cream-colored shirt. "Hang on a second, Brock. You've got this tucked inside itself."

"Take your time." He looked at me with unusual tenderness pouring out of his eyes, and my heart skipped a beat. *No, I don't think I'd better take my time. Just the opposite, in fact.*

Rob took another look in the mirror and nodded. "I don't know about you, but I'm done. Can I change now? I'm still sweaty. Don't want to get it all wet."

"Of course."

He disappeared into the other room, leaving Brock and me standing . . . well, a little too close. I reached for a box of safety pins and turned to anything and everything to make me look busy.

He drew nearer than ever, so close I could almost feel his breath on the back of my neck. Startled, I looked up. He gazed at me with those beautiful eyes, and I turned my head, determined to focus on other things.

"Sorry . . . I, um, have a lot of work to do."

"Go right ahead." After a bit of a pause—and perhaps sensing my discomfort—Brock shifted gears. "So, how did you and Marian meet, anyway?"

"Oh, Marian heard about Club Wed from her friend Sharlene. Sharlene was my very first customer after I took over the venue."

"Really? What sort of wedding did she have?"

"It was a Boot-Scootin' bridal extravaganza." I giggled, remembering what a night it had been. "And I think Sharlene was pretty happy with the way things turned out, because she recommended us to Marian. And the rest, as they say, is history."

"So, thanks to a woman named Sharlene, we now know each other." He stood near once again. The smell of his cologne wafted over me, making me a little nervous.

"I . . . I guess you could say that."

He took his finger and traced my cheek, which caused me to flinch.

"Do you believe in karma, Bella?"

"Karma?" *Um, no.* "What brings that up?"

Brock slipped his arm around my waist, drawing me close. "Sometimes I think I must've done something really great in a previous life to have things so good now. And when I meet a girl like you . . ." He took his fingertip and brushed it along my hairline, sending a shiver down my spine. "Well, let's just say I'm even more convinced."

I took a giant step backwards, my mind reeling. There were so many things I wanted to say, but I could hardly think of where to begin. I finally managed a few words. "Brock, you're a nice guy."

At once his expression shifted. "Gee, thanks."

As he came close once again, I took another step back. "And I'm sure you've got a thousand girls who would fall all over themselves to get to you."

He shrugged. "I'll admit there are a few out there who've tried, but there's something about you, Bella . . . You're different."

"Brock." I exhaled. Loudly. "Look. Here's the thing. I love D.J. Neeley, and D.J. Neeley loves me. I'm flattered that you're attracted to me, but that's about it."

His smile faded. "Ah. I see."

"No, I don't think you do. I think you're attracted to me—at least in part—because you see the love of God in me. And in my family. We're . . . well, we love each other and we love him. And that's pretty irresistible."

Brock stepped backwards, folding his arms at his chest. "What do you mean?"

"Tell me what's going on in your heart, Brock. In the deep places."

"The deep places?"

"I saw the look in your eyes that day on the Strand. You have a story. Beyond the Hollywood hype, I mean."

Brock grew silent, but I could see his Adam's apple bobbing up and down. When he finally spoke, his words stunned me. "It's not what you're thinking."

"Meaning, it's not a woman?"

"Oh, it's a woman all right. Just not what you're thinking." He paused a moment and then said, "It's my mom."

Okay, he was right. That wasn't what I was thinking . . . at all. "Your mom? What do you mean?"

He exhaled loudly, and I could read the "I don't really want to talk about this, but you're going to make me do it anyway" look in his eyes.

"What, Brock? We've been through a lot together over the past couple of days. You can be honest with me."

"Look." He turned to me with a hint of accusation in his eyes. "You're not going to get this. You've got parents who love you and the picture-perfect family. You're right about all of that."

I wanted to laugh at his assessment but held it inside when I saw the serious look on his face. Instead, I said quietly, "I never said they were perfect . . . just that you'd fallen in love with us."

"What's not to love? You Rossis are like something from a Norman Rockwell painting. I never knew what that was like. My dad left when I was two." Brock shifted his gaze to the floor. "And my mom . . ." He began to pace the room. "She wasn't around much either."

"Meaning . . . "

"Meaning she worked. Mostly nights."

I paused to think about that. Poor guy. Sounded like he'd missed the idyllic upbringing I'd enjoyed. Suddenly my heart grew heavy for him. "So, were you a latchkey kid?" I asked. "You stayed with a sitter?"

"No, you're not getting this, Bella. My mom worked nights . . . with men."

"Ooohhh." Yikes. After a moment's pause, I worked up

the courage to ask a couple of questions. "How old were you when you found out?"

He shrugged. "Maybe eight or nine? I just remember the first time she brought a guy home." He shook his head. "Anyway, let's just say I was ready to get out of there by the time I was in my teens."

"Do you have a relationship with her now?"

Another sharp exhale from Brock clued me in. "She's contacted me several times over the past four or five years. Ever since I won that first Academy Award. She wants money. She always wants money."

"W-what did you do?"

"I sent some the first time. And the second. It didn't take me long to figure out what she was doing with it. She's been drinking for years. When I talk to her on the phone, it's obvious. Most of the time, she can't even remember we've talked." Brock shook his head. "So, this happy family of yours . . . it's a little surreal to me."

Instead of giving a quick response, I chewed on his words awhile. "Can I ask you something?"

"Sure. I'm pretty much an open book."

"Have you forgiven your mom?"

"Forgiven her?" He turned to me with a hardened expression. "Forgive her for dragging me from apartment to apartment, school to school? Forgive her for leaving me alone late into the night while she was off doing whatever it was she did?"

"I'm not saying you should condone her actions. Just wondering if it's possible for you to release her so that God can heal your heart."

"God?" Brock shook his head again. "I should've known it would come down to that."

"Well, here's the deal. It does come down to that. It always comes down to that. If he spoke the world into existence, don't you think he can fix whatever pain you're feeling?"

Brock shook his head. "Listen, I'm sure this stuff is the norm in Texas. And maybe in the forty-eight other states. But in Hollywood"—he spoke the word as if Hollywood somehow qualified as its own state—"let's just say you'd be a minority and leave it at that."

"I'm sure that's true. But I know God wants to reach you, whether you're on Galveston Island or walking down the red carpet in Hollywood, California."

He rolled his eyes.

Shaking my head, I fought to think of what to say. "Brock, I'm going to answer the question you asked earlier."

"What question?"

"You asked me if I believed in karma. The answer is no. I don't. Want to know why?"

"No, but I have a feeling you're going to tell me anyway."

I tried not to let his words sting. This was too important. "People who believe in karma have the idea that their actions in some former life have somehow brought about the good or bad situations they're now going through, right?"

He shrugged. "That's the short version. There's a little more to it than that."

"The Bible teaches the opposite of that. We're given only one life. One. And what we do with it is so important. But even with that, my ultimate destiny isn't based on how good or how bad I am. It's about accepting what Jesus did on the cross. That changes absolutely everything."

Brock sighed. "See, there you go—"

I cut him off. "I don't believe in karma because doing so

would mean I'm totally responsible . . . for everything. I can't even imagine what it would be like to play God in my own life. I'm too busy just trying to be human."

And right now, staring into Brock Benson's pain-filled eyes, I felt more human than I had in a very long time.

17

That Lucky Old Sun

On Tuesday morning, Sophia awoke in a foul mood. I understood her angst, really. After all, the guys were leaving on their yachting trip today. Still, she went a little overboard with the drama as they loaded up my SUV. I'd never heard so much heaving and sighing.

Not that I really had time to think about Sophia's woes. My mind was still troubled from the conversation I'd had with Brock yesterday. How would we get past this awkwardness?

Minutes later, Rob was ready to leave. However, we couldn't find Brock. I walked through the various rooms of the house, hunting for him. Finally I heard his voice coming from the kitchen. I stepped inside and saw him standing next to Rosa, who was looking at a piece of paper.

"It's all about inflection," he said. "Inflection is everything."

"Inflection?" She looked at him, her brow wrinkled. "What do you mean?"

"I mean your phrases have to have some highs and lows. Otherwise you come across sounding monotone. Here, let's run that line again. And this time, emphasize the words *food* and *passion*."

She began to read the words from the paper she held in her hand. "I've been cooking most of my life, and food is my passion."

"Better," Brock said with a smile. "But I think you've got more in you. Think about when you were a young woman. You loved to cook?"

"Oh yes!" Her eyes sparkled. "And people in my village came from all around to taste my food."

"No doubt!" He smiled again. "That's the enthusiasm you need as you deliver the line, Rosa. Tap into those feelings you had as a young woman, when people would show up at your family's restaurant to eat something you cooked. Let that feeling drive your words. People will sense it and really believe you. That's what you want, right? For people to believe you?"

"Of course!" She delivered the line once more, this time sounding like a consummate pro. When she finished, Brock yelled, "Bellissimo!" then gave her a kiss on the cheek. "I think you're the best, Rosa. And I hope this gig on the Food Network opens lots of new doors for you. If anyone deserves that, you do."

Rosa gave him a hug and whispered, "Thank you."

See, Lord? He has a good heart. Can't you take that and build on it?

I knew, of course, that he could. I just wasn't sure if he needed my help doing it.

As we climbed into my vehicle, I tried to keep the conversation light. Still, as I caught a glimpse of Brock's eyes in the rearview mirror, I felt the tension reappear. Rob went on and on about their plans, particularly the part about the deep-sea fishing they planned to do, but I was only half listening. My heart ached for Brock. More than anything, I wanted him to understand God's love. But I knew he wouldn't listen to me now. He'd completely shut me down yesterday.

Lord, I blew it. I got in the way, didn't I?

D.J.'s words flitted through my mind. What was it he had said? *The seeds have been planted, Bella. God will take care of the rest.* Maybe the Lord would do just that over the next four days. I needed that time to focus on my bride-to-be and her big day.

We had no sooner backed out of the driveway than I saw Tony's car in the street. He ambled our way, and I gasped. "Brock, hide!"

Brock reached for the newspaper Rob had tossed in the backseat and opened it, covering his face. Tony rapped on Sophia's window, and she pushed the button to roll it down.

"Hey, Tony." She kept her voice steady.

"Hey, Sophia. Where are you going? I was hoping I could talk you into going to Moody Gardens today. They've got that new butterfly display, and I know you like that."

"Oh, that's so sweet." She paused. "But I have plans. We're taking Vinny and his best friend Rob to the pier. They're leaving on a yachting trip for a few days."

A look of sheer relief passed over Tony's face when he heard that "Vinny" was leaving. He squinted as he peered through the open window. Glancing back, I realized Brock had the newspaper up and was hiding his face.

"Hey, Vinny. Good to see you again." Tony gave an abrupt nod.

"You too, man." Brock brought the paper down, revealing only his eyebrows.

"Well, have a nice trip." Tony looked longingly into Sophia's eyes, but she rolled up the window so quickly he never had time to say anything else.

As we pulled away, Rob piped up. "Seems like a great guy, Sophia. And it looks like he's really hung up on you."

"You think?" She shrugged. "Maybe. But we're just friends."

Just friends, my eye. Before Brock had showed up, Sophia and Tony's affections for each other were clear to everyone in the Rossi family. Now, suddenly, she'd forgotten Tony even existed? Was my little sister really so easily swayed by a handsome actor with a mansion in Malibu?

Obviously.

Tony remained the topic of conversation as we made the trip to the marina, where the guys were set to meet up with the other groomsmen and board the luxury yacht belonging to Rob's dad. Growing up in Galveston, I'd seen a lot of yachts, but this one was impressive. The Marquis 55 LS stood tall and wide with sleek curves and ultramodern styling. The sleek white paint glistened under the morning sun.

"Whoa." I squinted against the glare the boat gave off. "She's a beauty."

"Thanks." Rob nodded in my direction. "My dad's sure proud of her. And I'm a little on the proud side too. Did you see what we named her?"

I squinted against the sunlight, smiling as I read the words *Maid Marian* on the side.

"Awesome. Hey, speaking of Marian, is she coming to see you guys off?"

"No." Rob chuckled. "She's having her final fitting for her wedding dress, and the last time I talked to her, things weren't going so well."

"Oh no! I'll call her soon, I promise."

"That would be great, Bella." He gave me a smile. "And in case I haven't already said it ten or twenty times, I think you've done a great job with all of this. You've made my bride's dreams come true. No small task, considering the sort of event we had in mind. But you've done everything and more."

"Thank you. That means a lot to me, Rob." I looked back at the words *Maid Marian* on the boat, suddenly struck by something. "So, if she's Maid Marian, does that make you Robin Hood?"

Brock snorted as he passed by with a suitcase in his hand. "He's Robin Hood, all right. Always stealing from the rich to give to the poor."

"Hey, I don't steal." Rob shrugged, then turned my way. "I'm involved with a couple of missions groups through my church—one in Nicaragua and the other in Ecuador. The kids in that part of the world are . . ." He shook his head. "Well, they struggle. We'll just leave it at that." He gestured to the boat. "Now, me . . . I've never struggled a day in my life. Grew up a spoiled rich kid. Went to work for my dad at seventeen. I've done pretty well for myself. So I balance things out by giving—as much as my heart tells me to give."

"The problem with his generous heart is he's always after me to join him," Brock said. "I've never been to Nicaragua."

"Yeah, but surely you can relate to kids who struggle." I gave him a knowing look, and he shrugged.

"We all have our struggles." With a curt nod, he disappeared onto the yacht with Sophia on his heels.

Rob's father approached. I liked the silver-haired gentleman right away. He chatted at length about his boat, the pride evident in his voice. When he finished, I asked if he'd give me a tour, and he agreed.

"Man." I let out a whistle as we descended into the boat's interior. The beautiful hardwood cabinetry clued me in to the fact that this was no shabby ship. And the crafty layout of the galley and bedroom space was pretty impressive too. The leather seats at the table were the real deal. No faux stuff here. Even the linens on the beds impressed me. Talk about luxurious!

"How many people does this thing sleep, anyway?" Sophia asked.

"Six comfortably. Eight uncomfortably." Rob laughed. "But there are just six of us counting my dad, so we're good to go."

I leaned close to Rob to ask the next question. "And your dad's a good navigator?"

"The best. I'm not half bad myself." He gave me a confident nod. "Don't worry, Bella. We've done this dozens of times before."

"Right. But never four days before your wedding. Have you given Marian your itinerary?"

"Yes, I left a copy with her. She can fax it to you. We plan to go pretty far south into the gulf, then spend some time deep-sea fishing. We'll have the radio going at all times, so we'll never be out of contact with others. Not to worry—we'll be back by Friday morning in plenty of time for the dress rehearsal Friday evening."

"Who, me? Worried? Do I look worried?"

He laughed. "I wish I had a picture of your face."

"Okay, I'm a little worried. I'd hate for the groom-to-be to get distracted by a big fish and forget to come home in time for his big day. I read *Moby Dick*, by the way. I know how long these fishing trips can be."

Instead of laughing at my little joke, Rob looked at me with such seriousness in his eyes that it threw me a little. "Bella, I'm going to tell you the truth. Marian is the best thing that's ever happened to me. I love her more than life itself. I can't wait to get back. So . . . no worries."

Relief swept over me, and I whispered, "Agreed."

We helped the guys unload their supplies, and I did a quick visual, making sure they had adequate life jackets. Out of the corner of my eye, I watched as Rob's dad checked their fuel and went over their navigational plans. Looked like he knew what he was doing. Not that I really doubted Rob. I just found myself fretting over such a risky venture this close to the big day.

When I heard unfamiliar voices, I looked down the pier to discover several groomsmen headed our way. I'd never met most of them, but Rob quickly remedied that. They looked like a stalwart crew, and my fears gave way to common sense. This was just a group of guys headed out for a fishing trip. Nothing dangerous.

No worries, Bella. God has this under control.

The guys went into full-out prep gear, and Sophia and I took our cue to exit the boat. We watched from the pier as *Maid Marian* revved her engines and headed out to sea. Hopefully both she and Robin Hood would return in one piece at the expected time.

Sophia and I left the guys at the marina and headed back home. She spent most of the drive staring out of the window, and I thought I heard her sniffle at one point.

"You okay?"

"Mm-hmm." She sighed with a bit more dramatic flair than usual, which was really saying something.

"What?"

"This is all just a foreshadowing of things to come."

"Huh?" Since when did my sister talk like that?

"Brock is leaving in less than a week, and I need to get used to the idea that he's going back to Hollywood. Back to the land of glitter and glitz, where the women are beautiful and the men are . . ." She started to cry. "Where the men are about as far away from Texas as the sun is from the moon!"

Wow. I needed to fix this—and fast. "You want to stop at Starbucks for a white chocolate mocha frappuccino?"

"Uh-huh." She followed this with another award-worthy sigh.

I understood her plight, of course. She'd fallen head over heels for Brock. Who could blame her? He was tall, dark, and handsome . . . and he'd invited her to the opera, for Pete's sake. Talk about a dream date!

Of course, she had no idea he'd expressed an interest in me just yesterday. All she saw was the handsome face, the broad shoulders, and the stylish clothing. Well, that and his millions.

Right then and there, I wanted to tell her. Wanted to share what had happened just yesterday with Brock. But I didn't tell her. Protecting my sister's heart was key.

Then again, I couldn't help but wonder if keeping this information to myself was the best way to protect her heart. On the other hand, if I offered her a white chocolate mocha frappuccino, she might just forget the whole thing.

Yep. Suddenly that sounded like the perfect option.

18

How About You?

On Tuesday around noon, I met D.J. at Parma John's for lunch. This was the first time in days I'd actually had a chance to kick back and spend time with my guy without thinking about the wedding. Or the Food Network. Or Brock Benson.

Anxious thoughts tumbled around in my head as I considered facing D.J. I'd wrestled with myself through the night, trying to figure out if I should tell him about Brock's advances. While I wanted to be completely open with my hunky cowboy, I wondered if he would flip out, maybe make too much of it. After a serious amount of prayer, I decided to drop it. To leave things in the Lord's hands. Surely he knew best. Besides, I needed to relax. Spend time with the man I loved.

When I walked into the restaurant, I found it crowded as usual. Tuesdays were always pretty crazy because of the Pennies from Heaven Special—a large meatball pizza. I couldn't wait!

As I made my way through the crowd, I saw D.J. waiting for me at the counter. I smiled when I saw his parents sitting next to him.

"Why didn't you tell me?" I asked as I drew near. My arms immediately went around Earline's neck, and she responded with her usual bosomy hug.

"We're headed down to the state park again," Dwayne Sr. said. "So I'm glad the weather is cooperating."

"It's our monthly meeting with the motorcycle ministry," Earline said.

That would explain their attire. Both Earline and Dwayne Sr. were wearing their jackets with the emblem SHADE TREE BIKERS—HITTING THE TRAIL FOR JESUS.

"I thought I saw a Harley in the parking lot but didn't make the connection." I nodded.

"That's our baby." Earline's eyes immediately filled with tears. "Oh my! I guess it *is* our baby, now that the boys are grown." She reached for a napkin and dabbed her eyes, then offered a winsome smile. "It keeps us busy, and that's a good thing."

"What are you guys eating?" I sat down on the barstool next to Earline.

"You have to ask?" D.J.'s eyebrows elevated.

"Nah." I knew they'd probably ordered the Pennies from Heaven. Everyone did.

"I'm not sure why we're eating anything at all." Earline laughed. "I had some of the folks from church over last night and made chicken-fried steak, mashed potatoes and gravy, and green beans. Oh, and homemade yeast rolls."

My mouth watered at the revelation. I'd tasted Earline Neeley's chicken-fried steak before and knew it was the best in the state. Probably in the country.

"You ate chicken-fried steak without me?" I offered what I hoped would look like a convincing pout, and Earline laughed.

"Next time I'll invite you. But I know how busy you are with the wedding and all."

"Speaking of busy, what did you think of your son in that opera performance the other night?" I asked.

Earline's eyes filled with tears once again. "Oh, Bella. It's the craziest thing. As a mom, you always pray for your kids. You want them to grow up and be all they're called to be." She paused a moment and shook her head. "I always knew Bubba could sing. From the time he was a little guy in church, he would sing his heart out. It was such fun to watch him because he never paid much attention to what people thought. Just gave it his all."

"Both of our boys are worshipers," Dwayne said. He reached for his cappuccino and took a swig, then glanced at D.J. "But Earline's right. You never know how things are going to turn out. Just because your boy can sing when he's little doesn't mean he's going to do anything with it when he gets older."

"Though, of course, you hope he will." Earline smiled. "But when I saw him on that stage the other night . . . when I saw him up there, singing his heart out, I realized that God had gifted him, not just so that he could minister to people in the tiny town of Splendora. God gives us gifts so that we can make a difference for the kingdom. And sometimes that means getting out of your comfort zone."

"I can tell you for a fact, Bubba was way out of his comfort zone." D.J. chuckled.

"I'm still not sure how I feel about my boy wearing tights," Dwayne said, shaking his head. "But I have to agree with

Earline about all the rest. It's nice to see your kids using their gifts." He reached over and slapped D.J. on the back. "That's why I'm so thrilled with what you're doing down here, helping folks rebuild their homes."

"Thanks, Dad." D.J. smiled at his father, then cleared his throat. "Actually, that brings up another subject. I've been wanting to tell you about this man I met named Willy Maddox. He's an African American pastor on the west end of the island. Both his church and his home were destroyed during the hurricane."

"Oh, D.J., that's awful!" Earline reached to touch his arm, such a sweet gesture that I paused to take note of it. "What's going to happen to him?"

"Several of us in the construction business are helping to rebuild his home. We're putting the finishing touches on it now. We managed to get vendors to donate most of the supplies to get the house fixed up. But the church . . ." D.J. shook his head. "That's another situation altogether. The whole thing's got to come down and then be rebuilt. It's going to be a huge project, and I can't afford to take it on by myself."

As I listened to D.J. pour out his heart, I was overcome with pride. How many men spent so much time focused on others and not themselves? Very few these days.

"What can we do to help?" Earline asked.

"Glad you asked." D.J. grinned. "Since you've got your motorcycle ministry meeting today, this is the perfect chance to mention it. When the time comes, we're going to need workers. Contractors. Laborers. Regular Joes. Anyone and everyone who can swing a hammer."

"But first you have to come up with the money?" Dwayne asked.

"Yes. That's a prayer request. But since you're going to be

with praying people, I'm sure you won't mind passing along the message."

"Not at all." Earline nodded. "But honey, let's don't wait till then to pray. Let's pray right now." She bowed her head and ushered up a Holy Ghost–anointed prayer, one that caused several people around us to turn and stare.

Not that I was looking.

When she finished, I smiled at her. "Earline, I want to be a prayer warrior like you."

With a wave of her hand, she said, "Girl, it's easy. Whenever someone tells you they need prayer, don't say, 'Oh, I'll be praying about that.' Stop right then and there and pray with that person."

"R-really?"

"Sure! Might be tough at first. And, of course, you might not always be in the best place to pray. But do it if you can." She giggled. "You know, I've prayed just about everywhere. In women's restrooms. Hospital waiting rooms. Hotel lobbies. Airport gates. You name it, I've been there. And here's the best part—God was there too. That's why it was so important to stop right then and join him!"

Jenna showed up with our pizza just then, and I pondered Earline's words. She was clearly a woman of great faith. And great courage. If she could stop in a ladies' room and pray with a complete stranger, she must be.

What kind of family was this—these Neeleys? They used their God-given talents for others. They gave freely. They put others first. They genuinely cared about people. They prayed for people, even in public places. They shared the gospel freely.

These were all things to aspire to. Oh, I wanted that kind of free-flowing faith, the kind that lived out what you believed on a day-to-day basis. Not that I didn't already have it, at least to some extent. But being with the Neeleys made me want to go deeper. To give more.

As I bit into the spicy pizza, I pondered all of these things. How could I begin again with the Neeley brand of faith?

Maybe, like our pastor said on Sunday, I just needed a fresh start.

19

Too Close for Comfort

Later that afternoon, I found Uncle Laz sitting at the dining room table alone, looking more downcast than I'd ever seen him.

"What's up?" I drew near. Surely this had something to do with Rosa.

"It's Sal."

I gasped as he mentioned his friend's name. "Is he . . . did he . . . ?"

"No." Laz shook his head. "Nothing like that. He's recovered from his stroke and wants Guido back. He said he's planning a trip down here in a few weeks to get him."

"Oh no!" My heart nearly broke for Uncle Laz. Though everyone else found Guido a bit of a nuisance, he'd taken a liking to the old bird. In fact, I had my suspicions Laz would really grieve when his colorful sidekick left.

"I guess it's for the best. I've been training Guido for weeks, after all. Hopefully he'll remember the plan of salvation and the Lord's Prayer. Those are the important things."

"What? You didn't ask him to memorize Leviticus too?" I grinned.

Laz gave me a hug. "I can always count on you to cheer me up, Bella."

"And vice versa."

As I walked away from Laz, I had to admit he'd needed more cheering up than usual lately. What was up with that?

I didn't have time to think about it for long. A knock at the door interrupted my thoughts. I answered it, surprised to find Phoebe and Dakota standing there. Talk about God's merciful timing! Thank goodness Brock was gone.

Something about this mother-son duo looked a little . . . off. Phoebe appeared dazed, but Dakota just looked mad.

Phoebe nodded my way. "Bella, would you mind if we came in? Dakota has something he'd like to say to you."

"Um, okay." I gestured for them to come inside, and within seconds Mama joined us.

"Phoebe! I didn't know you were stopping by. What's up?"

"Dakota has something he needs to say to Bella."

Mama offered a gracious smile. "Well, come into the living room. Let's get comfortable."

I had a feeling I didn't want to be comfortable. In fact, I had a feeling I might never be comfortable again.

As we settled onto the sofa, Phoebe reached into her oversized handbag and came out with a tiny camera, which she handed to Dakota.

"Go ahead, Son."

He groaned as he clicked the camera on. Extending his palm upward, he seemed to be waiting for something else.

She handed him a long cord, which he plugged into the camera. Then he walked over to our television and linked the camera to it.

"What is this?" Mama asked with a laugh. "Home movies?"

"Hardly." Phoebe gestured to Dakota, who flipped a switch on the camera.

Our television filled with a huge image of Brock and me sitting on the front porch. I gasped, then looked at Dakota, who shrugged.

"You think that's something, look at this one!"

The screen now filled with another image. In this one, Brock had his hand on my arm and was looking into my eyes. Great. I could almost read the caption in the newspaper now: IS THE PIRATE TAMING ANOTHER LADY?

"They get better," Dakota said.

The next one had to have been taken from his roof. It was a picture of Brock opening the car door for me. Great. The picture that followed was the two of us sitting next to each other in the front seat of my car.

I shook my head, not quite believing this. The kid had made invasion of privacy a full-time business.

"Just a couple more," Dakota said, messing with the camera.

I gasped as the photos of Brock dressed as Vinny DiMarco filled the screen. These were the shots Dakota had gotten at the opera. But why?

After those, a couple of shots of Brock and Rob playing basketball appeared. I groaned, realizing Dakota had followed our every move over the past several days. How much was his silence going to cost our family?

As the pictures cycled back around to the one of Brock

and me on the porch, Phoebe turned our way with a woeful sigh.

"First, I have to apologize. I would never allow my son to take pictures of anyone without their permission, especially someone like"—she pointed at the screen—"Brock Benson."

Oh man. We were sunk. Totally, completely sunk. And Rob and Marian were going to kill me, no doubt about it. This whole thing was sure to upset their big day.

"I should have known something was up when Dakota wanted to stay home from school on Friday," Phoebe said with a sigh. "He said he had the stomach bug."

"Hey, my stomach did hurt," he said.

"I had my doubts but left him anyway. There was so much to be done that day." Phoebe turned to my mom. "You remember, Imelda. That's the day I went up to the opera house to help some of the other ladies finish the programs. I think you went to town that day with Earline to go shopping."

"Of course. We found a fabulous dress. Did you see it?"

"Oh yes. It was beautiful." Phoebe paused. "But anyway, I left Dakota at home with the maid. She's watched him before, but, well . . ."

"What?" I asked, fearing the worst.

"I should have known he was up to something, because when I got home, I found him on the computer. He's never allowed to use the computer when I'm not home, and he knows that." Her words grew more forceful, and she gave Dakota a stern look. "Anyway, I didn't know what he was up to then, but . . ." She groaned. "I do now. It's been rather startling, actually."

I rose from the couch and began to pace the room, then looked at Dakota. "Just spill it. What did you do?"

He shrugged. "What anyone with half a brain would do."

Phoebe rose from the sofa with tears in her eyes. "I got a call this morning from the *National Enquirer*, asking for Dakota. They wanted to know about the pictures."

"No!" I turned to him, stunned. "Tell me you didn't! You sent them the pictures?" Suddenly I felt like I might faint. Or hurt someone. One or the other.

"I didn't send them anything." He laughed. "I'm not that dumb. I wasn't going to give them the pictures until we talked money. I figure they're worth at least a couple mil, don't you? I mean, c'mon! This is Brock Benson we're talking about. He's a hot commodity. Front and center in the gossip rags."

Ugh! I wanted to strangle the kid. Instead, I drew in a couple of deep breaths and turned to my mother. "What should we do?"

"I don't know." She laced her fingers and released a sigh. "I'm clueless."

"Well, I'm not." Phoebe walked over to the television and unplugged the camera, which she then yanked from her son's hand. "First of all, he's grounded for the rest of his mortal life. Second . . ." She fiddled with the camera, finally getting it to cooperate. "I'm destroying every picture."

Dakota let out a cry, but I had a feeling it was exaggerated. Likely he'd dumped the pictures on some flash drive or CD. I'd be sure to tell her privately to look for them. And she would also need to block his emails and phone calls before he could do further damage.

Still, I blamed myself for this. We'd taken a risk by sitting out on the front porch that day, and an even greater risk by driving Brock around the island. Once he returned from his yachting trip, we'd have to be much more careful. If we lasted that long. From the looks of things, the paparazzi would be showing up sooner rather than later.

As I pondered these things, Phoebe turned to Mama with tears in her eyes. "I'm horrified at what my son has done. I can't tell you how horrified."

"Oh, honey, don't worry too much about it," Mama said. "These things happen."

"No, you didn't let me finish." Phoebe drew a breath. "I'm embarrassed and ashamed, but I'm also upset—at you, Imelda!"

"W-what?" Mama stammered. "What did I do?"

"It's what you didn't do." Phoebe spoke in a passionate voice. "I cannot believe you—my best friend in the world—didn't tell me you had a movie star living in your house! It's simply not fair!"

"Oh, honey!" Mama threw her arms around the overly emotional Phoebe. "I wanted to! You don't know how badly I wanted to. But I was sworn to secrecy. Actually, we're *still* sworn to secrecy. Brock is here for the wedding Bella is coordinating this coming weekend. He's the best man."

So much for secrecy. Now Dakota had the photos *and* the story. No telling what he would do with this much information.

Somehow the conversation shifted. Thank God. Phoebe and Mama got to talking about Bubba's performance at the opera. Talking about that led to a conversation about how beautiful Mama had looked the night of the opening. Talking about that, of course, led to a conversation about the beauty secrets Mama had so recently learned from Twila and the other women. At this point, my mother was really in her element.

"Oh, Phoebe, come upstairs with me!" Mama grabbed her

by the hand. "I'm going to show you my secret stash of good-
ies. But you can't tell anyone what you've seen! Promise?"

"Promise!"

Seconds later they were headed up the stairs, where I knew
my mother would pull out the hemorrhoid cream, Pepto Bismol, and sugar—all important ingredients in her skin-care
regimen.

Well, let them have their time together. Mama had the un-
canny ability to forgive and forget very quickly. I understood
that. I could forgive, no problem. But, forgetting? That might
be a different issue altogether.

From across the room, I caught Dakota's eye. He had that
"What are you gonna do about it?" look, but that didn't faze
me. Oh no. He'd almost taken me down, but I was on to him
now. I wouldn't let this wedding be foiled by a ten-year-old.
No, I'd watch my back.

After I pulled the knife out of it.

20

Come Rain or Come Shine

Wednesday was spent making phone calls. I telephoned Marian, asking about her dress. She responded with a lengthy story about the alterations lady, who'd overcharged her and done a shabby job. I couldn't blame her for getting emotional. I'd be upset too, especially if I'd spent that kind of money on a dress. And besides, a bride had only one chance to show off her special gown. It had to be perfect.

"Did you get it taken care of?" I asked when her conversation finally slowed.

"Oh yes. I went to my future mother-in-law's house, and her sister fixed it. I should've just asked her in the first place but didn't want to be presumptuous."

"Be presumptuous, girl! It's your wedding day!"

She laughed, and then we talked about the construction of the castle.

"Have the people from the set design company come yet?" she asked.

"They're coming tomorrow morning," I said. "No worries. They'll get the exterior walls up first and will come back on

Friday to work on the inside. I understand from the pictures the guy showed me that they're using some sort of shiny teal fabric to create a river effect around the castle. And they're putting in gas lamps. It's going to be a ton of work."

"Wish I could be there," she said, "but I'm up to my eyeballs in RSVPs. You wouldn't believe how many people wait till the week of the wedding to let you know they're coming. Or not coming. It's nerve-racking!"

"Oh, I'd believe it, trust me. I'm in the wedding business, remember?"

"Oh, that's right." Marian giggled. "Well, I'd better hang up before I get caught up in chatting and forget I'm supposed to be getting my hair trimmed and my nails done. These are important things."

"Yes, they are. A bride has to look her best. Though"—I couldn't help but laugh as I said this—"I'm not sure nail polish is exactly authentic to the time period."

"I know, I know." She laughed. "But a girl's gotta do what a girl's gotta do."

"Tell me about it."

When I ended my call with Marian, I called to check on the wedding flowers. Marcella assured me she had everything under control, asking only a couple of questions about the floral arches. That done, I turned to the table linens and seat covers, making sure everything was clean and pressed. Oh, if only people realized how much work went into events like this!

The hours zipped by, and before I realized it, evening's shadows were falling. Yikes! Likely the whole family was sitting around the dinner table. I'd better get home—quick!

As I entered the house, I heard the sound of voices coming from the dining room. Sure enough, they'd started without me. Oh well. Maybe Rosa would forgive me just this time.

Thankfully, no one much noticed as I entered the room. Their eyes were fixed on Sophia, who looked like she'd been crying. I took my seat and filled my plate, wondering if she would say anything. When she didn't, I turned her way.

"What's happened?" I asked.

Sophia shook her head. "You . . . you haven't been listening to the radio?"

"No." My heart began to race. "What happened, Sophia? Tell me."

"There's a tropical disturbance headed for the gulf."

"No way." I almost dropped my fork. "Are you sure?" My gaze shifted from person to person at the table. Everyone had that same somber look. A gripping sensation took hold of my heart. Our little island had already been through enough. We didn't need another storm. And the guys . . . they were out there. Somewhere. What would happen to them if they got caught up in the midst of it? "How could this have happened?"

"I listened to the weather report just before dinner," Mama said. "The forecasters said the tropical depression came up so quickly, they never knew what hit them. It took everyone by surprise, including the experts."

"Wow."

"Yes, and they're predicting it will turn into a tropical storm just as quickly." Sophia's voice trembled, and I knew she was thinking of Brock. Who could blame her? I couldn't help worrying about him myself. And the other guys, of course.

"Not a hurricane?" I asked.

She shook her head. "No. I've been watching the Weather Channel, and they don't think it's that bad. But even a tropical storm could be catastrophic if the guys are in a yacht. Right?"

"Right." I shook my head, trying to erase the image. Not

only did my thoughts go to the men on the yacht, they traveled to the wedding as well. Would a storm prove to be our undoing? *Lord, help!* "When?" I asked, dreading the answer.

"It's expected to hit land tomorrow night."

"Surely they have access to the National Weather Service on the boat, right?" I looked to my pop for support, and he nodded.

"They should, hon. And if they think they're in trouble, they'll send out an SOS. More likely, though, they'll catch wind of what's happening—pun intended—and head back home. I'm predicting we'll see them tomorrow before the storm hits. They'll race it to shore."

"I hope so," Sophia whispered.

"Either that, or they'll head west to McAllen, near the Mexico border. The storm isn't supposed to go that far south."

"McAllen." I shook my head, trying to imagine how we could possibly have a wedding with the groom on the border of Mexico.

Over the next few seconds, I forced my thoughts into alignment. While I didn't have any control over this, I did need to spend some time figuring out how it might affect everything we'd planned. Provided the groom made it back in time, of course.

Okay, so the storm is coming ashore on Thursday. That gives us all day Friday and even part of Saturday to get things in order. The wedding isn't till Saturday night. We can do this. I know we can.

Still, I could hardly imagine putting up the castle on muddy ground. What was it the Bible said about building your house on sinking sand? Did mud count? Were we destined to fail?

Sophia's gaze shifted to the table. "I don't know what to do," she whispered. She looked up, her eyes filled with tears.

"What do you mean?" Pop asked, shoveling a bite of food into his mouth. "Do about what? You can't control the weather, baby."

Sophia's shoulders began to heave, and before long sobs erupted. As she finally came up for air, I heard her stammer, "I . . . I . . ."

"Sophia, what is it?" I looked her way, startled. While my sister was prone to emotional outbursts, something about this seemed different.

"I . . . I'm in love with Brock Benson," she whispered. "And I don't know what to do about it."

You could've heard a pin drop at that revelation.

"Well, honey . . ." Mama reached over and took her hand, giving it a comforting squeeze. "Who says you have to do anything about it?"

"Don't you see?" Sophia's gaze circled the table, drawing us in like flies to honey. "He could be swept out to sea. I might never see him again." She sighed. "That would be a Hollywood ending all right, wouldn't it? But I don't like that ending. I want another one."

Okay, now she was being dramatic. Was this really about him . . . or her?

"It's much more likely he'll come back, and everything will move forward as planned." Pop nodded, as if that settled the whole thing.

"Yes." She sighed. "But what if he comes back, does his thing in the wedding, then goes back to Hollywood and forgets that I even exist?"

"I somehow doubt he'll forget any of the Rossis," I said with what I hoped was a comforting smile. "It's more likely he's going to go on remembering us for years to come."

"Maybe. But which Rossi will he remember? You know?"

Ah. I got it now. She was worried he might have feelings for me . . . and that those feelings would somehow cause him to forget she existed. After my latest run-in with him, I couldn't really argue. Not that I wanted his attention. No, right now I just wanted to get him home so he could be the best man in a wedding. Nothing more.

Mama looked at Sophia with her brow wrinkled. I could tell she was worried about this latest revelation. "Sophia . . . Brock hasn't given you any indication that he . . ."

"A girl can hope, can't she?" My sister had an almost frantic look in her eyes.

"Yes, she can." I nodded, but I didn't say what was really on my heart. After all, Sophia was the sort to get her hopes up almost every time a handsome guy walked into her life. I'd seen her heart broken at least a dozen times since high school and didn't want to see her injured again, especially with someone who didn't share her faith. Besides, strange as it was, I still held out hope that she and Tony might actually continue their relationship.

The rest of the meal was spent in a somber frame of mind. Afterward, as Mama and Rosa headed off to the kitchen, Pop and Sophia settled on the sofa to watch the Weather Channel. I slipped out onto the veranda to call D.J. He answered on the third ring, his familiar twangy voice bringing joy to my heart.

"Bella, I was just thinking about you."

"Happy thoughts, I hope." I smiled as I took a seat on the porch swing. Somehow, just talking to D.J. made me feel better.

"Very happy thoughts. How are things on your end?"

"Everyone over here is fretting over the storm. Did you hear about it?"

"Yeah." He sighed. "I did. Hope it doesn't interfere with your wedding."

"Same here." Now I was the one sighing. "Just feels like everything is so hard. Nothing in my life comes easy."

"Yeah, but you appreciate things so much more when you have to work for them," he said. "And I know you, Bella. You're strong. You'll weather this." He chuckled. "Funny. Didn't even mean to say it like that. But you will get through this medieval wedding, rain clouds or no rain clouds. It's going to be great."

After several more consoling words from D.J., I finally headed back inside. By the time I ended the call, I felt much better about things. My pop gestured for me to join him on the sofa, so I placed my cell phone on the coffee table and sat down.

Nestled in my pop's arm, I felt like a kid again. We'd done this countless times through the years, after all—waited on storms to blow in. I always knew my daddy would protect me, of course, and it felt so good to hide under the shadow of his comforting embrace. But Sophia, who sat on Pop's other side, was on the edge of her seat, eyes and ears glued to the television. I watched in silence.

Sure enough, the forecasters were already predicting a tropical storm. And to make matters worse, reporters were headed to the island so that they could broadcast live. After our last big storm, this one would be of great interest to people around the country. All eyes were on tiny Galveston Island once again. And just in time for the wedding.

And the Food Network! I gasped as I remembered. Would the tropical storm keep the folks from the Food Network away? I hoped not. For the first time, I really prayed—fervently, even—that Rosa would still get her big break. She of all people deserved it.

Pop turned away from the Weather Channel and sighed. "So, we're about to be inundated with reporters from the mainland."

"Sounds that way." I shook my head, overwhelmed by all of this.

"And they're coming for a story."

"Yeah."

He shook his head, and I could almost read his mind. We were two peas in a pod when it came to things like this. He was likely thinking of the potential disasters that awaited us if the newshounds found out Brock Benson was out in the gulf with a major storm approaching. Surely they would be on that story in no time.

As if to somehow solve the unsolvable, Pop reached for the remote and clicked off the television.

"Hey, what are you doing?" Sophia looked at him, clearly irritated.

"The Bible says, 'You have not because you ask not.' Well, we're going to ask—for a miracle. We're going to pray that those boys come home safe and sound. And we're going to pray a hedge of protection around our home and the wedding facility too."

As Pop bowed his head to pray, I reached to take his hand. His strong, steady voice brought the same comfort and assurance it had given me as a child. Suddenly I was little Bella Rossi again, ear tuned to her daddy's loving voice.

A message for my current situation, perhaps?

21

Between the Devil and the Deep Blue Sea

The guy from Stages Set Design must not have gotten the memo about the incoming storm, because he arrived at the wedding facility on Thursday morning at 9:00, as planned. The huge moving trucks—three of them in all—lined Broadway. I stared in disbelief, wondering how or if we should move forward with this. According to the newscasters, we had only eight or nine hours until the outer bands of the storm came ashore. Until then, sunny skies reigned. But once the storm blew in, who knew what would happen? If the walls to my castle fell in, would I be held responsible?

Turned out Larry, the set-design guy, knew all about the storm. "Doesn't sound like it's going to be a big one," he said with a wave of his hand. "So we're better off getting the flooring and walls in beforehand. If we wait till after, the ground will be too wet. Not a good scenario. Trust me on this, okay?"

"Okay." So I'd been right with my sinking-sand theory. Getting the foundation in place before the storm was the better bet. Still, I had to wonder what would come of all of his hard work when the winds got to blowing.

I watched Larry and his guys work for a couple of hours, mesmerized by both their speed and the prevalent sunlight overhead. Seemed like that's how it always was—the sun seemed to shine brightest right before a big storm. What was up with that?

D.J. showed up at 11:30 to help with the castle construction. As I watched him work, my heart skipped a beat. Now this was a true knight in shining armor—always here when we needed him. And it didn't hurt that the boy had muscles that went on forever.

At noon, a couple of guys from the Food Network arrived at our house with papers for all of us to sign. There were liability waivers, privacy forms, and even some legal mumbo jumbo about how we wouldn't hold them responsible if something negative about our family aired on their program. That one gave me reason to pause, especially in light of all we were going through. I had no idea things could get this complicated.

As we signed the final form, Mama looked up at one of the men with a concerned look in her eyes. "So, you plan to move forward in spite of the storm? Is that right?"

"We're hoping it'll pass in time. Our main concern now is electricity."

Good point. Sometimes we went without power for days or even weeks after a big storm. Still, I hoped that would not be the case this time around. I made a commitment to pray specifically about the power situation.

I prayed for something else too. As the skies overhead darkened, I prayed with every fiber of my being for Rob, Brock, and the others. Marian had managed to get through to Rob on her cell phone earlier this morning, and he'd given us an update. They were trying to race the storm home, just as Pop had predicted. But would they make it?

At 4:00 D.J. joined me inside since Larry and his crew were leaving for the day. Soon after, Marian showed up at my door with all of her bridesmaids in tow. Her eyes were swollen and red. "Bella." She took a few steps into my house and threw her arms around me. "I haven't heard from Rob in over three hours. He's not answering my calls. You've got to help me. If something has happened to him, I don't know what I'll do."

I ushered all of the ladies inside but kept my attention on Marian. "Deep breath, honey. The first thing we're going to do is call the Coast Guard. They'll know what to tell us. Likely they know just where the guys are."

She nodded. "Rob's dad is an experienced navigator. He's made this trip dozens of times before and has fought a few storms. I'm not sure why this one has me so unnerved."

"It's only natural. And you have no control over things. That's always hard." I smiled before adding, "And, of course, there is that part about your wedding. Maybe you're a little nervous about all of that."

"You think?" A hint of a smile graced her lips, and I saw a sparkle in her eyes beyond the tears.

"I don't know much about traveling in a yacht," I said, "but I was there when they loaded up, and they've got plenty of supplies."

"Yes. And I know Rob." Marian looked a bit more confident now. "He's always listening to the radio with the National Weather Service information. They drone on and on, but trust me, he hears what he needs to hear when he needs to hear it. And they've got the ship-to-shore radio in case of emergency."

"Of course. And again, they've done this before."

Within minutes we heard the first peal of thunder. The entire Rossi clan—along with Marian and her entourage—gathered together in the foyer, the only room in the house without windows. Well, unless you counted the window on the front door.

Settling down on the floor, I rested my head against D.J.'s shoulder, whispering, "I'm so glad you're here."

"Me too. I wouldn't be any other place." He kissed me on the top of the head. "But I have to admit, it's a little different riding out a storm down here on the island. Splendora's so far north that we usually don't see much action."

"I'm hoping it won't be bad here either."

The bridesmaids chattered incessantly, but their conversation slowed as those first few raindrops fell. I could sense the tension in the room but tried to relax. Tried to put my mind on other things.

Just when I'd almost accomplished my goal, someone pounded on the front door, startling us all.

"Who would be out in the middle of a storm?" Pop asked, making his way to the door.

"Someone pretty desperate," Mama said.

Turned out it was someone pretty desperate—Tony, checking on Sophia. As he came rushing through the door—his clothes wet, his usually perfect hair in wet curls—my sister glanced up at him with a casual, "Oh, hey, Tony. What are you doing here?"

The whole Rossi clan released a collective sigh. When would she get it? After all these years of jumping from one boyfriend to another . . . after so many broken hearts . . . here stood a perfectly great guy—and handsome to boot—ready to pledge his love. Only she clearly didn't get it. Or didn't want to.

Strange how much had changed since Brock walked in the door. Two weeks ago, Sophia would've given her eyeteeth for Tony to show her this kind of attention. Now she didn't seem to see that he existed at all.

Tony took a few steps in her direction, but Rosa stopped him in his tracks. "You're dripping all over the rug, boy. Let me get you a towel." She sprinted out of the room, then returned with a large beach towel, which he used right away. Then he turned in Sophia's direction.

"Can I sit next to you?" he asked.

"What?" She looked up, appearing completely distracted. "Oh, sure. I guess so, Tony."

Less than ten minutes later, the howl of the wind met the first sheets of rain in what sounded like a musical performance. D.J. looked up at the ceiling and whistled. "Whoa. Hope she holds."

"She will," Pop said. "This house has survived dozens of storms over the years, and she's standing strong."

"What do you expect?" Laz piped up. "She's a Rossi! Of course she's still standing!"

We all had a good laugh at that one. I glanced over at Marian, who hadn't said a word since her call to the Coast Guard. She gripped her cell phone, waiting for that one call that would change everything for the better. Unfortunately, it never came. The bridesmaids more than made up for her silence, however. I'd never heard so much mindless chatter. You would think we'd all gathered together for a party, not a storm.

We sat huddled together for much of the evening, and I

kept a watchful eye on Marian. As the storm raged, I held my shivering Yorkie-Poo in my arms. Several times she let out nervous whimpers. I didn't blame her. I was scared too. Finally, as the winds slowed, she fell asleep in my arms, a comforted child.

Was this how God felt, perhaps, when I finally relinquished my fears and gave myself over to his protection during the storms of my life? Did he want to reach down and pat my head and say, "It's gonna be okay, Bella. Just sleep."

Likely.

At 6:45 the power went out. We were prepared with flashlights and candles. And, of course, Pop had an emergency generator. Not that he would use it. No, it would be reserved for tomorrow, if the power problems lingered.

I wondered about that for a moment. What if the storm passed but we were left without power for several days? Could we still hold the wedding?

Somehow thinking of that got me tickled. A true couple from the Renaissance era wouldn't have had electricity anyway. So, if they could do it, we could do it! Somehow.

Glancing over at Joey and Norah, I had to smile. The two were a picture of peace and tranquility, curled up in each other's arms. I'd never seen two people better suited to each other. Well, almost never. I reached up to give D.J. a kiss on the cheek, and he responded by drawing me close.

By 8:15 the worst of the storm had blown over. Most everyone in the room had dozed off, with the exception of Marian, D.J., and me. The winds eventually slowed. For that matter, so did my breathing. Again I realized just how anxious I had been. But now . . . well, the worst appeared to be behind us.

Or was it?

Suddenly our front yard came alive with lights.

"What is that?" I jumped up and peered out the window on the front door, squinting as I was met with a blinding glare.

"Did the power come back on?" Sophia asked, coming awake.

"No. The lights are coming from . . ." I squinted again. "Headlights?" Sure enough, a car had pulled into our driveway. Two more cars had parked in the street. The blinding light appeared to be coming from one of them.

"What is that?" D.J. asked.

We got our answer seconds later when the loudest banging in human history nearly knocked our front door from its hinges.

"I'll get it." D.J. headed that way and inched the door open. Seconds later he cried, "I don't believe it!"

The whole group of us rose as we heard the voices of Rob, Brock, and the other groomsmen. The bridesmaids all began to squeal at once, filling the foyer with their high-pitched voices.

Marian raced across the room and threw herself into Rob's arms, wailing at the top of her lungs. "I'm so glad you're alive!"

Sophia rushed to welcome Brock, who looked like something the cat had dragged in. She threw her arms around Brock's neck and began to weep. Loudly.

One by one the others were all led into the foyer, dripping water all over Mama's precious Persian rug. Rosa, being the practical one, went to look for towels. The bridesmaids were happy to help.

Joey and Norah headed off to the kitchen to make sandwiches. Always thinking of others, of course.

Tony looked at Brock and Sophia, apparently a little confused. Bit by bit recognition came into his eyes. "Wait a minute." He pointed to Brock. "You're not Vinny DiMarco."

Oh, yikes!

"Well, technically, I am," Brock said, extending his hand. "But these days I usually go by my stage name—"

"Brock Benson," Tony said, his jaw hardening. He glanced over at Sophia, then shook his head. "I get it now. I guess you have been a little distracted."

With a nod of his head, Tony disappeared out the front door . . . and into the storm.

My heart ached for him, but what could I do? Sophia sure didn't seem troubled by his disappearing act. She kept her attention on Brock.

As the guys toweled off, I asked the obvious question. "What in the world happened?"

"We raced the storm back home," Rob said. "Almost beat her, but those last few miles were rough."

Marian smacked him in the arm, and he responded with an "Ouch!"

"I've been calling you for hours on your phone and your dad's. Why didn't you answer?" she asked.

"I lost my phone. It went overboard about seventy miles out from shore when the winds picked up. We tried to reach you on my dad's phone probably twenty times, but the call wouldn't go through. It would act like it was going to . . . and then nothing."

"I tried on my phone too," Brock said. "Nothing. No service. We got to the marina over an hour ago, but the weather was just too crazy to drive here. We waited till things slowed down, then Rob's dad brought us over."

We would have continued the conversation, but the blinding light from outside grew even brighter. Brock walked over to the window and groaned as he looked outside.

"Rob, I think I was right about those cars." He turned back to face us. "They followed us from the marina. They must've picked up on our conversation with the Coast Guard. We had to give officials the names of everyone on board."

"So . . . the media knows you're here?"

When Brock nodded and said, "I guess," I swallowed hard. No telling what would happen next.

Turning back to the window, Brock shrugged. "I should've given them my legal name. No one knows who Vinny Di-Marco is. But under the stress of the moment, I just let 'Brock Benson' slip out." He released a sigh. "Not that it matters, really. They'll go away eventually. They always do." He turned to face Marian. "Still . . . the last thing I wanted to do was draw any media attention on the week of your wedding. I'm so sorry about all of this, Marian."

"Brock, I don't care about that anymore." Marian's voice broke, and she spoke through her tears. "I'm just so glad you guys are safe. I . . . I was afraid . . . I was afraid there might not be a wedding. I was afraid Rob was . . ." She dissolved into tears, and Rob swept her into his arms.

"It's okay, baby. We're safe and sound." He held her close for a couple of minutes and turned to all of us. "There's going to be a wedding, and it's going to be great."

Brock yawned, and I turned to him with a smile. "Looks like you could use some sleep."

"Yeah." He stifled another yawn. "A hot shower would be great too."

"With the power out, there's not going to be much hot water," Mama said.

At this, the guys flew into action. Brock hollered, "First

dibs!" then raced up the stairs with Rob and the other guys on his heels.

It didn't make sense to send the guys to the Tremont this late, and the condo Marian had rented was too close to the water's edge to be considered safe. No, they would all stay here—with us. Mama and Rosa took inventory, trying to figure out where everyone would sleep. They finally came up with a workable plan, one that used up every bed, sofa, and floor space.

By 10:30, everyone had eaten and the house was silent and still. D.J. and I sat on the bottom stair, and I leaned my head against his shoulder. He slipped his arm around me and drew me close.

"Tough night," he whispered.

"Mm-hmm." A shiver ran down my spine. "When I think of what could've happened to those guys out there . . ."

"I know." He grew silent for a moment, then added, "I was really worried too."

"You were?"

"Yeah. Spent a lot of time praying for them. Rob is a great guy, and Brock . . ." His voice drifted off.

"What about him?" I asked.

D.J.'s voice wavered a bit as he spoke. "Bella, I really like him. He's a lot of fun and a really talented guy. But we both know that personality and talent won't get you into heaven. I was worried that something might happen to him before . . ."

"Before he came to the Lord?" I asked.

"Yeah." D.J. drew in a breath. "I'm mighty glad he's back safe and sound. Hoping God can use this near miss to somehow get through to him."

"Me too." I leaned over and gave D.J. a kiss on the cheek. "You're sweet, you know that?"

He shrugged. "I am?"

"You are." I paused a minute, and my stomach rumbled.

"Hungry?" D.J. asked.

"Starved!"

We took one of the smaller flashlights and snuck into the kitchen, looking for something to eat.

"Thank goodness the lights are out," I said, reaching for some of my aunt's homemade cookies. "If Rosa knew we were in here, she would—"

"She would what?" Rosa's voice rang out, startling me.

"She . . . would tell me to take not just one cookie but two!" I grabbed them from the cookie jar and giggled. Pretty soon we were all laughing. And by the time we finished, I felt better about everything. The storm. The wedding. Brock Benson's spiritual journey. Everything.

Yes, tomorrow was definitely going to be a better day. I could feel it in my bones.

22

Young at Heart

By Friday morning the storm had almost passed, and—wonder of wonders!—the power was back on. Rob and his groomsmen headed off to the Tremont—minus Brock, of course. And Marian drove her bridesmaids back to the condo. As much as I'd loved having them all here, I enjoyed the peace and quiet even more.

After they left, I lay in my bed, curled up under the covers, listening to the last remnants of rain on our roof and a light breeze whistling at our windows. Though things were pretty tame now, the wind had really whipped up in the night. I could only imagine what the castle looked like. Was it even still standing? If so, could I really pull off a wedding there by tomorrow night?

I'd just started to play out the possibilities in my head for the hundredth time when the doorbell rang. Precious took this as a sign that we were under attack and began a yapping frenzy. When would the dog learn that incoming guests were just that—guests?

I managed to get her calmed down and went into the hall-way, where I found Pop heading down the stairs.

"Who in the world would come knocking at our door this early in the morning?" He yawned and slipped on his robe.

"Maybe someone needing help," I said. "Or . . ." I paused, thinking about the men in the cars last night. "Maybe the paparazzi looking for Brock. Better look through the glass before opening the door, just in case."

I followed him down the stairs and noticed the reflection of something shiny hit the glass panes on the front door. Through the glass I saw someone—make that several some-ones—in a shimmering haze of color. They were almost blinding, in fact.

Pop opened the door, and I gasped as I saw Twila, Jolene, and Bonnie Sue standing there in their sequined dresses. Jolene's beehive hairdo was lopsided, Twila's makeup was smeared all over her face, and Bonnie Sue looked like she'd been crying. Their bags were mangled, but they held on to them for dear life.

Precious took one look at the women and flipped. I'd never seen her yap with such vigor. Likely the sight of these be-draggled ladies scared her to death.

"Sister Twila!" I threw my arms around her. "Are you all right?"

I felt her trembling as she responded. "As all right as a person could be after a near-death experience."

I ushered them inside, and Pop and Joey helped with their bags.

"What in the world happened?" I asked, leading them into the dining room.

"Th-the tropical storm." Twila's voice trembled as she took a seat at the table.

"We were in the middle of the gulf on that big cruise ship," Bonnie Sue added. "And then the storm hit."

I gasped, realizing that in all of the chaos I'd completely forgotten the trio of sisters had also been in the gulf. *Lord, forgive me! I forgot to pray for them!*

"Our ship wasn't due here till Sunday, but they brought us back two days early." Twila slumped over, looking like she might pass out at any moment. "Don't know when I've ever been so tired."

"Me either," Jolene said, leaning against the wall. "I feel like I could sleep for a week."

"I just need to get my car and go home." Twila yawned. "That's why we came here first, to get my car. But it appears to be MIA."

"Ah, that's right."

"Where is it, Bella? Did the winds pick it up and fly it away?"

I smiled at the image of her pink Pinto sailing over the house. "Funny story." I hoped she would find it funny, anyway. "We took it to D.J.'s house on Bubba's wrecker so it wouldn't be in the way during the wedding tomorrow night."

"Oh dear." She groaned. "Why did you move it with a wrecker? Why not just drive it over?"

"For some reason, I couldn't find your keys all week. Mama didn't have them. Rosa didn't have them. And if you gave them to me, I must've somehow misplaced them. I hope you'll forgive me. And I hope you have a spare set."

"Sure. I always keep a spare. But I could've sworn I gave you my original." Twila fished around in her purse, coming up with the set of rhinestone-studded keys. "Oops." She sighed. "I guess I've made a real mess of things."

"Not at all. But you're stuck with us for the time being." I reached out to take her hand. "You don't need to be driving until you've had some rest. After you sleep, we'll go and get your car."

"Yes, we'll take care of that for you," Joey said. "You ladies should get some rest."

Just then I thought I caught a glimpse of someone on the front porch. Through the dining room window, I could make out a blue shirt and dark pants.

"Is that the Burton kid?" I turned to Joey. Moving into the foyer, I headed toward the front door. Pop, Joey, Twila, Jolene, and Bonnie Sue all followed along behind me, as if I were the Pied Piper. As I swung open the door, I came face-to-face with a strange man with a camera in his hand. A flash went off, nearly blinding me, and I let out a bloodcurdling scream. That didn't seem to faze him.

"I'm a reporter with the—"

He never had a chance to finish. I yelled, "Get off our property before I call the police!" then slammed the door in his face. The noise awakened just about everyone in the house. Mama and Rosa came sprinting down the stairs, still dressed in their nighties. They took one look at the trio of sisters and began to squeal with delight. Then Mama turned my way.

"Who was that at the door, Bella?"

"I . . . I think it was the paparazzi!"

Bonnie Sue looked as if she might faint as she heard the word. "P-p-paparazzi?" She looked at the other sisters. "Do . . . do you think they're after us?"

Joey snorted with laughter, then quickly tried to disguise it as a sneeze. Nice attempt, anyway.

Twila giggled. "I don't know, honey, but I guess it's possible." Turning to me, she explained. "We were a smashing success on the ship—with the passengers and the captain."

"Oh?" I wasn't sure what this had to do with the paparazzi, but I kept listening.

"Yes. And we had the prestigious honor of being asked to sit at the captain's table. How do you like them apples?" She beamed with delight.

"The captain's table?" Mama looked shocked. "How did that happen?"

I could hardly believe this news myself. To sit at a captain's table usually required knowing someone pretty important. Or *being* someone pretty important.

"Well, here's the thing." Jolene smiled. "One of the gals who judged the big karaoke event heard us singing and told him all about it."

"Singing?" This was news.

"Oh, honey . . ." Bonnie Sue giggled. "We were all the rage last night at the big karaoke final. But anyway, back to the story. The next thing you know, there we were, dressed in sequins, singing for the captain. It was the fancy night, you know."

"Fancy night?"

"Formal night," Twila said with a yawn. "They have at least one formal night per week on the ship, so we got trussed up like chickens in our opera dresses and moseyed in to meet the captain. He heard us sing, then asked us to sit at his table. But I think . . ." Twila leaned in to whisper. "I think he had his eye on Jolene."

"Oh, hush, Twila." Jolene giggled. "No doubt the man is just nice to everyone. But I must admit he's the handsomest man God ever did put on this earth. Oh, you should've seen him, ladies. He was tall and tanned, with a silver moustache and perfectly placed silver hair."

"Perfectly placed, humph!" Bonnie Sue laughed. "There's a reason it was perfectly placed. The man was wearing a hairpiece."

"Oh." Jolene's expression darkened. "Anyway, his name is Bjorn and he's from Norway."

"Of course." Mama nodded. "They're all named Bjorn." *They are?*

"Bjorn's wife died a few years ago," Twila said. "He's a widower now."

"Poor guy," I said. "So now he spends his days traveling the seas?"

"Yes, and he meets literally thousands of beautiful women," Bonnie Sue said. "But the fairest of them all—at least from what we could tell—was Jolene."

"Wow." I didn't know what to say, but Rosa sure did. She jumped on the story with full vigor.

"That's the most wonderful thing I've heard in years, Jolene! I'm so happy for you. In fact, I'm so taken by your story that I might just have to go on a cruise myself." Rosa took Jolene by the arm, giggling like a schoolgirl.

I could almost envision my aunt on a cruise ship. Of course, there would be that one little problem at dinnertime. She rarely ate food that she hadn't cooked herself. Still, if we could overcome that one obstacle, she'd probably have the time of her life.

Rosa apparently wasn't ready to let go of the story about the captain. "I'm trying to imagine what sort of courtship you would have with the captain of a cruise ship, Jolene," she said. "Will you have to live at sea if he asks you to be his?"

"Oh, I haven't thought about that." Jolene frowned. "I

don't know that I could ever leave Splendora. I love my friends and my church. They had a little chapel on the ship, but it's just not the same thing."

"What a barrel of pickles this is." Bonnie Sue sighed.

Jolene's eyes filled with tears. "Well, I don't suppose I have to marry the captain. I can just dream of him. He can be that one special memory I have of a beautiful cruise to the Caribbean."

"Jolene!" Twila shook her head. "It wasn't a beautiful cruise to the Caribbean. We were swept out to sea by a hurricane."

"Technically, it was a tropical storm," I said. "Not a hurricane."

Twila's eyes narrowed as she turned my way. "Honey, call it what you like, but when you're on the inside of a metal tube, hurling this way and that, a sprinkle can feel like a hurricane. We were trapped inside there like sardines, and I didn't think we were ever getting out."

"Thank God we found some other believers and went to prayer," Jolene said.

"Oh?" This piqued my interest for sure.

"Heavens, yes," Twila said. "You know what the Bible says about two or more being gathered together. So we went on a hunt for Christians. And by the time we were in the eye of the storm, we had a real prayer meeting going on. In the casino, no less. Even the captain joined us."

"That man can really pray." Jolene sighed. "That's how I knew he was the right man for me. Handsome and a good pray-er—the perfect combination."

I had to admit, I understood that last part. After all, D.J. was one of the best pray-ers I'd ever met. And it went without saying that he was handsome.

What could I make of this story? The poor ladies had almost been lost at sea and still managed to find the good in the midst of the bad. Unfortunately, it looked like they were fading quickly. I offered them two rooms—mine and Sophia's—and they headed upstairs for what I hoped would be a good long nap. After all, I had work to do. With the skies finally clearing, I saw my first glimmer of hope that this show—er, wedding—might just go on!

23

Send in the Clowns

Once the ladies were safely tucked into bed, I followed Pop, D.J., and Joey outside to check out the damage.

As was always the case on the day after a big storm—particularly one in early October—the air was hot and sticky. You could almost cut through it with a knife, it was so thick. I'd been outside only a few minutes when my clothes were soaked, not just with perspiration but with the air itself. I prayed this icky feeling would lift before the evening.

Looking around, I examined our properties—both the yard surrounding our house and the wedding facility. Thankfully, we hadn't lost any trees. I didn't figure the winds had been strong enough for that. But we did have a lot of broken limbs and piles of wet leaves, which the guys went to work cleaning up right away.

The ground was soggy, and my shoes were plenty muddy by the time I reached the area at the back of the wedding facility. Yet the castle was standing strong. She'd served as a fortress from the storm. I could hardly believe it. Looked like she was on a strong foundation after all.

Larry—my guy from Stages—arrived at 9:00 in the morning, took one look at the soggy area behind the wedding facility, and sighed. "Not the most ideal situation."

"But workable?"

"I guess. I'll keep you posted. Thank God we've already got the foundation in place."

"Yes, thank God for a good foundation." I smiled as I thought about his words. "How long do you think it will take?"

"Oh, maybe eight or nine hours."

"Yikes. Did I mention the rehearsal is at seven?"

"Mm-hmm. And did I mention that a tropical storm just blew in off the gulf?"

"Right. Got that."

Minutes later a truck pulled up in front of the Rossi home. I sighed as I read the words THE FOOD NETWORK on the side. Finally, the moment I'd been dreading. Rosa would get her foray into the spotlight, but would it interfere with the plans next door?

A young guy with a ponytail hopped out of the truck and put a hand over his eyes, squinting. I approached him, and he extended his hand. "Rosa Savarino?"

"No, I'm her niece. She's inside."

The man nodded and waved the rest of the crew out of the vehicle. One by one they came, until the house was filled with people, equipment, and pure chaos. Guido didn't take this interruption lightly. He squawked and squalled, making a general nuisance of himself.

I led our guests into the kitchen to meet Rosa, and introductions were quickly made. The producer, who introduced

himself as Shawn, gave instructions. "We're going to be setting up lights in the kitchen and the dining room. We'll film
in both places. We'll get several clips of you cooking, then a
few more of the whole family—and maybe a few friends—
seated around the table."

"What time do you think you'll be shooting that part?" I
asked. "Because I need to . . ." I didn't finish.

Shawn looked at his watch. "Maybe around six? We want
to catch the sun as it's going down so it really looks like you're
having a normal family dinner."

"There's nothing normal about our family dinners," Laz
said, passing by.

Shawn laughed. "Well, we want to make it look as normal
as possible, so we'll need everyone there. And we're going to
do some clips of family members talking about Rosa and her
cooking too," he said. "So get ready for that."

At this point, Guido took to singing "Amazing Grace."

"Laz, if you don't shut that bird up, I'm going to . . ."
Rosa didn't finish her sentence, probably not wanting to look
bad in front of the company. And the cameras. Already the
cameramen were at work, testing their lenses and checking
the lighting in the house. Anything we said from this point
forward could—and probably would—be used against us.
On a national television program, no less.

The makeup people swept in and spent a couple of hours
making Rosa look like an Italian beauty queen. They dressed
her in a sparkly top and black skirt and dabbed on some
makeup. I had to admit, she looked pretty snazzy. The only
concession she wouldn't make was with the hair. It went up
in a bun, as usual.

"She looks like the real deal with her hair up," I whispered
to the producer. "You want this to be authentic, right? Well,
that's our Rosa."

"Got it." He smiled. "She's really something, isn't she?"

"Oh yeah. And just wait till you taste her cooking. You folks are going to sweep her off to New York, and we're never going to see her again." A tight feeling gripped my heart as I uttered those words. Though I'd meant them in jest, it now seemed completely possible.

Shawn grinned. "We're counting on this meal being great. Do you know how much fast food we've eaten on this trip?"

I could only imagine.

"I'm telling you, Rosa is hands down the best Italian cook in the country."

Shawn motioned for me to keep talking and signaled for the cameraman to get some footage. Suddenly I was very thankful I'd touched up my makeup.

"So, what have you learned from your aunt over the years?" Shawn asked.

"Too much to share in a one-hour show!" I laughed. "She's always made cooking seem like so much fun. You should've seen the kinds of games we played growing up." I couldn't help the smile that crept up as I remembered every one. "Rosa would play 'Name That Spice' with us. That was our favorite."

"How did that go?" Shawn asked.

The memory was suddenly so real, I could almost smell the spices. "She would fill small plastic bags with different spices, most fresh from the garden. There was always oregano, of course. And basil. But then there were some trickier ones. Rosemary. Nutmeg. Fennel. Thyme." I closed my eyes, remembering what each one smelled like. I opened my eyes and smiled. "Anyway, she would line us kids up in the kitchen and give us a piece of paper with the names of the spices on it. We had to match the bags with the names on the paper, and the child who got the most right would get two desserts that night."

"Not a bad deal," Shawn said. "So who won?"

"Most of the time my brother Nick. He's a born chef, just like Rosa. Oh, and just like Laz. My uncle is great in the kitchen too. We're just a family of great cooks. Well, some of us, anyway. Not all."

"What about you?"

"M-me?" Yikes. No one had ever asked me about my cooking skills before—that I could remember anyway. Did I dare confess? "Um, yeah, well . . . I can't even boil water."

"How is that possible?" he asked.

"Easy. Rosa's so good that I'm afraid anything I attempt would always and forever be compared to her stuff. So, for now anyway, I'll go on being spoiled by her cooking."

"And if she ever moves . . . ?" Shawn asked the question I'd been struggling with just a few minutes earlier.

"I think we'll keep her." As I turned to the camera with a smile, I caught a glimpse of the clock on the wall: 10:30. I'd better get busy.

Pop engaged the producer in a titillating conversation about his lactose-intolerance problem. Great. Just what I wanted flashed on national television—my father's aversion to cheese.

Lord, help me. Please.

I headed out to the veranda, smiling as I saw D.J. working in the yard. He took a break and headed my way. He must've picked up on my anxiety because he started massaging my shoulders right away. I melted under his touch.

"Oh, man, that feels good."

"Stressed, huh?" he asked.

"Yeah. I've been dreading this day for a week now. I don't want anything to ruin the rehearsal tonight. But I don't want to hurt Rosa's feelings either. So I need your help."

"Whatever you need, babe. I'm here for you." He wrapped me in his arms and planted a kiss on my forehead.

"Okay, what about this. I'm going to come and go from the wedding facility to the house. That way I can keep an eye on the set construction guys and still let Rosa know I'm there for her. Whenever they get ready to film, I want to be right there, in the room. If they'll let me."

"I'm sure they will. But how can I help?"

"Let's just tag team, okay? Whenever I'm over there, you stay here with the family. Whenever I'm here with the family, you keep an eye on the castle."

He laughed. "Sounds funny. Keep an eye on the castle. But I'm fine with that. Anything you need." He released a yawn, and I sighed.

"I hate to ask you to help when I know you're so worn out, but I'm so glad you're here. I really mean that. I wouldn't have made it through the last week or two without you, D.J."

"Just the last week or two?" He gave me a rehearsed pout.

"You know what I mean." I gave him a kiss, in case he had any lingering doubts.

"So what's Vinny DiMarco going to do all day?" he asked, rolling his eyes.

I sighed. "No idea. Probably hide out. Seems like that's what he spends a lot of his time doing."

D.J. shook his head. "I wouldn't want to trade lives with the guy, that's for sure. I might be your average Joe, but at least I'm free to come and go as I please without paparazzi following me."

"First of all, you're not an average Joe. Not even close."
I gave him a wink. "Second, speaking of paparazzi, would
you mind keeping an eye out for them? I have a feeling that
with all the action going on around here, they're going to
pounce."

"Will do. But Bella, listen." He gave me a round of kisses,
then gazed into my eyes, causing my heart to do that crazy
flip-flop thing. "I want you to promise me you're going to
relax. You will get through this. God's got it under control,
so just take a deep breath, okay? No worries."

"No worries." I nodded, thanked him for his help, then
sent him on his way. As I watched him amble across the yard
in the direction of the wedding facility, I remembered the first
time I'd laid eyes on him, just a few months ago. Then, I'd
been attracted to his physical attributes, no doubt. He was
easy on the eyes, after all. But now I saw so much more. D.J.
Neeley's handsomeness started on the inside and worked its
way out.

Just then I heard a whistle from above. I looked up and saw
Brock leaning out of an upstairs window. Hmm.

"Want to do the scene from Romeo and Juliet in reverse?"
he asked. "I'm tired of being cooped up in my room."

"If you think I'm climbing up the trellis, you've got another
think coming." I laughed, then squinted up at him against
the glare of the sun. Yep, Brock Benson was handsome for
sure. But nothing could compare to the man in the cowboy
boots who'd just disappeared into the castle next door. D.J.
Neeley was the real deal.

Determined to stay focused, I turned to Rosa and the rest
of the family—at least for now. Soon enough I'd be trading
places with D.J. for round two.

We received another guest just before the cameramen

started setting up for their first scene. Eugene, our UPS guy. He arrived with a package in his hand for Laz.

"What's going on around here?" he asked, trying to peer around my uncle into the house.

"Pure chaos. Rosa's going to be on television."

"No kidding! Rosa? On TV? I should go and congratulate her." He took a few steps inside the house, smiling when Rosa greeted him.

"Eugene, you've come for my big debut! Thank you!" She threw her arms around him in an overly dramatic fashion, and I chuckled.

Laz didn't find it particularly humorous, apparently. He took one look at Eugene wrapped in Rosa's arms and rolled his eyes, muttering, *"A ciascuno il suo"* under his breath. I knew what it meant, of course—"To each his own." But I had a feeling Laz didn't really mean it that way. He was secretly saying that Rosa was *his* own. If he felt that way, why couldn't he just come out and say so?

Shawn watched this exchange, motioning the camera guy to capture it all. Likely he found it humorous that the UPS guy was so enthralled with Rosa's cooking. I wasn't sure if it was her cooking or Rosa herself. At any rate, Eugene turned as red as a beet as the camera panned in on him. He managed to get out a few flattering words about Rosa, then headed to the kitchen for his usual glass of iced tea before taking off.

Just about the time they were ready to start shooting, I noticed Jenna sneaking in the back door.

"How's it going with the food for tomorrow night?" I asked.

"We've got everything prepped and ready to be cooked. In fact, Laz is going to go ahead and grill some of the meat tonight, then rewarm it tomorrow. I'm taking care of all the side dishes and sweets. Things are under control, Bella. Don't worry."

"Oh, I'm not worried." I knew they could pull it off, no matter the obstacles.

Jenna looked around at the mob of people. "Man, this is crazier than I thought it would be."

"It's the Food Network."

"I know." She giggled. "Why do you think I'm here? I wouldn't miss this for the world!"

At this point, D.J.—who'd been going back and forth between the wedding facility and the house—joined us in the kitchen. I thanked him profusely for his help, then slipped my arm around his waist as we took our places to watch the filming.

Minutes later, Rosa sat behind the kitchen island with a mixing bowl in front of her. I could see the nerves written all over her face and ushered up a silent prayer that she would find peace in the middle of this storm.

I glanced over at the spot where Guido's cage usually sat. Mama had moved it into the living room. We'd had an ongoing debate about what to do with the ornery parrot when the Food Network people were in the house. Rosa had insisted the prayer cloth would do the trick, but Brock had spent the morning testing her theory. He just couldn't seem to grasp the idea that Guido was one bird underneath the cloth and another when it was lifted. Maybe God was trying to tell him something. Regardless, the bird had been spirited away to the other side of the house, so we were good to go without any interruptions.

Shawn gave her an affirming nod. "Okay, Rosa, take us through the process of making your garlic twists."

"O-oh, okay." Her hand trembled as she reached for the

bag of flour. "I . . . I'll do that." She started mixing up the ingredients, not saying a word.

"Cut!" Shawn called out. He turned to my aunt with a concerned look on his face. "You've seen the Food Network, right?"

"Of course! I record nearly every episode of *Iron Chef*. And *Everyday Italian*. And *Ultimate Recipe Showdown*. And *Diners, Drive-ins and Dives*." She went off on a tangent, listing her many favorites.

"You left out Paula Deen," D.J. said.

"Well, that's a given," Rosa said with a nod. "Anyone who's *anyone* watches Paula. She's the queen of the Food Network." Rosa dove into a speech about all of the many people she admired, her face awash with joy.

Shawn finally stopped her, albeit with a smile. "Great! Well then, you know that our chefs have to be animated. They have to talk as they cook. They fill us in on what's going in the mixing bowl as it's going in. That sort of thing."

"Right, right." She looked at him with a nervous smile. "Let's do it again."

They did another run-through, but she sounded stiff. Off in the distance Laz watched her. I knew he had his hands full today, cooking for the wedding. What was he doing here, anyway? Wasn't he supposed to be grilling turkey legs or something?

On the other hand . . . it suddenly occurred to me that *he* was the missing ingredient in Aunt Rosa's garlic twists. She never made them without arguing with him all the way through it.

Shawn cut the cameras once again, and I walked his way. "I, um, think I have your answer."

"Oh?"

201

"You want this to be real, right? As in really real?"

"Sure." He shrugged. "As real as we can make it."

"Okay, here's the deal." I explained—in front of Rosa, Laz, and all of the other tech people—that Rosa and Laz usually argued while she cooked. At first Rosa denied it, her cheeks as red as the Roma tomatoes on the countertop. Then she finally looked at Laz with a desperate look in her eyes.

"Help me out?" she whispered. "I need you to be mean to me."

"My pleasure."

The makeup lady moved to Laz's side and tried to dab some powder onto his cheeks before he stepped into the limelight. He almost knocked her down as he moved Rosa's way.

The cameras rolled once again, and Laz joined her in the clip, poking fun at her as she got the dough ready. Their bantering went back and forth as she put the garlic twists together. Laz—to his credit—got in lots of great jabs. Rosa struck back, at one point flinging bread dough onto his shirt.

At the end of the clip, Shawn hollered, "Cut!" then walked toward my aunt and uncle with a broad smile on his face.

"I don't believe it." He stared at the two of them. "You two are a match made in heaven. How long have you been married?"

"Oh, we're not married." Laz took a giant step backwards, his hands now trembling.

"You're not?" Shawn shook his head and then looked at me. "Thought you said she's your aunt."

"She is." I nodded.

"And he's your uncle?"

"He is." Another nod.

"Mm-hmm." Shawn shrugged as he turned back to Rosa and Laz. "Well, whatever. I just know the chemistry between the two of you is priceless. The fans are going to love this episode." He looked at the bread dough, then asked, "How long before you put that batch in the oven so we can continue filming?"

"I have a batch ready to go," she said. "I'm prepared."

"I'll say." He gestured to the cameraman once again, and they filmed Rosa and Laz as she twisted the risen dough into knotted rolls. Then Rosa dipped them in melted butter, informing the audience that it had been prepared with fresh garlic and oregano. Those beautiful twists went into the oven, and Laz looked at her with a grunt.

"What, old man?" she asked.

"You're making me hungry."

Rosa snapped him with a dish towel, and a boyish grin lit his face. He reached over and grabbed her by the shoulders and did the most unthinkable thing I'd ever seen the man do. He planted a kiss squarely on her lips. Then he turned around and walked out of the scene.

I looked at Mama, wanting to shout but not wanting to interrupt the sacredness of the moment—if one could call a scene on the Food Network sacred. Laz had kissed Rosa . . . in front of his entire family and, well, the nation. I gripped D.J.'s hand and watched my aunt to see how she would respond.

"I . . . I . . ." Her cheeks looked like they might catch fire any second. "I think I'm going to have to murder that man in his sleep!" She reached for one of the twists and took off running. The cameras followed her as she let the dough fly. It hit Laz in the back of the head. He turned with a crooked grin.

"You won this battle, Rosa." He nodded, peeling the dough out of his hair. "But I'm pretty sure I won the war."

She stood there with a look of awe on her face. Finally,

Shawn yelled, "Cut!" He looked at Rosa, completely mesmer-ized. "That's the best television I've seen in years. Did you plan all of that ahead of time?"

"Um, no." She shook her head, then reached for a dish-cloth and went to work scrubbing bits of dough from the countertop. "We did not."

"Then I've stumbled into the love scene of the century!" Shawn laughed. "You two are priceless. I can't believe my luck!"

He instructed the cameraman to keep filming and gave Rosa a few instructions about closing out the scene, which she did. But I could see the look in her eyes. Half terror, half joy. All laced with the glistening of tears.

Well, who could blame her? When you'd waited over fifty years for your first kiss, you had a right to get a little misty.

24

Goin' Out of My Head

After the incident with Laz and Rosa, I decided anything was possible. Not only would we pull off this wedding on the heels of a tropical storm, it would be the best wedding anyone on Galveston Island had ever seen.

If we could just avoid the paparazzi. We had two more visits that afternoon from reporters. One of them posed as a Food Network employee, but we saw through his bag of tricks. The other one hid in our bushes, scaring the daylights out of me as I came up the front stairs.

Brock kept his distance upstairs, but I felt bad for him. Was this how he lived, hidden away from people? Sure didn't seem like much fun.

Thankfully, Twila, Jolene, and Bonnie Sue managed to sleep through all of the chaos. Who could blame them? They'd had a rough voyage. And D.J.—sweet D.J.—went back and forth from our house to the wedding facility, doing anything and everything I asked him to do. At 4:30 I snuck up on him helping Laz and Jenna with the turkey legs.

"Hey, you." I wrapped my arms around him and planted a kiss on him that he wouldn't soon forget. "Thank you so much for all your help."

"Anything for my girl." He returned my kiss, this time more passionately than before. He stared into my eyes, his baby blues making my heart flutter. "What's the plan for tonight? You've got the rehearsal, right?"

"Yeah." I sighed. "I was hoping to catch a few minutes with the family for dinner first, but I don't think that's going to happen. The Food Network is counting on a huge crowd gathered around the dining room table." I paused, then looked at him. "What about you? Do you want to stay for dinner with the family or hang out over here with us during the rehearsal?"

"Hmm." He shrugged. "Do you need my help with anything during the rehearsal?"

"Not that I can think of."

"Then I guess I'll have dinner with your family, if that's okay with you."

I gave him another hug. "I'll try to sneak over for a few minutes between the rehearsal and the rehearsal dinner to get in on the action. I don't think the bride and groom will miss me very much if I do."

"It's a date." He kissed the tip of my nose, then dove back into his work.

At 5:00 I made my way next door to check on the castle. I found Larry and his workers hanging the gas lamps and putting in the tables and chairs. I could hardly believe their progress.

When I arrived back at the house, I found Twila, Jolene,

and Bonnie Sue snacking on Rosa's garlic twists and gabbing with the men from the Food Network. Well, if one could call flirting gabbing. Thankfully, they'd changed into regular clothes. No sequins here. No sir. They still looked a little groggy but appeared to be in good spirits.

Twila took to pouting when the oldest camera guy said they needed to go out back to get some footage of Uncle Laz's garden while there was still sunlight. For a minute there I thought she might follow him, but she restrained herself. Brock chose that moment to walk into the room.

"Is the coast clear?" He looked around to make sure the television cameras had moved elsewhere.

"They're out back," I assured him.

Brock had donned a pair of black slacks and a fabulous dress shirt in an amazing shade of blue. He'd also spent a little extra time on his hair, from the looks of things. And his skin glistened from the tan he'd acquired while out to sea. Gone were the taped-up glasses. The man who stood before us was pure Adonis, no doubt about that.

Twila, Jolene, and Bonnie Sue took one look at Brock and turned to me, squealing with delight.

"Bella! You did it!" Twila said. "We weren't even gone a full week, and you've turned the ugly duckling into a swan."

"More than a swan." Jolene let out a whistle. "I don't know how you did it, Bella, but you've almost made him look like . . . " She paused, then shook her head. "Like a movie star."

"I've been reading *People* magazine," Brock whispered as he settled onto the sofa between the ladies. "Don't tell anyone, okay?"

"I read *People* magazine too," Bonnie Sue said. "But only for the news stories."

"Of course." Brock nodded, then leaned back against the seat, allowing the women to talk about him at length.

Thankfully, this Brock-a-thon didn't last long. Marian arrived at the front door with tears in her eyes. The bridesmaids fussed over her as I ushered them inside. She tossed her cell phone into her purse and turned my way.

"What is it, honey?" I asked the question with fear and trembling, unable to take much more.

"I've got some terrible news." Her voice trembled, and she paused to draw a deep breath before continuing. "The madrigal group that was supposed to sing at the wedding tomorrow night . . ."

"What about them?"

"They can't come. Their lead singer had to have her gallbladder removed. She's in the hospital in Houston."

"Can't they sing without her?"

"Apparently not. And I've been counting on them. It was going to be one of my favorite parts! What are we going to do?" I noted a hint of desperation in her voice.

Twila sat straight up on the sofa. "Honey, leave it to me."

"Leave it to you?" Marian turned her way with a confused look on her face.

Twila grinned. "You probably don't know this, but Jolene and Bonnie Sue and I used to sing together at county fairs and such. You should've seen us at the last one. We were quite the rage. Drew in a real crowd."

"Ah." A look of sheer terror came over Marian as she took in this information. The bridesmaids, to their credit, didn't say a word, though their eyes spoke volumes.

Twila nodded. "And we had quite a repertoire back in the day."

"Oh heavens, yes." Jolene giggled. "We did everything from Elvis songs to Sinatra. And a few Gershwin tunes, for the older folks."

"In three-part harmony," Bonnie Sue threw in.

Mama happened to walk in at this very moment. She looked at the women and nodded. "Earline told me all about your singing abilities. She said you were once offered a contract."

"Yes." Bonnie Sue sighed. "But Twila made us turn it down."

"Why?" I asked.

"Because the company wouldn't let us sing Christian songs. And I told the girls, if we can't sing about the Lord, they can just forget it!"

"Amen!" the other two women chimed in.

"We do occasionally sing secular music," Twila said. "Remember, I told you we sang karaoke on the cruise ship." She giggled. "And I hate to brag, but we brought the house down. That's why the captain was so taken with us. We got to sit at his table."

"I'm sure you were wonderful," I said, trying to keep this conversation on the positive side. "But this wedding is medieval. We're talking music from the 1500s and 1600s. And it's a cappella, which would be tricky under the best of circumstances."

"Don't underestimate the power of God working through us!" Twila said. "Do you have any samples?"

"I have a CD in my car," Marian said with a hopeful look on her face. "Would you like to hear it?"

"Sure."

Minutes later, I listened in a state of disbelief as the trio of sisters joined voices to duplicate one of the songs they'd been listening to on the CD. It was remarkable, really. They sounded just like the real deal. Better, even. Why had I doubted them? The bridesmaids went crazy—in a good way—and I could read the relief on Marian's face.

"You're hired." She extended her hand in Twila's direction, beaming from ear to ear.

"But . . . what will we wear?" Jolene asked, tugging at a loose hair. "The things we packed for the cruise won't work for a madrigal presentation."

"Oh, that's right." Twila took a seat on the couch, her brow now wrinkled in concern. "They didn't have sequins during the Renaissance era, did they?"

"No." Marian bit her lip and sighed. "I don't know what to do about that part."

"Oh, I know!" Mama said. "The opera house has a huge wardrobe room filled with costumes from every production over the past ten years. You ladies come with me and I'll get you suited up in no time." She glanced at her watch. "*The Marriage of Figaro* doesn't start for another couple hours, so we have time. C'mon." She grabbed her purse and headed for the foyer.

"But . . . I'm not a small girl," Jolene said with a pout. "I doubt any of those costumes will fit."

"This is the opera we're talking about here." Mama turned back with a smile. "I can assure you we'll find costumes to fit. Now come with me, ladies. We can listen to that CD on the way over. In fact, I'll even have Francois, our vocal coach, give you a few pointers. And when we get back to the house, we'll talk about how to do your hair for the big night."

"Just one problem." Twila's words stopped us cold. "If we hang around for the wedding, we'll have to look for a place to stay tonight. Should we book a room at a hotel?"

"I doubt you could get a room," I said. "They fill up mighty quick whenever we have a storm."

"What are you talking about? Hotel?" Mama looked stunned. "You're staying at the best hotel of all. The Villa de la Rossi. You can have Sophia's room, and she can sleep in Bella's."

I tried to envision the three women all sleeping in Sophia's double bed but stopped myself before the chuckles took hold. The trio disappeared out the front door on Mama's heels, laughing and talking all the way. I could hardly imagine what they would come back looking like.

At 6:00 the guys from Stages arrived on our front porch looking winded but pleased.

"I can't believe we got it done," Larry said. "But the castle is up, everything is functional and looking good. I'll have to come back tomorrow to put in the fabric for the river. The ground's too wet right now."

"Understandable." I laughed. "Looks like God provided a little river of his own." I offered them my thanks, then sent them on their way. Afterward I checked the front yard for paparazzi. No doubt a few were hiding on the roof or under the azaleas. Nah. The place looked clear.

Marian and the bridesmaids headed next door, chattering with abandon. I watched as Rosa and Laz took control of the crowd, ushering them into the dining room for an Italian feast. I was starving but wouldn't be able to stay. I planned to sneak back over after the rehearsal, so I asked Rosa to save some food for me. She willingly obliged. I gave D.J. a kiss, told him to enjoy his dinner with the family, and headed back to the wedding facility with Brock at my side. We made our exit out of the back door of the house, just in case any lingering reporters hovered nearby.

By 6:20 the bridesmaids were going strong, their nervous energy igniting a flame in me. By 6:40 the groom and groomsmen had arrived. At 6:45 almost everyone was in place. I'd never heard so many *oohs* and *aahs* coming from one crowd. Seemed none of them had ever been in a castle before. At least, not one this realistic.

I called everyone to order. "Folks, we're going to start out front, walking through the ceremony from start to finish. Follow me, and I'll talk you through the processional part."

We went to the front of the wedding facility, where I spent some time telling everyone how the carriages would arrive and what would happen once they did. That done, we went around the side of the building to the front of the castle.

As we stood there facing it, I noticed tears in Marian's eyes. "You okay, hon?" I whispered.

"Mm-hmm." She turned to me, brushing away a tear. "Bella, I can't believe this is happening, especially after all we just went through. I don't know how to thank you."

"I don't control the weather!" I laughed, then pointed upward. "So I can't take credit for the storm passing."

Marian smiled. "I know. I didn't mean that. I'm just so excited! I've dreamed of this day since I was a little girl. And you've done it. You've given me what I asked for . . . and more!"

I had a few tears as well. Marian and I had come a long way together. She'd put her trust in me, and I'd done my best to give her the moon. The very thought of how much we'd accomplished together made me misty.

But no time for that—we still had a rehearsal to pull off!

I stepped inside the castle, marveling at how authentic it looked. Apparently the bridal party found it pretty impressive too. I'd have to send Larry a thank-you note. Or name my firstborn child after him. He'd pulled a rabbit out of a hat, no doubt about it.

As the others gawked over the facility, I found myself distracted by some familiar voices.

"Yoo-hoo!"

I turned to find the trio of sisters standing behind me with grins on their faces.

"Ladies! You made it. How did the search for dresses go?"

"Oh, Bella!" Jolene took my hand with a grin. "I'm going to look like a princess!" Her smile faded a wee bit as she added, "Well, a plus-sized princess, but a princess nonetheless."

"Your mama is a miracle worker," Twila said with a wave of her hand. "She found the perfect dresses for all of us. And she was right! They carried our size!"

"Just a few minor alterations," Bonnie Sue added, "and we'll be ready for tomorrow night."

"Oh, and that vocal coach!" Twila giggled. "He gave us some awesome pointers." Her cheeks flushed. "And he said some very flattering things. In fact . . ." She leaned in to whisper. "He asked us to audition for the Gershwin review they're doing in February. Can you believe it?"

"Actually, I can." Reaching over to embrace Twila, I realized just how many talents she and the other ladies possessed. My initial reaction to both their size and the way they dressed had almost prevented me from seeing them as the shining stars they really were. But no more! The Splendora trio would shine on the stage tomorrow night, and I would shout their praises from the rooftop.

"We're here not just to sing, honey," Twila said, tucking her arm through mine. "We're here to support you—in prayer, and by doing whatever else you need."

"Really?" I looked at her, relief sweeping over me. "That's so awesome."

"Well, what is the body of Christ for, anyway?" She gave me a tender kiss on the cheek. "Now, let's get this show on the road, girlie!"

I turned to look at the castle filled with people ready to celebrate. Yep. We'd better get this show on the road.

25

That's Life

The evening flew by at warp speed, and—short of me worrying about paparazzi appearing at every turn—everything came off without a hitch. Strange in light of the chaos in the days prior. And the funniest thing—I never once thought about the Food Network trucks. Were they still in front of my house? Had they destroyed the ambience of the evening for anyone in attendance? If so, no one had complained. No, they were too busy congratulating the bride- and groom-to-be and celebrating the upcoming nuptials. Why had I even worried?

As we left the castle, ready to load everyone up into limos to head to Moody Gardens for the rehearsal dinner, I glanced at my house. Through the open curtains in the dining room windows, I could see a mob of people gathered around the table. Likely Rosa and Laz were still entertaining their guests with cameras rolling. I could almost envision it now. Rosa was probably having the time of her life. And Laz had probably been offered an exclusive. Maybe even his own show. *Lunch at Lazarro's.* Something like that. I got carried away thinking about the possibilities. In fact, I could barely wait to sneak inside for a couple of minutes before leaving for the rehearsal dinner. And I needed to get in one last kiss with D.J. before heading out to face the rest of my evening.

I glanced at the road, noticing the Food Network trucks had been moved. A couple of cars sat in their place. Unfamiliar cars. Still, nothing glaring. Likely Mama had asked the crew members to pull their trucks around the corner to the side street so as not to interfere with my plans. God bless her. All of that worrying for nothing.

I thought about that for a moment. I had spent a lot of time worrying over the past few weeks, hadn't I? And for what? A strange calm settled over me, and I breathed a huge sigh of relief. Another couple hours and the rehearsal dinner would be behind us. Then I could focus on one thing—the bride's big day.

The first limo arrived, and Marian climbed in with her ladies-in-waiting. I could see the second limo arriving from off in the distance and knew the guys would soon load up and head out. Funny. I hadn't thought about Brock all evening, but in that moment I wondered how he was feeling about all of this. His best friend was about to get married, after all. And his stay on Galveston Island would soon come to an end.

I didn't have much time to ponder the question of how he was feeling. At that moment, the bride's father pulled me aside and handed me an envelope.

"Just a little tip," he whispered in my ear. "I know it took a miracle to pull this one off, Bella, and I want to thank you for making my little girl's day possible. This really has been a dream come true . . . for all of us." He gave me a big teddy-bear sort of hug, which brought tears to my eyes. Oh, what a wonderful confirmation. All of my work had been worth it. His wife—a beautiful woman with sparkling green eyes—grabbed me and whispered a thousand thank-yous in my ear. I couldn't recall ever feeling better about things.

They headed off to their car, a fabulous black Porsche, and I called out, "See you at the restaurant." Just one thing left to do—head inside and let my family know I was leaving for a couple of hours. Then on to the restaurant I would go to spend a much-needed and much-deserved evening relaxing.

As I crossed the lawn, I watched a fellow get out of a white Crown Victoria and head my way. He nodded in a somewhat cavalier sort of way, and my skin began to crawl. Another reporter. Hadn't they caused enough trouble already? How in the world did Brock live like this? These guys were such a nuisance!

The limo that held the groom and groomsmen started to pull away from the curb. I waved, which seemed to draw the attention of the man approaching me with a notebook in his hand. Great. Just what I needed.

Just act like you don't see him, Bella.

I kept walking, though my nerves suddenly got the better of me. I noticed the limo pausing. Thank goodness. Likely Brock saw what was happening. But what could he do about it from inside?

The man with the notepad drew close and nodded. My heart leaped into my throat. How could I handle him on my own? It would be foolish to try. He was a professional, after all. And I was never very good at these sorts of things.

"Looks like you've got a lot of action going on around here tonight." The man nodded in the direction of the wedding facility, then pointed to my house. "You live here, right?"

"Mm-hmm." That was all he was getting from me.

Keep walking, Bella. Keep walking.

"I saw the Food Network trucks. What's going on? Some sort of TV shoot?"

"No comment." I continued walking across the lawn, but I was very aware of the fact that one of the windows in the limo was inching its way down.

"I just wanted to ask you a few questions so I can do a better job of serving you."

"Serving me?" Oh, that was priceless.

"I'm an undercover officer." The fellow gave a brusque nod. "We've been keeping an eye on your place ever since we heard Brock Benson was staying here. We started by circling the block and just observing, but when we saw the Food Network trucks, we doubled our efforts."

"Brock Benson?" I tried to play innocent. He wasn't getting any information out of me. Not this time. I'd messed up plenty of things in the past, but not today.

"Sure. Of course." The guy looked a little perturbed at my response. "We've known he was staying here since yesterday when the Coast Guard informed us. To protect him, of course."

"Right. The Coast Guard called you to protect him. Great story." He might be able to fool a less savvy person, but I wasn't buying his twisted tale. Like the others from earlier in the day, this guy was with the media, no doubt about it. He'd sniffed out a story. Well, I wasn't having any of it. "You're really funny." I laughed. "But I'm not in the mood for humor right now. So if you don't mind, I think you need to get out of my yard." I turned away.

"Excuse me?"

"Look, I know who you are. You're a reporter. Paparazzi."

I shook my finger in his face. "You think you're so smart, pulling a fast one over on me. Well, listen to this and listen good. Just because I'm a woman doesn't mean you can take advantage of me." My courage rose with each word. Maybe I had more chutzpah than I knew. It was starting to feel good. Mighty good.

The reporter shook his head. "Ma'am, you've got the wrong idea. As I said, I'm an undercover officer. That's my car over there." He pointed at the Crown Victoria, then flashed a badge.

I shrugged. "Where did you get that? At the costume shop? Look . . . what's your name again?"

"Warren James."

"Warren. You look like a great guy. And I know you've probably got a family to support, so you could really use the story. Whatever news rag you're working for will probably pay you a pretty penny if I cooperate with you. I know that. They might even pay me a little something for my time. But I'm not playing your game. You're not getting any information out of me."

"Information?"

"Yes, information. And furthermore, if you don't leave me alone, I'm going to call the police and report you for impersonating an officer. That's a felony, you know."

"Well, yes, but ma'am, I—"

I got right up in his face, the frustrations of the day giving me more courage than usual. "I have a lot on my plate right now, and I don't want to have to deal with this. You understand? Now get off my property right now." I jammed my index finger against his chest, giving him a little shove.

What happened next will be forever seared in my memory. I saw the silver glint of handcuffs as he whipped them out from under his coat. Heard the click as he opened them. Felt the sting of pain as he grabbed my wrists. Everything after that began to move in slow motion. Why was this crazy reporter going to such lengths for a story? And how could I stop him?

Just then, Brock's voice rang out. "Unhand her, you infidel, or I'll take your head off!"

Interesting. Sounded a lot like a line from one of his movies. Or was I just imagining that?

The reporter turned, a stunned look on his face. He reached to his side to grab something.

Brock continued, his voice ringing out. "What are you staring at? Are you just going to stand there or get out of here like I told you to?" He took a few aggressive steps toward the guy. I watched in what seemed like slow motion as Brock doubled up his fist, pulled it back, and let it fly. He caught the guy squarely in the jaw. The first time. The second punch was a belly whop. I could see the look of pain on Brock's face as he withdrew his hand from the fellow's midsection.

The reporter shouted a few obscenities, then reached to his side and came up with . . . what was that? A toy gun?

Nope. At second glance, I realized it was anything but.

Next thing I knew, the man was shoving me into the back of what really turned out to be an unmarked patrol car. I could see Dakota Burton taking pictures up on the roof across the street. Great. He'd probably sell them to the *National Enquirer* before midnight.

My mother came running from the house with a trail of people behind her. Rosa approached with a ladle in hand and raced in Brock's direction, hollering in Italian about saving him from the evil that surrounded him. Then D.J. came flying across the yard, headed right for the officer. I knew my hunky cowboy could take him down in a minute but prayed he wouldn't attempt it.

The officer looked his way and shouted, "Stand back, or I'll have to call for backup."

That stopped D.J. in his tracks. By now the veranda was filled with people, including the cameraman from the Food Network. I could see the camera hoisted on his shoulder but didn't have time to process it just yet. No, my mind was on other things.

The officer clucked his tongue at me. "It didn't have to go down this way, ma'am. I just wanted to ask you a few questions about the crowd inside your house. I was assigned to watch over your family today, that's all. And Mr. Benson. But now . . ." He turned back to Brock, who stood on the lawn frozen like a statue. A handsome statue, but a statue nonetheless.

At this point, the wail of a siren pierced the air. A Galveston County sheriff's car pulled into our family's driveway. Before I could say "paparazzi," the police swarmed Brock. In that instant, I decided it would probably be easier just to faint. The wooziness swept over me in nauseating waves. Then everything went black.

26

Something Stupid

I was probably out for only a minute or so, but when I came to, I felt sure I'd dreamed the whole thing. In my nightmare, a man posing as a police officer arrested me and threw me into the back of his patrol car, where I fainted. Brock had been arrested as well, and D.J. stood gaping through the patrol car window.

Hmm. Turned out I really was sitting in the back of a patrol car, my hands cuffed together. And I could tell from the look of panic in D.J.'s luscious blue eyes that this wasn't a dream. The nightmare was a reality—in living color.

Through the window, I could see my mother standing on the lawn, wailing. And I caught a glimpse of Aunt Rosa off in the distance, sprinting across the lawn with the trio of Splendora sisters on her heels.

Laz came tearing out of the house with Guido on his shoulder. The parrot—probably spooked by all of the chaos—took off flying, landing on a female police officer's shoulder. She let out a shriek, which threw poor Guido into a frenzy. He flew off once again, this time running smack-dab into the light pole. Down he went, dazed but otherwise unharmed. Laz ran his direction to rescue him.

Why did all of this feel like it was moving in slow motion? Who had tampered with my internal clock?

In the midst of the chaos, I suddenly heard barking. Oh no, Precious! She'd taken hold of the female officer's pants leg and was pulling her this way and that. Turned out that little Yorkie-Poo was stronger than she looked. Would she end up in jail too? Did they have a holding cell for disobedient dogs? My heart broke just thinking about it.

Pop took a few tentative steps toward the patrol car—likely to offer words of reassurance and comfort. Or maybe to tell me he'd find someone else to run the family business. However, my arresting officer stopped him in his tracks. Through the window I could see the two men arguing.

I could see something else too. Sophia had pasted her body to the patrol car holding Brock. Even with my car door closed, I could hear her wails.

This, of course, was all being filmed by the cameraman from the Food Network. Well, by him and about three other paparazzi types who'd appeared from out of the bushes. Suddenly our lawn was an ocean of cameras.

Squinting, I tried to make out D.J.'s face. He looked shell-shocked. And what about Rob and the other guys? How would they react to the news that the wedding coordinator and the best man had both been arrested?

A shiver ran down my spine as I thought this through. Poor Marian! What would she do when this story broke? Would it destroy her big day?

The crocodile tears that followed were probably as much

from the stress of the past few weeks as anything. But once they got to flowing, I couldn't get them stopped. For a few minutes there, I thought I might flood the backseat of the patrol car.

Only one saving grace in all of this—Earline wasn't here to watch it go down. I shuddered, thinking about how she might've responded to all of this. Any hopes I'd ever had of becoming her daughter-in-law were washed out to sea with my tears.

The officer climbed into the patrol car and got on the radio, telling the folks on the other end of the line that he had a 2862, whatever that was. I shrugged and wiggled my shoulders, trying to get comfortable. Seemed that wasn't going to happen anytime soon.

"I . . . I'm s-sorry, O-Officer," I managed through the sobs. "I didn't mean to give you such a hard time. I really, really th-thought you were a r-reporter. Besides, I don't know why I'm being arrested. I barely touched you."

"You shoved me." He looked at me in the rearview mirror, likely wondering if he'd arrested some sort of nutcase. Maybe he would skip the jail and just take me to the insane asylum. "Where I come from, that's called assault."

Assault with a deadly finger? My mind reeled. "I weigh a hundred and fifteen pounds dripping wet. You barely moved when I shoved you." Yikes. Had I just admitted to shoving the man?

"Look at the trouble you stirred up. If you'd just left well enough alone, Brock wouldn't have attacked me. Now I have to arrest both of you."

"P-please, officer!" I tried. "He was just protecting me." I tried to wipe my eyes with my shoulder—my hands being incapacitated and all—but didn't do a very good job. "Besides,

224

I was trying to explain . . . I thought you were a reporter. We've been dealing with them for days now, ever since they got word Brock Benson was staying here. One of them was hiding in the bushes and almost gave me a heart attack, and another one"—I shivered as I remembered this one—"well, he was up on the roof, looking down at us. He tried to tell us he was a lighting guy for the Food Network, but they'd never seen him before."

"Mm-hmm."

"Look at our lawn. You'll have all the proof you need. They're everywhere. Oh! Look at that one! He's a big strapping guy, just like yourself." I gave him a smile, which he ignored.

"Good try."

"Please, sir. You have to let me go."

"Why do I have to let you go?"

"Because I'm coordinating a wedding tomorrow night."

"Yeah, right."

"Oh, but I am. And it's the most important wedding of my career. You wouldn't believe the amount of money the father of the bride has invested already." I thought about the envelope I'd just shoved in my pocket. The tip from Marian's father. Likely it was a pretty big chunk of change. What would happen to it now? Would I ever see it again? Worse yet, would the officers think it was dirty money? That I was a drug dealer or something to that effect? I shuddered just thinking about it.

"Doesn't matter to me what you had planned this weekend," the officer said. "You're headed to the Galveston County jail, so you'll have to clear your schedule."

Clear my schedule? Was he kidding?

I tried a different tactic. "Do you have daughters, Officer?"

225

"Two of them. One in junior high, the other in elementary school."

"Imagine if one of them was getting married tomorrow night and the whole thing fell apart due to a simple misunderstanding. Please, I beg of you, let me get back to work, doing what I need to do. Otherwise . . ." I couldn't finish the sentence. I didn't want to think of the otherwises.

"I'm sorry, ma'am. It's too late. We can sort all of this out at the station." He paused a moment, then looked my way, his brow knotted. "Let me just ask you a question."

"Yes, sir."

"What's the deal with the Food Network trucks and all the lights? That's all I really wanted to know in the first place."

"Oh." I sighed. "My Aunt Rosa's going to be on national television." I looked out of the window as a news truck pulled up. Instantly a man with a camera ran toward the patrol car, shining his light in my face. I groaned, then turned back to the officer. "Looks like Aunt Rosa's not the only one who's going to end up on national TV." Though somehow I had a feeling she'd come across looking a lot better than I would.

Not that I had time to think about it. Within seconds, the officer radioed the jail that we were on our way, then he started the engine.

"We're off to see the judge," he said, peering at me in the rearview mirror. "This is sure to liven up his day. Can't wait to tell the wife and kids about all of this." He laughed. "They're never going to believe it."

Very funny.

I did my best to get comfortable, but the cuffs were cutting into my wrists. Glancing out of the window, I noticed that Brock's patrol car had pulled out onto Broadway behind mine.

The paparazzi were chasing his car down the street, cameras still rolling. Well, the paparazzi and Sophia, who turned out to be a pretty good runner.

Within minutes it all faded away. I closed my eyes and prayed—not just for mercy but for the bride-to-be. What would happen if they didn't release me in time for the wedding? Surely things would move forward without me. Mama would likely take over as wedding coordinator. She could do it. I'd watched her coordinate hundreds of weddings through the years. Pop would help, of course. And the others would all do their part. Yes, this wedding would move forward, with or without me.

Of course, this wasn't the greatest disaster. No, Brock Benson's potential absence from the festivities was a far bigger issue. Rob and Marian would be without their first knight, and this would surely devastate them. I groaned as I thought about Brock and his arrest on my front lawn. This would not bode well for him—or his career. How would he ever explain this to his agent? And his fans—what would they think when they learned their heartiest pirate had been taken into custody by a female officer barely five feet tall? Likely they would laugh him out of Hollywood.

We arrived at the sheriff's office minutes later. I saw Brock come through the door, but that's where our time together ended. The next hour was spent booking me. I'd always wondered about those people who got their mug shots taken. Most of the time they looked just plain awful. Like they weren't even trying. Then there was the occasional smart aleck, who tried to make their mug shot look like a photo op.

Hmm. I'd be that one.

The police officer had just instructed me to stand with my toes touching the little yellow line when I snapped, "Hold it!"

He looked up, a surprised look on his face. "Yeah? You need something?"

"Mascara. And lip gloss."

He laughed, then snapped the photo with my mouth half open and my eyes half closed. Well, great. That would make a pretty picture for the national news. And the national news was just where I was bound to end up, what with my ties to Brock Benson.

That took my thoughts in several different directions at once. Would people assume I was Brock's girlfriend? Likely Dakota Burton would be willing to offer proof with the photographs he'd taken. Lovely. I could only guess what those headlines would do to poor D.J.

As I thought about D.J.'s reaction to all of this, my heart twisted. This past week had been tough enough on him already. I'd sensed his discomfort about Brock all along, of course, but what would happen now?

Finally the moment arrived. I was placed in a holding cell with three other women. Well, if one could call them women. One of them—a girl named Kate—looked like she'd barely passed her thirteenth birthday. Turned out she was eighteen. And a drug dealer. Go figure. Bridget was more of a mystery. The fortysomething sat curled up in a corner, staring at me. Every time I'd start to say something, she'd holler out, "The end is near! The end is near!"

Alrighty then.

The only one I could really connect with was a lady named Linda, who'd been picked up for shoplifting at the local Walmart. She told me her entire life story over a three-hour period—how her husband had taken off and left her to raise their four kids on her own. How she'd lost her job. My heart broke for her. In fact, the more she talked, the more I wanted to do something for her. But what?

As her story continued, I looked around the jail cell, curiosity getting the better of me.

So, this is what the inside of a jail cell looks like. Mama would have a fit if she knew I was sitting on this bed even for a minute. No telling who slept on it last night. Or the night before.

I contemplated all of the people who'd once shared this tiny space. Where were they now? Had they been set free?

Linda continued on with her story, then turned to Kate, who decided to share a little of her personal testimony as well. That's what this was, after all. Testimony time.

Finally they turned to me.

"So, what are you in here for?" Kate asked, her arms crossed at her chest, as if she dared me to top her story.

I pondered her question a moment before answering. "You know, I'm not sure. I guess you could say I smarted off to a cop. Is that a crime?"

"Depends," Linda said. "Were you carrying a weapon?"

"Heavens, no! Just a Coach purse and a tube of lip gloss." *And a deadly finger.*

"Hmm. I don't think that counts." Kate shrugged. "So, he arrested you for no reason?"

"Well, I sort of shoved him. I guess, anyway. I don't really remember it all now. It's a blur. See, the whole thing was a case of mistaken identity. I thought he was one of the paparazzi. I'm still not clear on who he thought I was." Then I spilled my guts to these women—my sisters, my jailmates. Told them everything—about Brock, about the wedding, about the Food Network. Everything. And why not? Who could they blab to, anyway?

By the time I finished, they sat with mouths hanging open.

"So you're telling me Brock Benson is here?" Kate whispered. "In this very jail?"

"Yeah." I yawned. "But I probably shouldn't have told you that. And maybe I shouldn't have mentioned the wedding either. I probably invaded the bride's privacy by doing that." As I mentioned the wedding, tears sprang to my eyes. I'd ruined a perfectly good wedding by letting my temper get the better of me. And just when things were going so well.

They were going well, weren't they? Just a few hours ago I'd walked out of the castle, feeling like a queen. On top of the world. And now, here I sat . . . the village idiot. In the stockades.

The perfect ending to the perfect night.

27

In the Still of the Night

As my evening in jail progressed, I thought about so many things. All of the highs and lows of my life. The mistakes. The joys. The problems. The things I'd overcome. The things I had yet to overcome.

For whatever reason, I was reminded of Twila, Jolene, and Bonnie Sue. I thought about how they said they wanted to take me on a cruise. The idea hadn't held much appeal at the time, but now it seemed like the most glorious idea in the world. We would sing karaoke together and sit at the captain's table. I would wear sequins and learn to ice-skate. Then, when we stopped at one of the ports, we'd take an excursion. Go snorkeling. Or scuba diving. Afterward we'd head back to the ship and dive into the all-you-can-eat buffet.

If I ever got out of here.

Thinking about food made my stomach growl. Closing my eyes, I dreamed of Rosa's chicken cacciatore. Oh, I could almost smell it now as it bubbled on the stove. And the garlic bread! If I squeezed my eyes really tight, I could practically taste it. Yes, it would surely soften the heart of even the toughest cop.

Thinking of Rosa got me thinking about Mama. Thinking about Mama got me thinking about Pop. And thinking about Pop caused a lump to rise in my throat. Surely having a daughter in jail was breaking his heart.

And D.J. . . . I couldn't get him off my mind. What a great guy he was. He was likely worried sick. Suddenly the tears began to fall.

"Go ahead and let it out," Linda said, taking a seat next to me on the cot. "It really will make you feel better." She handed me some toilet paper, and I blew my nose.

Kate shrugged. "I'm not so sure about that. Might just make you feel like a wimp."

I didn't care. When a girl needed to cry, a girl needed to cry. No apologies warranted, none offered. So I sat there in the Galveston County jail, bawling like a baby.

When the river finally dried up, I found myself thinking about the story of Paul and Silas and their stint in prison. Their voices raised in joyful song had brought them freedom. Maybe it would work for me too. It was worth a try, anyway.

With a tentative voice, I started to whisper the first worship song that came to mind—"Amazing Grace," Guido's favorite. Seemed appropriate, all things considered.

After just a couple words, I stopped cold. I was struck by something so profound, it startled me. Guido had spent his entire life behind bars. No wonder he sang that little song! Was this what his view was like? I peered through the metal bars and began to sing again, this time allowing my voice to rise in intensity.

Linda gave me a curious look, then slowly joined me, adding her voice to mine. Before long we were even trying a little harmony. Not too long after that, we were going strong, our voices perfectly blended.

Then Kate—who turned out to be quite the vocalist—joined in. I could see the tears in her eyes, especially when we hit the "I once was lost, but now am found" part. This wasn't the first time she'd sung "Amazing Grace," and I had a feeling it wouldn't be the last.

And then there was Bridget. She continued to stare at us, occasionally muttering, "The end is coming!" under her breath. Oh well. Maybe she was right. Or maybe she would join us for the second verse. Didn't really matter right now. Only one thing mattered—a trio of women bonding in the Galveston County jail.

We wrapped up the song, and a holy hush fell over our little cell. Well, except for Bridget's occasional mutterings. I thought again of Guido, how he spent his days behind bars. Might work for parrots, but not human beings. Suddenly I could hardly wait to get out of here, not just for the obvious reasons, but so I could tell Guido that I understood his plight.

Slow down, Bella. Don't lose it!

A lump rose up in my throat. Though I tried to swallow it, the crazy thing wouldn't go away. Fine. I'd just live with a lump in my throat. Who would know, anyway?

I continued to hum the song as I stretched out on my cot. Though I wanted to sleep—the hope of still going home in the morning front and center in my brain—I could not. Every time I closed my eyes, I saw the look of horror on D.J.'s face. Envisioned the phone conversation with his mother as he shared the news with her. Pondered the things I would say to him the first time we saw each other once I was sprung loose from this place. *If* I was sprung loose from this place.

At 6:00 a.m.—according to the clock on the wall, anyway—an officer arrived at my cell with a key in hand. He used it to open the door and gestured for me to rise from my little cot.

"Ms. Rossi, you're set to appear before the judge in a few minutes."

"O-oh?" I sat up and ran my fingers through my matted hair. I could feel a line of tightness down the edge of my lip, a sure sign I'd been drooling. And my eyes ached. I'd finally slept—less than an hour in all, so I must look a fright. Still, the judge had probably seen worse. I hoped.

I wished my cellmates well, pausing as I took Linda's hand in mine. "I want you to contact me when you get out. Promise?" Turning to Kate, I said, "And you—remember what we talked about, okay? I've got pretty broad shoulders if you ever need to chat. You know where to find me."

"Club Wed." She spoke the words along with me.

"Sorry I don't have a card on me," I said. "But it's on Broadway, just a few blocks from the Moody Mansion."

"Got it." Kate shrugged. "And thanks. It was great to meet you."

"You too."

I wanted to say something to Bridget too, of course, but she'd finally drifted off to sleep. For the sake of the others, I didn't disturb her.

The officer led me to the small courtroom—if one could call it that. You'd think the judge wouldn't get much business, this being a Saturday morning and all, but he had a roomful of criminals to attend to. Chief among them was Brock Benson, who was the first to approach the bench. We were called up together, a fact that surprised me. The judge looked at both of us . . . and he didn't look happy. Great. We were off to a wonderful start.

"I want you to know, I was up all night reading the letters that came in on behalf of the two of you." He yawned.

"O-oh?" I looked at him, stunned. "From who—er, whom?"

"Let's see." He squinted through his bifocals. "I see a woman who refers to herself as Sister Twila here. Must be a nun. Would you like to hear what she has to say?"

Brock shook his head. "Maybe not, sir."

The judge shifted through the stack of papers. "And then there's one from a Sophia Rossi. Maybe you'd be interested in her pleas on your behalf."

I groaned. "That's my sister."

"Mm-hmm." He reached for another. "This is an interesting one. It's from Bartholomew Burton, one of our island's most prominent attorneys."

That certainly got my attention. Dakota's dad had written a letter? Hmm. Likely Phoebe had put him up to it. But what could he possibly have to say that would help me now?

"Says here he's happy to represent you should we choose not to drop the charges." The judge peered over his glasses. "Interesting. Burton usually doesn't take clients unless he thinks they're innocent. Wonder what that says about you." He cleared his throat. "But the rest of his letter is what got to me. Burton has written quite a soliloquy about your efforts on his son's behalf. Says you've turned his boy's life around. Made him a better citizen. He says you're quite a role model."

I pondered that for a minute. Had I really turned Dakota's life around?

In that moment, I knew . . . Bart Burton hadn't written that letter. Dakota had. But why? Why did the kid want to see us released? So he would have another photo op, perhaps? I was on to him, no doubt about it.

The judge grinned as he pulled out another letter. "This was a nice one. A gentleman named Lazarro Rossi."

"My uncle." I sighed, wondering what Laz had said on my behalf.

"I see." The judge lifted the letters one by one. "This one's from a florist."

"My sister-in-law."

"This one"—he held up a lengthy one—"is co-authored by seventeen people who all claim they work for the Food Network."

"They do, sir," Brock said with a sigh. "That's the truth."

"Oh, I don't doubt it." The judge continued to thumb through the letters. "Here's one from a set design company in Houston. Three guys named Larry, Bob, and George. Sound familiar?"

"Oh yes. They're great guys. Hard workers," I said.

"They say the same about you." The judge kept shuffling the letters. "But the notes on your behalf don't end there. Here's one from a woman who drove all the way down from Splendora. Her name's Earline Neeley."

My heart twisted at that revelation. Earline had written a letter on my behalf?

"This is a very kindhearted woman, and she apparently loves you a lot," the judge said, looking over Earline's letter. He peered at me over his glasses. "Bella Rossi, you have a lot to be thankful for."

"Oh, don't I know it, sir."

"Yes, you have what most people don't—a huge family and a great support system. Every one of these letters speaks of love, family, and safety. I think it's best if I send you back to the safety of that family this morning."

"Y-you're going to let me go?" I asked, not quite believing it. "Really?"

"Yes." He turned to Brock. "And about you . . ." Looking through the stack once more, he came up with a letter in familiar handwriting. "There was one in particular that swayed me on your behalf. Do you know a Dwayne Neeley Jr., young man?"

"D.J.," I whispered.

Brock nodded. "I do, sir. Great guy. He works here on the island."

The judge nodded. "Well, he's greater than you know. This is the most impassioned note I've ever read. He sings Bella's praises for quite some time, but when it comes to you . . ."

"What?" Brock asked. "What did he say?"

"He explained that you could do more good out of jail than in. That you're a very good man with a high profile who has the opportunity to change lives for the better, if given a chance. That you likely got carried away protecting Bella—"

"That part is true, Your Honor," Brock said. "I did think she was under attack. And, again, I thought I was punching a reporter, not a police officer."

"Yes. And about that . . ." The judge sighed and put the letters down on his desk. "The next time someone tells you he's a police office, don't question him."

"Right," we said simultaneously.

"And when you're asked to give a police officer information, give it. Even if it seems unreasonable at the time."

We echoed each other with a "Yes, sir."

"And whatever you do, don't ever lay a hand on a police officer."

"Well, in my case, sir, it wasn't exactly a hand. Just a finger."

"Regardless." The judge nodded, then banged his gavel. "Case dismissed. Next!"

As I turned to leave the room, the judge called my name once more. Turning, I gave him a curious look. "Yes, sir?"

"Interesting coincidence." His brow wrinkled. "My daughter's boyfriend proposed to her last night. You won't believe where she wants to get married."

I couldn't stop the smile from erupting. "Oh?"

"Yes. Something about a Southern plantation wedding."

"Oooh!" I practically squealed. "I've been hoping someone would choose that package. You'd think, living in the South, that lots of people would want a Southern wedding. Oh, tell her to call me, sir." I reached down to give him a card, then realized I still didn't have my purse. "Hmm. I'll have to get back with you on that."

"Oh, we know where to find you. Trust me."

As the next poor fellow made his way to the bench, I celebrated. Glancing at the clock on the wall, I realized I still had the whole day ahead of me. Praise the Lord, I'd been set free! Now, if I could just get the bride to forgive me, we'd have a wedding!

28

My Way

Funny how the sun looked so much brighter when you saw it for the first time on the outside of a jail cell. It almost overpowered me with its goodness. Its radiance. Its warmth. Made me want to sing, to dance, to clap my hands for joy. Instead, I knelt down and kissed the sidewalk.

Which, I'm sure, made an awesome photo for the reporter with the camera in his hand. And he wasn't alone. Looked like the newshounds were out in force. Not to catch a glimpse of me, of course, but to see what Brock Benson had to say after his night in the slammer. They rushed him, almost knocking him down. I marveled at the fact that he didn't retaliate in any way. Instead, he paused and flashed a winning smile.

Yep. He was a consummate actor.

"Brock, can you tell us why you were arrested?" a reporter asked, shoving a microphone in his face.

"It was just a misunderstanding," Brock said, using beautiful diction and a pronounced stage voice. "And I am happy to report, all charges have been dropped. But to answer your question, I was rescuing a fair maiden in distress." He pointed to me, and I curtsied.

"Just like the scene in *The Pirate's Lady!*" another reporter said, extending a boom microphone. "Right?"

"Only without the pirate ship," Brock said with a Hollywood wink. "And this lady"—he turned my way and took my hand in his—"is fairer than the fairest."

Suddenly I felt a little nauseous. He'd gone a bit over the top. And I wasn't sure how D.J. would perceive any of this if he read about it in the paper.

"So, a love interest, then?" the first reporter asked, sticking the microphone in my face.

I heard the clicking of cameras as the reporters turned my way. Yikes! Did they really think I was involved with Brock Benson?

Before I could say "No," I caught a glimpse of D.J. through the crowd. Waving my arms, I shouted, "D.J.! Oh, D.J.! I'm so sorry! I love you!"

He came sprinting my way, parting the crowd as he aimed himself in my direction. I lunged into his arms, planting a thousand kisses on him. Apparently the paparazzi found this somewhat entertaining. I could hear the continual clicking of cameras as they went off all around me. Finally I came up for air.

"Thank you for springing me!" I said. "It was your letter—and the letters of all my friends and family—that did the trick."

"We love you, Bella," he whispered. "And we'd fly to the moon for you."

Brock turned to D.J. and extended a hand. The cameras starting clicking once again.

"I'm really grateful," Brock said with a sheepish look on his face. "You didn't have to do that, but I'm glad you did."

"It was an easy letter to write." D.J.'s voice grew more serious. "You're a great guy, Brock. And I really meant it when I said you could use your notoriety for good. So I'm glad the Lord saw fit to release you."

Brock flinched at the word *Lord* but didn't say anything.

At that moment, the most bizarre thing happened. I heard three very familiar voices ring out.

"Yoo-hoo! Bella, girl!"

Twila. Marvelous.

"Move on over and let me through!"

Bonnie Sue. Terrific.

"Hey, handsome! Scoot over and let me pass."

Jolene. Could things possibly get any better?

They arrived at my side, all giggles and smiles. As Bonnie Sue laid eyes on Brock, she let out a squeal. "Brock Benson! I can't believe it's really been you all along. Vinny DiMarco, my eye! Shame on you for pulling the wool over our eyes!"

"Sorry, ma'am," he said with a shrug. "Just role-playing. It's what I do. Besides," he leaned in to whisper, "my legal name really is Vinny DiMarco. Though I hope you'll forgive me for deceiving you."

"Oh, nothing to forgive." She gave him a hug. "We're old friends now, and friends always forgive."

Before anyone could respond, Twila interrupted. "Ready to fly this coop?" she asked. "We brought the Pinto."

"Th-the Pinto?"

"Yeah." D.J. shrugged. "Here's what happened. Sophia brought them to my place in her car last night. Then they picked up the Pinto, and we all drove back to your parents' place, where we spent the night writing letters."

"And eating garlic twists," Jolene threw in.

"Yes. But now we're rabbit trailing." D.J. grinned. "Anyway, I told your folks I'd come and fetch you in my truck, but when I went out to the driveway, the Pinto was blocking my truck. When I asked Twila to move it, she suggested they bring it here." He leaned down and whispered, "The ladies wanted to take you home in their chariot. So, here we are."

I looked at D.J. with one of those "You've got to be kidding, right?" looks, and he just shrugged. "Well, after your time in the back of an undercover patrol car, I figured it'd be a refreshing change. And when are you ever going to have the opportunity to ride in a pink Pinto again?"

I whispered, "Hopefully never!" then followed behind him through the throng of people.

We made our way through the crowd, cameras still flashing, and arrived at the bright pink Pinto on the side of the road. Unfortunately, it was double-parked. We'd better make a clean exit before a traffic cop showed up.

"Hmm. Not quite sure how we're going to do this." Twila looked at all of us and then at the little car. She seemed to be sizing up the situation. "I guess I could drive and Jolene and Bonnie Sue could go in back. Brock, you could squeeze in between them."

The look on his face was priceless.

"Bella, you and D.J. can ride up front."

"Both of us? In one seat?"

"No problem." D.J. looked at me with a lopsided grin. "I carried you through the night with my prayers. What will it hurt to carry you home on my lap?"

"That's the most romantic thing anyone's ever said to me!" My eyes filled with unexpected tears.

Man. I really needed to get some sleep.

We somehow managed to get everyone into the car. The camera guys had a field day with the photos of Brock in the backseat between Jolene and Bonnie Sue. The ladies made a big production out of it, and in the end, so did Brock. They even did a couple of fun poses.

I, on the other hand, was horrified. For one thing, I stunk. I'd spent the night in a jail cell. How could I sit on D.J.'s lap? He scooted into the seat, and I inched my way next to him, finally realizing we could both fit side-by-side if we squished a little. "There. That's not too bad."

Twila gave the crowd a wave as she revved the engine. "Let's get the heck out of Dodge!" she cried out, then took off toward home. A few minutes later, when we were out of the sight of the cameras, Twila sighed. "Bella, I'm sorry you spent the night in jail. It's wholly unfair, and I told the officer that myself."

"You talked to the police?"

"Of course!" She laughed. "And the sheriff too. I called him this morning."

"No way."

"Yep. Told him what a tragic mistake that policeman had made. He had a good laugh at it, of course. It's just plain silly."

"He laughed?" I could hardly believe it.

"Oh yes, he did," Bonnie Sue said. "The man can laugh."

"And then that judge sprang you like a broken lock." Twila giggled.

"Thank goodness! I still have to coordinate a wedding!" Glancing at my watch, I took note of the time: 9:40. The day was still young. I ran my fingers through my matted hair and tried to scrape the dried drool from my chin. "I must look like something from a horror movie."

D.J. looked at me with a smile. "Well, not any horror movie I've ever seen, though I think we've already established that I don't get out to the movies much."

"That's fine with me. In fact, after this week, I don't care if I ever see another movie."

As we made the drive through town, I noticed everyone was chattering except Brock. I turned around to face him. "A-are you ever going to forgive me for ruining your career?"

"Ruining my career?" He laughed. "Bella, this is the best thing that's happened to me in years. And I'm sorry if I seem like I'm down. I just have a lot on my mind. Spending the night in a jail cell gives you a lot of time to think."

"Tell me about it."

He exhaled loudly and then looked at me, his eyes a little misty. "I have something to confess."

"O-oh?" *Please don't tell me you've fallen in love with me in front of my boyfriend. That would be really awkward.*

"As much as I hate to admit it, you were right."

"Right about what?"

"All of that stuff you said about me falling for your family. Or, rather, falling for the idea of having a family of my own."

"Ah."

"Don't you see? When I look at your family, I want that. I want parents who love their kids . . . and brothers and sisters who fight. I want people gathered around a dinner table, talking about the weather and arguing about politics. I . . . I want what you have."

"And God wants you to have that too, Brock." I gave him a sympathetic look. "I honestly believe he's going to give you a great wife and a houseful of kids . . . if that's your desire. But as much as you want those things, he wants something even more."

"What's that?" Brock said with a curious expression on his face.

"Your heart." I whispered the words, hoping he understood my full meaning. "Brock, he wants your heart."

"She's right," Bonnie Sue said. "And it doesn't do any good to run from God. Ask me how I know."

"He's gonna catch you anyway," Jolene said. "So you might as well stop where you are and turn his way. Makes things so much easier."

Though I didn't know their individual testimonies, I somehow knew the ladies were speaking from experience. Turning back to Brock, I said, "Think about the wedding. That whole Renaissance theme."

"What about it?"

"Do you know what *renaissance* means?"

He shrugged. "Shakespeare and art?"

"No." I shook my head. "*Renaissance* means 'rebirth.' Starting over. That's what happened in the Renaissance era. Art, music, architecture . . . they all experienced a rebirth. They came alive again. And that's what God wants to do with you. In fact, I'm convinced that's why he brought you all the way from sunny California to soggy Galveston Island. You're at a fork in the road, Brock. And I'm hoping you turn the right way." When he looked at me with tears in his eyes, I whispered, "I'm just saying, maybe it's time for a little renaissance of your own. Maybe God has orchestrated all of this—you being here, the medieval wedding theme, and so on—to get your attention."

"If that's the case, then he went to a lot of trouble just for me." Brock laughed, and I could tell he was trying to make light of things.

"Oh, trust me. He's gone to a lot of trouble for you, all

right," I said. "When he went to the cross, he had you in mind."

Brock grew silent at this statement, but I could hear the wheels turning in his head. It was D.J. who finally spoke up, his words gentle but firm.

"You think that jail cell was tough . . . it doesn't even compare to spending a life without him."

More silence from Brock.

I turned back to D.J. and started humming. "Amazing Grace," of course. Just couldn't help myself.

29

From This Moment On

I arrived at the house, ready to face the music. No telling how my parents would greet me. Still, as that Pinto pulled into our drive and I laid eyes on our beautiful Victorian home, gratitude swept over me. The words *"A ogni uccello il suo nido è bello"* tripped their way across my lips. I knew the literal translation, of course—"To every bird, his own nest is beautiful"—but for me, today, it only meant one thing: "There's no place like home."

I made my way inside with fear and trembling taking hold. Would my family ever let me live this down? Likely they would get a lot of mileage out of this story. Thankfully, the Splendora sisters gave me the courage I needed to step through the front door and face my parents head-on.

As soon as I stepped through the door, Pop grabbed me and hollered, "My little prodigal!" I groaned, then he hugged me and whispered in my ear, "It's okay, Bella Bambina. I still love you. You're my little ex-con, but I promise not to treat you any different from the others." When I groaned again, he said, "Besides, you're not the first one in our family to get arrested."

"True." I'd forgotten that my brother Armando had done a little time in the slammer for unpaid traffic tickets. And then there was that incident with Rosa. Once, on a trip back to Texas from Napoli, she'd been held in police custody for hours. Turned out she was a dead ringer for a murder suspect back in Italy.

No, I wasn't the first Rossi who'd spent time behind bars. But I hoped I'd be the last.

I turned to Mama, who greeted me with a horrified look on her face. "Bella, you spent the night in jail for accosting a police officer?"

"Accosting a police officer?" I repeated, dumbfounded. "Is that what they said?"

"Yes. Didn't you realize what they were charging you with?" Pop asked.

I shook my head. "This whole thing is just a fog now. I figured they charged me with stupidity for not recognizing a police officer when I saw one."

"No!" My mother paled. "They said you actually attacked that officer!"

"Really?" I thought about it. "I guess I did touch him with my index finger. If that's considered an attack. But I guess the real culprit was Brock. He took a couple of swings at the officer. But I know for a fact he thought the guy was the paparazzi."

Pop laughed. "Well, thank God it's behind us now."

"Not really." I plopped into a chair and sighed. "I've ruined Marian's wedding day."

"Of course you haven't," Joey said as he entered the room.

"Don't you know—it's part of the show, for someone always ends up in the stockades at a Renaissance wedding."

"Really?"

"Sure! You were just playing along. Tell them it was part of the act, that you wanted to add to their special day."

I laughed at that one. "Okay. But I'll tell you the truth, it wasn't much fun."

Joey reached over and gave me a hug. "Yes, but think of all the stories you now have to tell your children and grandchildren."

"No doubt they'll reenact the story of their mom's big night in the slammer."

"I'm sure your kids will run around shouting, 'Unhand her, you infidel!'" Joey chuckled, and I joined in.

"True." I turned to Earline, who'd been in the kitchen with Rosa. She rushed my way and swept me into the folds of her ample bosom.

"I'm so sorry to put you through all of this," I whispered.

"Oh, my baby girl!" She slipped an arm over my shoulders, and her eyes filled with tears. "Don't think a thing about it. It was a misunderstanding. And from everything I've heard, you handled yourself like a champ."

"Except that one part where I shoved a police officer."

"Well, there was that." She paused and gazed into my eyes with such love that I felt inclined to give her another hug. She gave my hand a squeeze. "I wrote a beautiful letter on your behalf, Bella."

"Oh, I know, and I'm so grateful!" I sighed. "The judge told me all about it. But I still can't believe you drove down here the day after a storm to get that letter to him. In the night, no less."

"Rain, snow, sleet, or hail . . ." Earline paused a moment,

perhaps trying to decide how to end the little poem. "The love of a mother-in-law never fails."

Did she just say "mother-in-law"?

I reached to hug her once again, energized by her words. I whispered, "Thank you for letting your son date an ex-con."

Earline laughed. "You know, I never thought I'd hear someone say those words, but they're not as frightening as one might imagine, especially under the circumstances." She gave me a pensive look. "Honey, you spent the night in jail for a crime you didn't really commit."

"Technically I did commit a crime. I touched that police officer with the tip of my finger."

"Well, yes. But it wasn't much of a crime. Still, you know what it's like to be locked away from those you love. Likely you'll have more sympathy for people behind bars." She reached for my hand, a delighted look on her face. "Oh, I know! You could start a prison ministry!"

"W-what?"

"Sure! Up in Dayton there's a women's prison. Now that you've done time, you could minister to the women who are incarcerated for real. You've walked a mile in their shoes." She grinned. "Well, maybe not a mile. More like a few yards. Or at least a small city block." Earline chuckled.

"I guess I have."

"I'm a firm believer that the Lord allows us to walk through certain valleys so that we can better relate to others who are going through the same. So don't be surprised if he puts you to work in some way you don't expect."

"Um, okay."

I thought about Earline's words as I showered. Pondered them as I scrubbed my hair for the umpteenth time. Toyed with them as I conditioned and eventually toweled dry. Was the Lord asking me to take my experience and run with it? Use what I'd learned to help others?

My mind reeled backwards to the three women I'd spent the night with. They were just average, ordinary women whose lives had spun out of control. Sure, they'd made some poor choices. But in the end, weren't they just women like me? Didn't God look down on them with the same love, the same devotion? And didn't he want someone to reach out to them with a hand of love?

"Lord, show me what to do, and I'm there. Just be specific, Father, because I have a tendency to . . . well, you know what I have a tendency to do. I jump in with both feet before I'm really sure about what I'm doing."

The next few minutes were spent getting dressed for the day and putting on makeup. I could hear the voices of the others downstairs raised in laughter. Whenever the Rossis and the Neeleys got together, everyone had a blast. Add the trio of sisters to the mix, and watch out! Likely they'd be partying all day.

Not that I had time to party. No, I had far more important things on my plate. Glancing in the mirror, I double-checked my makeup. There were no telltale signs of lack of sleep, except for the dark rings under my eyes. I could remedy those with a little more makeup. I scrambled around in my makeup bag for some corrective cream, then dabbed it over the dark spots.

"There. Not bad at all." As I gave myself one final glance, I heard a knock at my door. I opened it to find Sophia.

"Aunt Rosa sent me up to get you. She made a special breakfast to welcome you home." A bit of an edge crept into her voice at the word *welcome*. "So, welcome home, I guess," she continued, her features a little too tight.

"Thanks." I sat on the edge of the bed and gestured for her to do the same. Oddly, she did not. "What's up, Sophia?"

"I'm just upset, that's all."

"Why?"

"You can do no wrong, that's why. You spend the night in jail, and everyone welcomes you back with open arms."

"Of course. We're family. And besides, I didn't really do anything to warrant going to jail. It was just a misunderstanding."

Sophia rolled her eyes.

"What?"

"Nothing. Only, this is what it always comes down to. Life is so easy for you. It's Bella this and Bella that. Bella gets the wedding facility. Bella gets the handsome cowboy. Bella gets the Hollywood hottie."

"Hang on just a second there, Sis." I shook my head. "For your information, I don't want a Hollywood hottie. I've got everything I need in D.J." I wanted to give her a piece of my mind, to tell her that she was completely out of line. Still, after a night of almost no sleep, I figured it would be safer not to overreact. No telling what I might say or do.

Sophia crossed her arms at her chest. "Look, I know D.J. is great. He adores you, no doubt about it. But I've seen the way Brock looks at you, Bella. He thinks you hung the moon. He won't even . . ." She dabbed at her eyes, the first sign that she was about to blow. "He won't look my way for more than a second when you're around."

"I didn't do anything to cause that, Sophia, and you know it."

"I know." She dropped down into a chair. "That's the part that makes me so angry. You're just so . . ." She grunted. "Just so perfect. And everyone knows it."

252

"Perfect? Oh, that's priceless. You didn't see me when I came in from my night in jail, but pretty much everyone else did. My hair was matted and my face was covered in dried drool. Very lovely."

"Doesn't matter. No one ever sees your flaws. Only you. Everyone else finds you completely wonderful."

"Everyone but you." I drew near and looked into her eyes.

"That's the problem." She sniffled. "I agree with all of them. You are completely wonderful."

"And completely flawed, like everyone else in the world." I paused, then released a sigh. "Look, Sophia, I don't have a clue why some things come easily for me. But I know that God has only given me the things he thinks I should carry. That wedding facility . . . it's the joy of my life. I wake up in the morning thinking about it and go to bed thinking about it."

"Oh, I'm not jealous of that."

"You're not? Then what?"

"It's the guys, Bella. That's what it comes down to. You're going to end up with your happily ever after, and I'm . . ." She began to cry in earnest now. "I'm going to end up an old maid."

"Sophia, you're only twenty-three."

"Doesn't matter. The handwriting is on the wall."

"What about Tony?"

Her eyes lit up, if only for a second. "What about him?"

"He's been hanging around here ever since I broke up with him."

"Yeah, but don't you see? Even Tony is your leftovers. Your hand-me-down."

I laughed at that one. "Sophia, he's a great guy, and not a hand-me-down. He's the fella who's been waiting in the wings, hoping you'd come to your senses about Brock Benson."

"Really?"

"Really. But you've been a little . . . preoccupied."

"Seriously preoccupied." She sighed. "But who can blame me? The lights of Hollywood were shining in my eyes! I saw Brock as a potential boyfriend, but it was a little silly, I guess. He's not going to date a Texas wildflower when he can have a Hollywood rose."

"Oh, I'm not so sure that's an accurate comparison. You're the prettiest girl I know, Sophia. Your hair is amazing. You've got the best figure on the block. And your skin is absolutely divine. I'd kill for skin like that."

"Pepto Bismol facial peel," she said.

I sighed. "Sophia, I think you're missing my point. I'm trying to tell you that I have plenty of reasons to be jealous of you too. You're gorgeous inside and out."

"Really? You think so?" A hopeful look crossed her face.

"Yes." I grinned. "And if you don't believe me, ask Tony."

A shy smile lit her face. "I do think Tony's a great guy. But I guess I'm just easily distracted by things of beauty. And we have to admit, Brock Benson is *definitely* a thing of beauty!"

"Amen, Sister!"

We had a good laugh, followed by a warm embrace. I had been anticipating having this conversation for some time now and was grateful to have it behind me. Maybe now we could move forward in our sisterly relationship, growing closer than ever before. I hoped so, anyway.

Once we'd made up, I practically sprinted down the stairs, anxious to have breakfast with my family and then get this ball rolling. So many thoughts went through my mind at once. Jail. The women I'd met. The conversation I'd just had with

Sophia. The rings under my eyes. The chat in the car with Brock. The wedding.

The wedding! Could I really pull this off?

When I reached the kitchen, D.J. approached and swept me into his arms. "Mmm, you smell good. A lot better than before."

"Yeah, the jailhouse stench is gone, replaced with almond soap and honeysuckle conditioner." I grinned. "Thought it might be more appropriate." I looked at him with a sigh. "D.J., I don't know how to thank you for coming to fetch me out of prison."

"Technically it was jail. And not really the big jail, just a holding cell." He shrugged. "Nothing to brag about."

"Yeah, I guess. But I can't believe you're still talking to me, let alone dating me."

He put a finger over my lips. "You're my girl, Bella Rossi, plain and simple."

"Okay then." I gazed into his eyes, the butterflies now in a dancing frenzy in my stomach. "D.J., I don't know if I've said this enough, but you are truly my knight in shining armor."

"And you," he whispered as he kissed the tip of my nose, "Bella, you are the love of my life."

30

Let's Face the Music and Dance

I started the afternoon with a phone call to Marian, who'd spent the night at the rented condo with her ladies-in-waiting. Somehow I had to get her to forget about my arrest and focus on her big day. She answered the phone with a lilt to her voice.

"Bella!"

"Hey, girl! Are you ready for the big day?"

"Oh, am I ever!" She dove into a lengthy conversation about all of the fun she and the girls had had after the rehearsal dinner, but I stopped her.

"Listen, about last night . . ." I swallowed hard, ready to make the appropriate apologies.

"Oh, Bella, Rob told me."

"He—he did?"

"Yes. And I'm sorry you weren't feeling well. You should have told me! I felt a little bad going ahead with the rehearsal dinner and the party without you there, but . . . the show must go on!"

"Y-yes. The show must go on!"

"It did make me a little sad that Brock decided not to come, but I guess I understand it. He didn't want to be seen out in public with the paparazzi on his trail."

"Ah." I stopped with just that one word.

We ended the call on a happy note. I'd have to remember to thank Rob later. He hadn't lied, that much was for sure—I hadn't been feeling well last night. Oh, but today I felt wonderful!

By early afternoon I had the castle area completely prepped and ready. Pop helped me put on the tablecloths and chair covers. Unlike more traditional weddings, the guests would actually be seated at their tables during the ceremony, while the wedding party took the stage at the front of the room. I'd carefully selected the tablecloths and chair covers in soft shades of yellow and green, based on Marian's request. Everything had an outdoorsy feel about it.

At 4:15 Marcella arrived with the bridal bouquets. I gasped as I laid eyes on the arrangements. She'd worked wonders with the Texas wildflowers, bundling them into rustic-looking bunches for the bridesmaids to carry. And the wreaths! I'd known all along the bride and her ladies-in-waiting would wear flower wreaths in their hair, but I had no idea they'd turn out this beautiful.

"Look, Bella. What do you think?" Marcella put one atop her head, and I gasped again. She'd chosen sweetheart roses and delicate sprigs of baby's breath.

"They're gorgeous."

"Oh, just wait till you see the archways and the center-pieces. They're still in my van."

I started to let her go but then stopped her. "Marcella, thank you for writing that letter."

Her cheeks flushed. "You're welcome. It was an easy letter to write."

"You know, I haven't told you this yet, but I think you're doing a fabulous job with the flower shop. It's just the right fit."

"Oh, thank you." She flashed an embarrassed smile. "Though I'm not sure the timing was the best. I'm still dealing with a little morning sickness." She rubbed her tummy. "But the work is a nice distraction. And I'm having the time of my life."

I grinned at her. "You are a creative soul, honey. And you married into just the right family. We need you."

She gazed at me with sisterly love. "No, Bella, I need you . . . all of you." Turning back to the matter at hand, she said, "Now, where do we begin?"

"Let's start with the centerpieces for the tables," I said. "Pop and I already have the cloths on, and the tables are looking a little bare. I don't want anyone to come in early and find them that way."

"Right. I'll be right back." Marcella scurried outside, and I realized I still had some work to do myself. Time to get dressed! I raced across the yard, hoping I wouldn't interrupt anything of importance at the house. Thankfully, I was able to sneak up the stairs without being noticed.

I ran into my room and grabbed the dress Mama and I had picked out weeks before at a costume shop on the mainland. The beautiful gown was an authentic medieval-style dress. I'd chosen a soft pink, hoping it would complement my skin tone. The rose-colored bodice was made of crushed velvet. I loved the crisscross ties that laced through the decorative button at the front. But my favorite part, by far, was the sleeves. They were chiffon and draped in a bell style. My only complaint? I couldn't wear my boots. Bummer.

Glancing down at my feet, I rethought the proposition. Who would see my feet, anyway? I made a quick decision to slide them on. Ah. Much better.

With every hair and boot in place, I darted back down the stairs and across the lawn. I arrived at the back of the wedding facility in less than a minute, a world record.

Stepping back, I looked over the castle with its beautiful faux river. Exquisite, inside and out. Truly, with the exception of the round tables and their accompanying chairs, I felt like I'd stepped back in time several hundred years.

Marcella and I worked together getting the centerpieces in place and putting the rest of the flowers in the large walk-in refrigerator inside the wedding facility. When we finished, she helped me in a thousand other ways. God bless her!

Uncle Laz and Jenna arrived at 5:30, ready to set up the buffet area. They'd done most of the cooking in advance, but the serving dishes had to be put in place, and they were pretty meticulous about all of that, particularly when they'd never done a wedding of this sort.

Jenna rushed my way and gave me a warm hug. "You spent the night in jail!"

"I did." No denying it.

"I wish I'd been there with you. It's no fair. All the good stuff happens to you!"

"Are you serious?" I quirked a brow, and she laughed.

"Kidding! But still . . . I'll bet you have tons of stories."

"Enough to fill a couple of books," I said. "But nothing we're going to talk about today. Today it's all about the bride!"

"Of course!"

Jenna fussed with tablecloths for the buffet tables and counted out silverware while Uncle Laz brought in loads and loads of food. Peering under the foil on a rectangular platter, I noticed the roasted quail. Yum. Looked very authentic. So did the beef, which they'd skewered. And those turkey legs! Though I'd argued with Rob about having them, they did smell amazing. I could almost envision the costumed guests walking around during the reception, turkey legs in hand. Very . . . authentic!

I knew Laz and Jenna's work would continue as the wedding ceremony progressed. By the time the "I dos" had been said, everything would be ready. The fruits and cheeses would be beautifully displayed, providing the guests with an appetizer before the main event. Then the real festivities would begin.

But enough about the food. I needed to find the bride-to-be!

At 6:15 I stuck my head in the bride's room to see how Marian was faring. I gasped when I saw the champagne-colored Juliet gown—hand-beaded crushed velvet with exquisite gold trim. I'd seen it on the hanger, of course, in all of its splendor. But now, seeing it on the bride . . . well, there were no words to describe it. Or her. She simply radiated beauty, from her adorned hair to her tiny, corseted waist to those delicate cream-colored slippers.

Her ladies-in-waiting were doing the very things ladies-in-waiting were wont to do—fussing with her hair, touching up her makeup, and so forth. Off in the corner, Marian's mother stood with camera in hand, flashing pictures and blubbering like a baby. Yep. Just your typical wedding thus far.

"Marian!" Stepping into the room, I approached with ginger steps. "You are by far the prettiest thing I've ever seen." I reached to touch one of the dainty faux pearls on the bottom of the flowing chiffon and lace sleeves. "You must feel like a princess. You certainly look like one."

"Bella, you're sweet." She took my hand. "But I haven't forgotten you run a wedding facility. You have to tell all of your brides that."

"Maybe, but I'm not exaggerating here. You are, in fact, the most gorgeous bride I've ever seen." I gestured for her to turn around so I could see the veil. From the front it looked like a simple floral circlet, but the back revealed something altogether different. Flowing layers of chiffon cascaded down Marian's back, trimmed off with some delicate beads.

"I still can't believe I ordered this dress and veil from the Internet." She sighed as she examined her reflection in the mirror. "Oh, Bella, I've known exactly what I wanted since I went to the Texas Renaissance Festival for the first time as a girl. I knew what the dress would look like. I knew what the bridesmaids would wear." She reached to take her sister's hand. "And I knew exactly what the ceremony would be like. The only problem was, I could never find someone to walk alongside me in all of that. Every other facility I tried said it couldn't be done."

"We called over a dozen facilities," her mother said. "None of them would let her bring in a castle."

"Oh, trust me, it wasn't the easiest thing I've ever done, but I love a challenge! And it's worth it . . . for you. Besides, I live for this sort of thing. You know that."

"I do now. And I'm so grateful." Her eyes filled with tears, threatening to destroy her perfect makeup job. "You were the only one who took me seriously. And now look where we are."

"Yes, now look. So what is it about a medieval wedding that felt right to you?" I asked her. "Why did you decide to go this route?"

"Oh, that's easy." Marian's eyes lit up. "The costumes are glorious. Breathtaking. And the trumpet fanfare, the carriage procession, the sword arch for the bride, the ribbon circlets . . . Oh, Bella, it's any girl's dream. She dresses as a princess and walks the aisle—past people she loves—toward her prince. It's Cinderella all over again, only there's no wicked stepmother. And everyone gets to go to the ball, absolutely everyone."

I glanced over at Marcella, who placed a flower garland atop one of the bridesmaid's heads. "Bella, could you hand me a hairpin?" she asked.

"Of course."

The dresses that the ladies-in-waiting wore were beautiful, in a soft shade of lavender with exquisite trim. But they didn't compare to Juliet herself. No, I had truly never seen anything like our bride-to-be.

After I helped Marcella, I rushed to get Joey, who had taken on the role of photographer. He entered the room, took one look at Marian, and stopped with his mouth open. "Oh, wow."

"I guess that's good, then?" she asked.

"Mm-hmm." He snapped a picture. "Kind of reminds me of that opera the other night. Seems like we've had a full-out Renaissance week."

"It's cool, isn't it?" She smiled, then turned back to the mirror to check her makeup once more.

Glancing at my watch, I took note of the time: 6:30. "I noticed you have a few guests already."

"My parents," Marian said. "And Rob's."

"More than that. A handful of people just came in. They were costumed, by the way."

She smiled. "I knew it! Probably half or more of the guests will be. Took some doing to convince my aunt Mildred, but I think she'll go along with it. I hope."

Somehow thinking about her aunt Mildred reminded me that I hadn't checked up on the trio of sisters. After asking around, I was told—by Jenna, who was putting the finishing decorative touches on the buffet table—that they were in the kitchen, practicing their tunes.

I knew, of course, that Mama had been hard at work on Twila, Jolene, and Bonnie Sue. Mama, the makeup queen. I knew I could trust her. Still, I was half-terrified, half-intrigued to see what they looked like. Surely with my mother at the helm they wouldn't go overboard.

When I entered the kitchen, I gasped. Truly they looked stunning. Twila wore a fabulous coral dress, completely appropriate to Renaissance times. Jolene—whose hair was absolutely perfect for the time period—looked stunning in royal purple. And the light blue really complemented Bonnie Sue's eyes. They were like three plus-sized Barbie dolls in Renaissance attire. Only prettier.

"What do you think of my hair?" Jolene patted her 'do, and I nodded.

"Who did that?"

"Oh, I did." Sophia appeared from around the corner with a smile on her face. "Didn't take me long at all. I just looked up a couple of sites on the Internet and followed the instructions. Besides, when you have great hair to start with, it's a breeze."

Jolene beamed. "Oh, thank you, honey. Want to know the secret to my hair's natural beauty?"

"Of course!" I said.

"It's all about the product." She leaned in, her eyes narrowing as she whispered, "Mane and Tail. You buy it at the feed store. Makes the hair silky smooth."

"And puts the giddyap and go in your day," Bonnie Sue said with a giggle.

At this all the women got the giggles. Jolene finally got herself under control, claiming her bladder couldn't take the excitement.

Seconds later Rob popped his head in the door. "Hey, Bella. I've been looking for you."

I approached him with a smile. "Rob, I owe you. Marian doesn't know that I got arrested."

"And she won't . . . till this is over. You should've seen the trouble the bridesmaids went through to keep her from the television and newspaper, though."

"I'll bet." I gave him a hug.

"You know the story hit the national news, right?" Rob added. "My parents saw it on several major networks."

I groaned. "Seriously, Rob. I'm so sorry all of this happened. I don't know what else to say."

"Don't say anything. I saw the whole thing, Bella. Not your fault at all. And everything is moving forward according to plan, so I'm a happy man."

"I'm glad."

"I just wanted to ask about the fireworks. I know we planned to have them if the weather cooperated. Looks like it's sunny and dry."

"Right. There's no sign of rain this evening. The storm has passed."

As the words passed my lips, I breathed a sigh of relief. The storm really *had* passed, and not just the one in the gulf.

I'd somehow made it through the planning of this wedding, the ordeal with Brock, and a night in jail. And I'd felt God's presence in the very midst of it, so I could attest to the fact that there truly was an eye in the middle of life's storms. No doubt about it.

But I didn't have time to be philosophical right now—I had a wedding to get to. And quick!

31

Love and Marriage

At ten minutes till seven, we were ready to roll. I sent the bridal party out of the side door to prepare for their grand entrance, then made my way to the front of the facility, where I got my first glimpse of D.J. in his medieval attire.

I let out a whistle. "Man. You look like you hopped straight off a movie screen into real life. Only . . . better."

"You think?" He turned, showing off the deep blue doublet and black leggings.

Yummy.

He gestured for me to spin too. I did, feeling like a little girl at play as my gown swished around my ankles.

"You're the prettiest thing I've ever seen." D.J. drew me close and kissed my forehead. "And that dress is like something from a magazine."

I felt my cheeks turn warm. "Thank you, kind sir." I curtsied, overcome by a sense of giddiness. "You ready for tonight? Feel like playing a medieval deejay?"

"I'll give it my best shot."

We made our way through the throng of people, and my gaze shifted upward to the sunset. It was breathtaking—a real treat, especially after the storm. Good thing, because the entire crowd—guests, anyway—stood outside the front of the wedding facility, awaiting the arrival of the king and queen.

As trumpeters played a magnificent fanfare, the carriage procession began. I could see the first carriage coming our way from the south end of Broadway. Thankfully, the police escort kept any would-be onlookers at bay.

Wait a minute . . . police escort? I looked at the officer, stunned to find the same fellow who'd arrested me last night. Go figure.

"D.J., do you see who that is?" I whispered.

"Mm-hmm. I talked to him earlier. He's really a pretty nice guy, Bella. I think you'll like him once you get to know him."

"Probably. If he ever forgives me for the way things went down."

Oh well. No time to think about that right now.

The carriage paused at the end of the driveway, and Rob's four groomsmen climbed out, dressed as knights, of course. Brock was the last one out of the carriage and created quite a stir with his arrival. His medieval attire really, truly made him look like a knight. And not just any knight—this was one worthy of the king's presence.

I shifted my gaze to the next carriage. I already knew it would carry the bride's ladies-in-waiting dressed for the night. One by one, the beautiful bridesmaids exited the carriage in their Renaissance gowns, greeting guests with hands extended. They were followed by a darling little flower girl, who made quite a production out of tossing the flower petals on the ground. Who could blame her? This was the opportunity of a lifetime.

Mama slipped into place behind me and whispered, "Bella, they look beautiful."

"Don't they?" I whispered back. "And what do you think of the carriages? Very fairy-tale-like, right?"

"Very. The whole thing is like something straight from a movie." She gasped as Rob arrived, not in a carriage but on horseback. "Oh my goodness!"

The beautiful stallion was decked out in attire fitting for royalty. The groom tipped his feathered hat at his guests as he neared the grounds, then leaped from his horse, joining them for a few rowdy cheers and boisterous slaps on the back.

"Congratulations to the happy groom!" D.J. called out, using his best deejay voice.

The crowd went crazy, following his lead. All part of the fun, of course.

Finally, the moment we'd all been waiting for was upon us. Even Rob didn't know what was going to happen next, but I did. Marian's father had arranged for a Cinderella carriage drawn by four magnificent Clydesdales to bring the bride up Broadway. I could hear the *clip-clop* of their hooves as they rounded the side street less than a block away. The guests gasped as the coach drew near. Twinkling Christmas lights caused it to sparkle against a now-darkening sky. The timing was perfect, just as we'd hoped it would be.

The trumpet fanfare continued as Maid Marian eased her way out of the carriage with her father at her side. With tears in his eyes, he led her to Rob, whose face lit up with a glow paralleling the lights on the carriage.

Tears sprang to my eyes. I turned to grab D.J.'s hand. "This is how it should be for every girl. Just like a fairy tale!"

As the trumpeters ended their fanfare, the four knights created a sword arch for the bride and groom to walk under. Once they made it through, Rob and Marian led the way around the side of the wedding facility to the castle in the back. With the sun now dipping off in the west, the castle had a magical glow about it. I could never have pictured it looking this perfect, but it did. If I used my imagination, I could almost see Camelot.

We made our way into the castle, where the guests took their seats at appointed tables. Unlike traditional weddings, the bride and groom went about greeting their guests, toasting the occasion and laughing with great cheer. I'd never seen such enthusiasm prior to the ceremony, and I'd been to quite a few weddings over the years. This was truly something to behold. And while the guests and wedding party were playing a game, they were quite serious in their accolades of the bride and groom. Seemed everyone thought this was a match made in heaven.

Funny. I paused to think about that. When you were perfectly matched, others knew it. You didn't have to convince them, did you? No, they just knew the two of you were meant to be together. And tonight, with so many witnesses in attendance, there was an overwhelming sense of support for Rob and Marian's decision not just to wed, but to wed in this fashion.

Finally the moment arrived. A string orchestra took the stage, along with Marian's pastor, a short, balding fellow with a whimsical smile. He wore medieval attire appropriate to a man of the cloth, but I could tell the neck piece was bothering him a little.

As the music shifted gears, Rob and his knights took their places next to the pastor. Then, as the violinist began a lyrical piece that sounded lighter than air itself, the ladies-in-waiting began their walk up the center aisle, followed by the flower girl, who'd now run out of petals.

I watched from the back of the room as the violinist played her introduction to *The Wedding March*, my heart beating so fast I thought I might faint. Sure, I'd been to hundreds of weddings, and the walk up the aisle always got to me. But we'd planned something special for this particular walk up the aisle, and I wanted it to go smoothly for everyone involved.

At that very moment, the bride's and groom's family members lifted beautifully decorated archways to cover the aisle. Then the guests rose from their seats as Marian began her walk toward her groom-to-be, crossing under each archway as she went.

I whispered a prayer that the rest of the ceremony would go as planned. Somehow I just knew I didn't need to fret over this one. Everything would be picture-perfect. And when all was said and done, there really would be a happily ever after.

32

The Best Is Yet to Come

True to my predictions, the wedding ceremony came off without a hitch. And though I'd never coordinated a royal event such as this, I felt like a pro in no time at all. In fact, I was feeling so confident about it that I almost forgot all of the work involved. Then again, that was always the case. No sooner did one wedding end than I was ready to go again with another. I barely remembered the work. Or the cost. No, all that mattered was the event itself.

And this was quite an event!

When the vows had been taken, D.J. introduced himself to the crowd as the town crier, then kicked into gear, inviting the guests to stay for the king's feast. Already Jenna, Laz, and Nick were putting appetizers out on the beautifully decorated tables, with D.J.'s parents scurrying along behind them, offering assistance. I knew the hot foods would follow, but not until the photos had been taken.

Scurrying around, I located Joey. Looked like I didn't need

to worry. He had the wedding party organized up front in no time and snapped pictures with joyful abandon. I knew he lived for nights like this. And apparently his fiancée Norah enjoyed it too. She helped him get the people lined up, making the process that much easier. They made a great duo.

While that was taking place, the guests loaded up on appetizers and punch, and the orchestra began to play. I knew it would be only a matter of time before the real party began.

Glancing over at Twila, Jolene, and Bonnie Sue, I gasped. They were making the rounds from table to table, doing some sort of comedy routine. Would Rob and Marian kill me or find this humorous? Hopefully the latter. The guests seemed to be enjoying the ladies' antics, at any rate.

When the pictures were finished, the wedding party took their seats at their table of honor on the stage. They were served by young women dressed in authentic peasant attire. The guests were served next. I could hear folks oohing and aahing over the quail and the beef kabobs. But ironically, the thing they seemed to enjoy most was the turkey legs. Go figure. Rob had been right about that. I'd have to tell him later.

The party really got going as the bride and groom rose to dance their first dance. D.J. announced them, of course, doing a fabulous job as town crier. The words "Come one! Come all!" had never sounded so good.

The violinist played a lively little jig, and Rob and Marian danced a well-rehearsed number that might very well have come out of Renaissance times. This was followed by the father-daughter dance and then the money dance, which seemed to go over well with the crowd. At D.J.'s bidding, the guests danced with Marian, tucking fifty-dollar and even hundred-dollar bills into the palm of the first knight, Brock

Benson. My honey did such a fine job drawing people in that Brock soon had to remove his cap to contain all the money.

A few minutes into the money dance, I noticed something rather unusual. Uncle Laz was walking around with Guido on his shoulder. I'd heard Rob tell him he should but didn't think he would actually do it. Of course, with Laz dressed in rogue-looking attire, the bird seemed a fitting accompaniment. Guido greeted folks with an "Arrr!" and a "Whatcha lookin' at, wise guy?" Thankfully, the guests found him delightful entertainment. Occasionally a guest was given the plan of salvation by the somewhat scatterbrained bird, but that was okay too.

I walked into the kitchen to check on Jenna and Nick, who were serving up the quail. Jenna looked pretty snazzy in her peasant frock. For that matter, so did Nick. I'd seen my brother dressed in a suit before, but never medieval attire. He looked over at me with a sigh. "Don't ever ask me to wear tights again, Bella. They're all twisted up . . . and let's just say that's not exactly making this a stellar evening. I'd like to focus on the food, not untwisting my pantyhose."

His words got me tickled. I went over to him and planted a kiss on his cheek. "Nick, I wish I could promise you wouldn't ever have to wear tights again, but I can't. I can only say how grateful I am that you—all of you—have been so willing to play along to make this evening spectacular. The food is great, your costumes are great . . ." Tears filled my eyes. "I really do have the best family on Planet Earth."

"Yes, you do," my mother said, entering the room with a tray in hand. "And don't ever forget it!"

Like I could do that.

Pop came in, grabbed a turkey leg, and took a bite. I gasped. "Pop!"

"What?" He played innocent.

"That's for the guests."

"What do I look like? Chopped liver?" He took a couple of hefty bites, then left the room, turkey leg still in hand.

I glanced at my watch, stunned at the time. "Oh man. I've got to find the Splendora sisters. It's almost time for them to take the stage."

I found Twila gabbing with one of the guests, showing off her new outfit. Tapping on her shoulder, I whispered, "You're on, ladies. Dazzle us with your madrigal tunes. Oh, and have fun!"

Maybe I shouldn't have added that last part. After D.J. introduced them, they made quite a production out of getting to the stage, flirting with several male guests along the way. As the trio moved toward center stage, they fussed with each other's hair and makeup, making a big scene about that too. The audience found it entertaining, thank goodness.

Then the music began. Their first number was out-of-this-world good. So good, in fact, that a guest asked for their card. I'd never heard such tight harmonies before.

After a few madrigal tunes, things took a bit of a turn in an unexpected direction. Twila had apparently worked on a little jester-like comedy routine for the women to do. I watched it all, laughing so hard tears ran down my face. Still, I wasn't sure how the bride would respond to this impromptu addition to her wedding. I looked at Marian, and a wave of relief washed over me. She, too, was laughing. In fact, I'd never seen her look happier.

Then again, why wouldn't she be happy? It was her wedding day, after all. The day she'd waited for . . . for years.

I grew a little sad thinking about that. I hadn't known D.J. for long. Just over three months. But I was nearing the place where I was ready for a commitment. Did he feel the same, or were we destined to date forever?

The orchestra began a jolly piece of music, and D.J. invited the guests to round dance. Marian had explained this part to me in detail, claiming it was the perfect opportunity for young men to meet ladies. Not to mention check out their dancing skills.

I watched with surprise as Brock went over to Rosa and extended his hand. Would she really dance with him? With flushed cheeks, she accepted his invitation, and within seconds they had joined the others on the floor. Rosa didn't really look confident with the round dance, but she seemed to be taking it in stride.

I searched through the crowd for a sign of D.J. Oh, if only things would slow down so that we could join the dance. Not that the wedding planner necessarily needed to be dancing. There were other things I should be attending to. Like the wedding cake, for instance. The bride and groom were supposed to cut the cake before the round dancing! How could I have forgotten?

As the dancing ended, I signaled the trumpeters to sound the call for the cutting of the cake. D.J.—now completely in his element as town crier—went to the stage to speak to the people about the tradition, something he and Rob had arranged in advance. The court jester, a lively fellow dressed in typical jester attire, acted out D.J.'s words as he spoke.

"Wedding cakes have an interesting tradition," D.J. said, using a more dramatic voice than before. His British accent wasn't very good, but at least he was giving it his best. "Back in Roman times, a small loaf of bread was broken over the bride's head for fertility."

That got a chuckle out of the audience. Brock elbowed

Rob, who flushed. The jester pretended to break a cake over the head of one of the guests, which caused even more laughter.

"In the Middle Ages, guests would bring small cakes to the wedding ceremony and stack them on top of each other."

I signaled for the ladies-in-waiting to enter the stage, each carrying a white cake. They looked a little nervous, especially the poor bridesmaid who carried the bottom layer. It was quite large. She managed to get it onto the table without dropping it, and I could read the relief in Marian's eyes.

One by one the cakes were stacked, the largest on bottom and the smaller ones above. The audience took great delight in this process, and I could hear the clicking of cameras around the room.

In the end, the cake stood four layers high. Well, five, if you counted the tiny cake on top, which the flower girl placed with D.J.'s help. I stood back and looked at how changed the table looked. Funny how such a thing of beauty could come from so many people working together. In a sense, that's what had happened with the wedding facility. I could never have pulled off this wedding if not for my parents and my siblings, not to mention Laz, Rosa, and Jenna. Yes, we'd stacked our cake layers—symbolically speaking—and the outcome looked pretty tasty.

At this point, D.J. grinned. "Would the bride and groom come to the stage, please?" Marian and Rob climbed the steps to the stage, taking their places on either side of the small table. "To symbolize good fortune and prosperity, the bride and groom would kiss each other over the top of the cakes. Without knocking them down, of course."

This got another laugh from the crowd.

"Rob and Marian, let's have a little smooching!"

The photographs that followed must've been priceless. They made it over the top of the cake—barely—and kissed, but Rob's doublet laces got hung up in the cake topper. When he stood up, the topper was dangling from his chest with icing all over it. The crowd went nuts, of course.

They also went nuts over the cake, which was the tastiest thing I'd ever eaten. In spite of her busyness, Rosa had still managed to pull off a great wedding cake. Nothing new there, but she'd never made one the same week she debuted on television. The woman was a wonder!

D.J. joined me and we shared a piece of cake. I'd just taken my last bite when Bubba swept through the door. I was pretty sure it was Bubba, anyway. He was still in his Figaro costume—decked out from head to toe.

As Bubba drew near, I looked at D.J., confused. "What in the world?"

"It's a surprise for Rob and Marian," D.J. explained. "Brock asked us to do this after hearing Bubba sing at the opera. He asked Bubba to entertain us here tonight."

"So here I am!" Bubba grinned.

"Oh, that's wonderful!" I took his hand and gave it a squeeze to show my delight at this news. "Are you singing in Italian?"

Bubba nodded. "Yeah. I've got a couple of songs from the show that will do. I have to sing fast, though, because we're on intermission at the opera house. I need to get back as quick as I can."

"I don't believe it! You left the show to come here?"

"Yep." Bubba took his place before the crowd of wedding guests and began to sing. Everyone—and everything—came to a grinding halt. Marian moved my direction with a stunned look on her face. "Oh, Bella! Why didn't you tell me? He's marvelous. Just perfect!"

"I didn't know he was coming. Brock arranged all of this. Well, Brock and D.J."

"That D.J." Marian giggled. "He really is something, isn't he, honey?"

"Oh yes." He was something, all right. And like a true knight in shining armor, he always rushed in to save the day, even when I didn't know I needed saving.

"He's a keeper, Bella," Marian whispered in my ear. Then she glided back across the room and took her groom by the hand. Seconds later they were on the dance floor, waltzing to the song Bubba crooned.

I looked at D.J. and extended my hand.

He looked a little flustered. "Oh, I'm not a dancer, Bella. You know that."

"Yes, and Bubba thought he wasn't an opera singer either. The truth is, we don't have a clue what we're capable of until we try."

He took my hand with a boyish grin. "I can't argue with that logic. Maybe by the end of the evening I'll be a ballroom dancer."

He swept me into his arms, and I felt like a princess as he twirled me around the dance floor. When the song ended, D.J. looked up at the stage, a terrified look on his face.

"What is it, babe?" I asked.

"I, um, have to do something."

He took off running, and I started to ask him if the clock was about to strike midnight. Maybe he'd leave a glass boot behind. For whatever reason, he took the stage next to Bubba. Then the two of them began to sing the most amazing Italian love song I'd ever heard in my life.

"Bella!" Jenna approached, her eyes wide. "I knew Bubba could sing, but . . . D.J.?"

I couldn't respond because I didn't want to miss even one second of their performance. Finally, as they rounded the chorus for the second time, I turned to Jenna. "I should've known. I've stood next to D.J. in church dozens of times and heard him worship. I knew he had a strong voice, but I never pictured this."

Two cowboys from the piney woods of east Texas, standing on a stage in medieval attire and singing opera. Would wonders never cease?

Earline drew near with tears in her eyes. "Bella, I can't thank you enough. Look at the transformation in my boys. Bubba has never been happier, and D.J. . . ." She released a sigh. "He's turned into quite an amazing man. I'm so proud of him."

"Me too." I could barely get the words out over the lump in my throat.

When the song ended, Bubba made a run for the door, hollering his congratulations to the bride and groom. I whispered a prayer that he would make it back to the opera house in time for the second act. D.J. slipped back into town crier mode and introduced the court jester, who took the stage once again, his silly antics bringing more than a few smiles. The whimsical fellow was followed by a juggler in colorful attire, then a real sword-swallower, each one introduced with great fanfare by my Splendora sweetie. I squeezed my eyes shut, refusing to watch the sword-swallower, especially when he lit the swords on fire.

Over the next hour or so, things got a little rowdy. People ended up in the stockades—this part staged, of course. Somehow D.J. kept things under control. I'd never seen him more in his element. Who would have known it? My D.J. really was born to be a deejay, even a medieval one.

I was happy when the moment arrived for the fireworks. Nick and Joey had been working on this for hours, I knew, and it would be perfect. The trumpeters got our attention once again, and I watched, my heart racing, as D.J. summoned the guests to the area in front of the stage.

"His Highness and Her Highness would ask you to join them in the courtyard for the royal display of fireworks. Afterward they will board their carriage, hand in hand, for the first time as a married couple!"

He left the stage and headed my way. The guests began to spill out into the area around the castle, which, under the twinkling stars, looked as real as any castle from medieval times. Joy wrapped itself around me as those first fireworks lit the night sky, merging with the shimmering stars above.

D.J. slipped into place behind me, wrapping his arms around my waist. I turned to face him, my heart soaring with the excitement of the moment. Fireworks flew overhead, but they were nothing compared to the ones going off in my heart as D.J.'s lips met mine for a kiss sweeter than tiramisu.

Surely no one would mind if the town crier and the wedding planner spent a little time smooching under the stars. Right? We were only following the script, after all.

33

After You've Gone

On the morning after the wedding, Marian surprised me with a phone call. I laughed when I heard her cheerful voice.

"Aren't you supposed to be on your honeymoon or something?" I asked.

"We're leaving tomorrow for Bali. But I wanted to call you to say thanks for everything you did."

"Oh, honey, you're welcome."

"I, um, picked up a newspaper this morning," she said, then giggled. "And I happened to catch a few minutes of the national news too." She paused. "Bella, why didn't you tell me? You spent the night before my wedding in the Galveston County jail?"

A groan erupted. "Yeah. Sorry. I didn't want anything to ruin your day. I wanted it to be about you. No distractions."

"Well, I'm glad no one told me. It certainly would have

been a distraction. But it's still pretty humorous. From what I hear, you beat up a police officer."

"That's what they tell me." I sighed. "But don't believe everything you hear. I'm really just a girl from Galveston Island who made a teeny-tiny mistake. At exactly the wrong time. In front of, well, pretty much everyone in America."

I shuddered as I replayed the moment in my mind. No telling what those cameramen had done with the footage they'd shot on my lawn that evening. Likely they were speculating about Brock Benson's love life on the talk shows at this very moment. Nothing I could do about that.

Oblivious to my thoughts, Marian kept going. "Well, you still managed to pull off the wedding of the century, and that's what matters!" She laughed. "And your Splendora friends were the life of the party, weren't they? Absolutely priceless!"

"Um, yeah. I hope you're okay with that."

"Okay with it? They were my favorite part!" She laughed long and loud. "Seriously, I think you're so blessed to have such great friends and family, Bella. They're wonderful. And those women were the icing on the cake. They looked amazing and sounded even better."

"I have to agree. Thank you for including them."

"Oh, honey, you're welcome! I'm just thrilled you did this for us. This was your first exposure to a medieval wedding, right, Bella?"

"Right." I had done a lot of research online but had never actually been to a medieval wedding until now.

"What did you think? Did you enjoy it?"

"Oh yes! I'd wanted to plan a medieval wedding for ages, but I wasn't sure I had it in me."

"You have it in you, all right. And think of how much

easier it's going to be next time, now that you have this one under your belt."

"Yes." I paused a moment, reliving the entire night. The gowns. The twinkling lights on the Cinderella carriage. The castle. The dancing. The cakes. Overcome with emotion, I shared my heart. "Oh, Marian, it was glorious. I think I loved it because it was absolutely fairy-tale-like. Sent me back in time and made me think that miracles were possible. That men really could be chivalrous and ladies could be elegant and . . . well, valued."

"Yes. Women were certainly different back then."

"Maybe not so different." I thought about D.J.—how he always treated me like a princess. "I guess the real difference is in figuring out that we're all royalty. We're God's kids. So the whole princess theme is very real. That's why it resonates with women so deeply. We're waiting for Prince Charming to sweep us away, of course, but that's just a symbol of God sweeping in and loving us in spite of our flaws. He doesn't see our warts. Or our wrinkles. He only sees that we're his little princesses. And he wants us to hang out in his throne room."

"Well said." Marian sighed. "And I agree on every point." After a brief pause, she asked about Brock. "Is he still at your place?"

"Until tomorrow afternoon. Joey's going to drive him to Houston to catch his flight back to L.A. around noon."

"Bella . . ." Marian paused, then her voice seemed to catch. "I want to tell you something about Brock."

"What about him?"

"Rob and I have been praying for him for years. He's Hollywood on the outside, but I've always believed God wanted to break through that shell and do a work in his life."

"Agreed."

"One of the reasons I jumped on board with the idea of Brock staying with your family was because I knew he'd spend those ten days surrounded by people who love the Lord, people who could share the love of Christ with him."

I sighed. "Marian, I don't know that we were the best choice. The Rossis are a little, well, offbeat. I hope we didn't do more damage than good."

"Oh no. The fact that your family is quirky is what made this so perfect. He needed to see that Christians are normal, that they still go through the usual ups and downs. That they're not stiff or pretentious."

"Yes, but getting arrested and being filmed by the Food Network?" I shuddered. "We've left a lasting impression on him."

"You have," she said, "but I'd be willing to bet it's not the impression you're thinking. He shared a few things with Rob out there on that boat. I think he's making progress."

"Even more since his night in jail," I added. "I heard all about it on the way home."

"Sounds like God is getting through to him. But I'm telling you this so you'll pray. Brock Benson's got the world at his fingertips, but what does it profit a man if he gains the whole world . . ."

"Only to lose his soul." We spoke the words together.

"Right." Her sigh was followed by an unexpected giggle. "Um, Bella, I have to go. A certain someone thinks I'm taking too much time away from him." Another giggle followed, and I did my best not to think about what might be evoking it.

"Marian, go enjoy your honeymoon. Oh, but just let me say one more thing—you were absolutely ravishing last night."

"Th-thank you." With a series of giggles, I lost her. The

phone went dead, and I stared at it, smiling. Oh, what would that be like? To wake up next to the man of your dreams? To have him so infatuated with you that he couldn't even be away from you long enough for a phone call?

A familiar voice drew me away from the phone. D.J.!

"When did you get here?" I rose from the sofa to give him a hug.

"Oh, about a minute ago. Aunt Rosa let me in."

"You came in the back?"

He nodded, and we sat together on the sofa. "Yeah. I parked my car in the driveway, so it was just easier to come in the back. Rosa and Brock are in the kitchen, talking."

"He's really going to miss her cooking," I said. "Poor guy."

"Oh, I wouldn't worry too much. From what I could tell, she was giving him the recipes for his favorites. In alphabetical order."

"Wow. He cooks?"

"Who knows!" D.J. laughed. "For all we know, he might hire a cook. But at least he's got the recipes now. He'll be taking a piece of Texas with him."

"He will." I nodded, thinking of Marian's words. I decided to spill my guts to D.J. "I have to admit, I was a little enamored with Brock when he first showed up."

"I figured."

"He's a Hollywood star."

"Right." D.J.'s eyes narrowed. "Are we going someplace with this?"

"Yeah." I leaned against him, placing a few tender kisses on his cheek. "I just need you to know that my heart is completely sold out to you, Dwayne Neeley Jr. You're my knight in shining armor. My prince. You're the Romeo to my Juliet.

You're the one I've dreamed of since I was a little girl. You're the one with my glass slipper."

"Are these fairy-tale analogies going to go on much longer?" D.J. grinned. "'Cause if they are . . . "

"Nah. I'm done now. But I just needed you to know I'm in love with you. Head-over-heels, can't-walk-straight, don't-know-what-I'd-do-if-anything-ever-happened-to-separate-us in love. In case you didn't already know it."

"You love me?" He looked stunned. "I had *no* idea." The look on his face was so serious, I slugged him. D.J. laughed, then wrapped me in his arms. "You're a nut, Bella. Seriously, I've never doubted your love for a minute, even with an Academy Award winner in the house vying for your attention."

"Really?"

"Yes. And just so you know, I've loved you from the minute I met you in that wedding facility of yours. The only problem with you saying all those things about me—other than the fact that about half of them are exaggerated—is I want to respond with something equally as grand, but I can't."

"What do you mean?"

"I want to tell you how much you mean to me, but I'm not as good with words, which really frustrates me. You painted a really pretty picture there with all that fairy-tale stuff. I would try to come back at you, but I don't think I could do it justice."

"You'll never know unless you try."

He looked me in the eyes, and for the first time I noticed his tears. "Bella, I thank God *every* day for you. When I wake up in the morning, I praise him from the bottom of my heart that he brought you into my life. And when I drop into bed at night, I tell him all over again. I'm not sure what I ever did to deserve you. Maybe that's what makes you such a gift—there's nothing I could have done to deserve someone as great as you. But I can't live without you, Bella. And I don't plan on trying."

I reached up with a fingertip and brushed a tear from his cheek, my heart pounding so hard against my ribs that it actually hurt. "That was more beautiful than any fairy tale," I whispered. "I don't think you could've done a nicer job of saying it."

"I'm just a country boy from Splendora, Texas," he said. "I'll never be in the movies. But I'm fine being who I am. And where I am. As long as you're with me, I'm content."

"Then you can count on being content forever. Because you're not shaking me. Ever."

He winked, then whispered, "Best news I've heard all day."

As his lips met mine for a kiss that rivaled any on a Hollywood screen, in the next room Guido took to singing, his voice adding just that right ambience for our special moment. In fact, "Ninety-Nine Bottles of Beer on the Wall" never sounded so good.

34

Just the Way You Are

When D.J. and I came up for air, I giggled, then gave him another peck on the cheek. Off in the distance, Rosa shouted, "Someone shut that bird up before I strangle him!" and I laughed.

"I guess we'd better do something about Guido before Rosa hurts him."

D.J. shook his head. "She wouldn't hurt that bird. In fact, I think she's crazy about him."

"Oh?"

"Sure. He's a part of Laz. And you know how she feels about Laz." D.J. grinned. "Not that she's come out and said it, mind you, but I think it's pretty clear."

"Yeah." I cradled into his embrace. "Why do you suppose it's so hard for some people to tell each other how they feel?"

"Not sure, but I'm glad that family trait didn't trickle down to you." He kissed the tip of my nose, then rose and grabbed my hand. "But Guido's starting to get on my nerves now, so let's go see if we can help him shift gears to another song."

"He only knows one other song."

"Exactly."

We entered the kitchen to find Guido in his cage in front of the window. He was down to eighty-eight bottles of beer, and Rosa looked like she might very well strangle him. Brock sat on a barstool, scribbling down a recipe, and acknowledged us with a grunt as we walked into the room.

"Tell me again how you prepared the chicken parmesan." He looked at Rosa, perched and ready to write her response.

"I start with the most tender chicken breasts I can find, and then pound them down to the perfect size, shape, and consistency."

"Okay. Got it." He looked up, ready for more.

"Afterward I deep-fry them and coat them in a meat gravy."

"The best on the planet," I threw in. "That first bite is always worth waiting for, but you've got to do it right. Get a decent-sized piece of chicken and plenty of sauce. And cheese."

"Oh, the cheese!" Rosa's face lit up. "I use mozzarella, of course, then add hand-grated Parmesan on top."

"The whole concoction is a cheese lover's delight," I said.

"Or a lactose-intolerant person's worst nightmare," my pop said, entering the room. He filled his coffee cup, then left us to our own devices.

Brock looked up at Rosa. "Thanks so much for sharing your secrets. I'm taking them with me back to Hollywood. Hope it's okay."

"As long as you give credit where credit is due." Aunt Rosa winked.

"Oh, I will," he said. "I'll tell everyone about you."

Rosa laughed. "I don't mean me, Brock, I mean the Lord. He's the one we need to give the credit to."

Brock looked a little confused by that.

I made my way over to Guido's cage and began to sing, "Amazing grace, how sweet the sound . . ." Guido picked up on my lead and added, "That saved a wretch like me!" He sustained the word *me* for quite some time, his voice warbling. I laughed. Turning back to Rosa, I said, "See? He's not so bad."

"I just wish he would make up his mind, is all," she said. "One minute he's a believer, the next minute he's singing about bottles of beer on the wall and calling people names. That bird straddles the fence, and it's driving me crazy. There's only so much a person can take, after all."

D.J. seemed to find that pretty humorous. "Well, we're working on him, but these things take time."

That got Brock's attention. He glanced up at us with a perplexed look. "What is it with you people and that song, anyway?"

"'Ninety-Nine Bottles of Beer on the Wall'?" I asked.

"No." He shook his head. "'Amazing Grace.' You were singing it in the car the other morning on the way home from jail, and the bird sings it all day long. Is that the only song your family knows?"

"Pretty much." I grinned. "Unless you count all of those Dean Martin songs coming from Laz's room. Or the Sinatra tunes Rosa plays all day. But even they don't compare." I turned to Rosa and shrugged. "Sorry."

"No, you're right." Rosa looked up from her recipe box. "Don't get me wrong, I love Ol' Blue Eyes. I'd marry him today if he asked me."

"Which would be tough, since he's currently crooning his tunes from the great beyond," D.J. whispered.

"But even Sinatra at his finest can't touch me like the words to 'Amazing Grace' can." Rosa lifted her apron and dabbed her eyes. "There's something about those words. They've stood the test of time."

She held us all spellbound with her dissertation on the song. I'd seen Rosa worked up before, but not like this.

Turning to Brock, she offered up an explanation. "See, I was just a little girl from Napoli who never really knew where she fit in."

"That's hard to believe," Brock said, offering her a sympathetic smile.

"No, it's true. I wasn't pretty like so many of the girls, especially like my sister Imelda. But I always knew the Lord loved me anyway, despite any flaws."

"You were just a kid." Brock shrugged. "He wouldn't be much of a God if he didn't love an innocent kid. Right?"

"Yes, but here's my point." She leaned her elbows on the island and looked into Brock's eyes. "I'm *still* his kid all these years later. And I still have flaws. But he loves me just the way I am. He's not like a man. I don't have to get all fancied up to impress him. It's his grace . . ." Rosa's eyes filled with tears. "Well, it's that grace that frees me up to be who I was called to be. It's that grace that reminds me I'm his child. If not for that grace, I wouldn't be here. Life is just too hard."

You could've heard a pin drop. I'd heard a lot of sermons in my life, but none like this. Rosa's words cut straight to the heart. Brock rose from his seat and began to pace the room. For a minute no one spoke a word.

"So . . ." He finally broke the silence. "That part about being lost and then found . . ."

291

We all looked at him, but no one interrupted.

"I'm not saying I really think I'm lost. But if I did, how would I go about getting found again?"

"You'd have to do the very thing that's the hardest to do—put your trust in someone other than yourself," I said. "And you don't have to worry about fixing anything yourself. He wants you . . . just like you are."

"So I guess that whole karma thing has to go right out the window if all of this stuff is to be believed."

I nodded. "Yeah, that's what I was trying to say the other day. If we could save ourselves, that would be one thing. But we can't."

"And there's no point in trying," D.J. added. "We're totally dependent on God, which is what makes the grace part so important. He does for us what we can't do for ourselves."

"I'm telling you, this would never fly in Hollywood." Brock continued to pace. "But there's something about all of you that's . . ."

"Different?" Rosa asked, wrinkling her nose.

"Yeah." Brock paused, then smiled. "But in a good way. In a way that makes me want to rethink the last twenty-eight years of my life. You know what I mean?"

"I know what you mean." Rosa reached over and touched his arm, such a gentle gesture that it took me by surprise. She really was softening lately.

Brock walked over to Guido's cage and stared him down. To his credit, Guido did a pretty good job of staring back. Then the most amazing thing happened. Without even being prompted, Guido began to sing "Amazing Grace" once again. When he got to the words, "I once was lost, but now am found," he paused, then continued his stare down with Brock.

If that didn't convince a guy, nothing would.

35

The Good Life

Less than five minutes after Guido's final rendition of "Amazing Grace," Brock fell to pieces right in front of us. He told us everything—about his childhood, his journey out of the pit he'd lived in with his mother, the eventual move to Los Angeles . . . everything. We let him talk, knowing it was the best thing for him, what with confession being so good for the soul and all. Besides, this was his testimony, and I had a feeling he'd be using it a lot from now on.

When he finally paused to take a breath, Brock turned to D.J. "What do I need to do?"

"Do? Hmm." D.J. paused, a reflective look on his face. "Well, you can start by just having a conversation with God like you've had with us. You're going to find that he's really easy to talk to."

"I wouldn't have a clue how to do that."

Over the next couple of minutes, D.J. talked Brock through the basic plan of salvation in layman's terms. No sermonizing. I'd never been prouder of my sweetie. And when Brock bowed his head to pray, the whole room grew silent. Even Guido seemed to fall under the spell of the holy hush.

My heart thumped madly as all of this transpired. Somehow God had taken the chaos of the last few days and used it for his glory. *You did it, Lord. You really did it.* Why had I ever doubted? And how wonderful to see the role D.J. had played in all of this. He had such a natural way about him. No preaching. No condemnation. Just a simple, honest conversation with a life-altering message attached. I had so much to learn from him.

As I turned to face Brock, I found myself unable to hold back my tears. "I'm so excited for you. This is going to change . . . well, everything."

"I have a feeling you're right." He raked his fingers through his hair. "But I'm not sure where to start. There's got to be something I can do." He paced the room.

"Something you can do?" I asked. "You've already done it, Brock. You've asked Jesus to be the Lord of your life. That's the best decision you'll ever make."

"I know, but now that I've done that, I feel like there's something more he has for me. Remember that stuff you told me about putting others first? I've had it backwards all along. It's time to change that. It's not about me, is it?"

"Well, you're supposed to love others as you love yourself," I said. "So I suppose it would be impossible to love others if you didn't love yourself first."

"Trust me, I've spent a lifetime loving myself." He shook his head. "But I get the feeling that needs to change. I can't just say I'm a Christian and not do anything. You know? For one thing, I'll have to turn down the role I've just been offered in that next movie. Totally not the kind of message I want to send to people, now that I'm . . ." He looked at me and quirked a brow. "What is it I am again?"

"You could call it any number of things—born again or saved being at the top of the list," D.J. said. "But I think I would just say you're a Christian. You're a believer in Christ."

"Okay. I'm a Christian. Good enough." Brock continued to pace, finally turning to me. "Bella, I have a lot of money."

"Right. I know. I mean, well, I figured . . . I don't really know anything about your finances."

"I'm always giving to charities to make myself look good, but I'll have to reconsider some of that. Saving the whales isn't exactly the theme of my life. Helping people . . . now *that's* more along the lines of what I'd like to do. How can I help people, Bella?" He took a seat on the sofa next to me with a pensive look on his face. "Where do I start?"

"Hang on a minute." I flashed a smile. "Deep breath, Brock. You don't have to figure out all of this in an instant."

"You're right." He exhaled, but I could still see the worry lines etched on his brow.

"What are you thinking?" I asked.

"I'm leaving soon, but I have so many questions. Could I call you . . . or D.J.? Would that be okay?"

"Of course. And don't forget about Rob. Once he gets back from his honeymoon, I mean." I grinned.

"Right, right."

We spent the next couple of hours answering Brock's questions, my heart racing all the while. At the end of it, he couldn't seem to hold back his enthusiasm. The more he heard about living for Christ, the more he felt he needed— wanted—a project.

"There's got to be something I can do." He paced the living room, finally pausing to look at me. Snapping his fingers, he said, "I know!"

"What?" D.J. asked.

"It's so obvious. I've met so many great people here on Galveston Island. And I can see that the island is still recovering after the storm. Maybe I could help."

I grinned. "Great idea. It's been quite a while, but some people are still not back in their homes."

"I told Bella all about a guy I know on the west end," D.J. said. "An older man whose home was almost destroyed. He's a pastor, but his church building was completely obliterated. The congregation is meeting in a school right now."

"Okay, that's it." Brock nodded. "I'll build him a church. What kind of money are we talking here? One million? Two? I can make out a check today. Just let me know."

D.J. laughed. "Brock, we're talking about a small congregation here. Maybe a hundred people or so. And they already own the property. It just needs to be cleared and rebuilt. We're probably talking two hundred and fifty thousand dollars, and that would include cleanup. For that matter, if my company takes on the job, we can probably do it all for less than that. I'd like to contribute in some way too."

Oh, my heart wanted to jump out of my chest. Now here was the man I loved! He would do just about anything to ensure that that pastor would get the thing he wanted most—a place to share the gospel.

"You've got it." Brock nodded. "Who do I make the check out to?"

D.J. laughed again. "Before we get into all of that, why don't I take you to meet Pastor Willy? I think you two are going to be great friends. He can fill you in. Sound good?"

Brock nodded. "Yes, and I guess we'd better take care of this today, since I fly out tomorrow."

My heart twisted at his words. Brock Benson had become so much a part of our lives that I could hardly imagine him leaving, especially now.

We climbed into D.J.'s truck and headed to the west end of the island, where we found Willy Maddox sitting in the front room of his house, watching a televised sermon. He greeted us with a look of sheer delight, his smile bright against such beautiful dark skin. "Well, well . . . to what do I owe the honor, young man?"

"I've brought a friend who wants to meet you."

"Have you now." He turned to me, and I giggled.

"Technically, I'm not the one he brought to meet you, but I'm happy to be here, just the same." Extending my hand, I made introductions. "I'm Bella, D.J.'s—"

"Oh, I know who you are, no doubt about that." Willy laughed. "You're the love of D.J.'s life."

I felt my cheeks warm and snuggled against D.J.

"This boy can't say enough about you, Bella." Willy grinned. "It's a pleasure to finally meet you. But who have we here?" He turned to Brock. "There's something familiar about you."

"The name is Brock Benson." Brock grabbed the man's hand and gave it an enthusiastic shake. "I'm from California."

"Well, hello, Brock Benson from California. What brings you out to the west end of Galveston Island today? And why are those people with the cameras following you?"

I turned back and looked through the open door, stunned to see that a news truck had pulled up in front of Willy's house.

Brock groaned. "No way. Did either of you see them earlier?"

"Nope." I sighed. "But you know what? Let's get them in on this. The more attention we can draw to the people in need on the island, the better, at least to my way of thinking."

"But I don't want anyone to know what I'm doing." Brock crossed his arms at his chest. "Does that sound dumb?"

"No. Not dumb at all. We don't have to tell them you're going to pay to rebuild the church."

"W-what?" Willy stared at him, his eyes now very wide. "You're going to pay to rebuild my church?"

"If you will let me, sir. It would be an honor."

"Son, come and sit with me a minute. It's important that we talk. I need to know why the Lord has laid this on your heart."

The two of them sat on the sofa, and I took D.J. by the hand. "Ready to talk to the press?"

"I guess." He sighed. "But I'm not very good at this."

"Oh, you'll do just fine."

As we walked to the news van, a cameraman jumped out and began to film us. Strange, but in that moment I had the weirdest flashback of the night I'd been arrested. Was it really only two days ago? Thankfully, this guy looked pretty harmless, but the harried reporter who jumped out of the van behind him did not. He thrust a microphone in my face.

"So, what can you tell us about Brock Benson?" he asked. "What's he doing out here on the west end of the island?"

I did my best to play it cool, hoping I could keep my voice steady. "Like so many of us, he is concerned about the welfare of those whose lives were touched by Hurricane Ike. Several of us are linking arms to do what we can." I gestured to D.J.

"But if you want to know about a real hero, you'll have to talk to this guy right here."

D.J.'s jaw grew tight, and I could read the fear in his eyes. Jabbing him in the ribs with my elbow, I added, "He really has a heart for people and is in the rebuilding business. So if you have any questions, he's your guy."

As those last words crossed my lips, I stared up at my cowboy, my knight in shining armor. He was indeed my guy. And I would love him no matter how many storms life threw our way.

36

These Foolish Things

On the morning after Brock Benson left for Hollywood, I slept in. I couldn't recall ever being more exhausted. I ached from the top of my head to the bottom of my toes. Even my brain hurt.

The activities over the past couple weeks had finally caught up with me. The wedding. The storm. The Food Network gig. Jail. All of it. So when I finally awoke, I could barely talk myself into getting out of bed. Only when I received a call on my cell from a potential client—ironically, the judge's daughter—did I garner the energy to sit up and think about the day ahead. We agreed to meet at 11:00 at the wedding facility, so I'd better get up and running. It was already after 9:00.

Looking around my room, I sighed. I usually prided myself on keeping things tidy, but I'd really let things go over the last two weeks. Well, my version of letting things go, anyway.

The room never got really bad, even when life was completely out of control.

Determined to make the most of the morning, I peeked inside my closet, looking for something to wear. Some folks—my brothers, for instance—accused me of being anal. I didn't consider myself anal. Of course, the hanging clothes in my closet were color coordinated, but weren't everyone's? And I did have all of my summer things and winter things clearly separated for ease of selection. That only made sense.

I gravitated toward the section of brown and bronze tops. With October fully upon us, I could get away with fall colors. And I always loved the darker colors. They seemed to work well with my skin tone and dark hair. Besides, the air had turned cool over the past couple of days, and I needed something a little warmer.

I yawned and stretched, then looked down at Precious, who still lay curled up on the bed. "Feeling lazy today, girl? What happened to our work ethic? Did it slide right out the window?"

For some reason, saying the words *work ethic* made me think of Brock Benson and the conversation we'd had about how hard Aunt Rosa worked. I wondered if he was back at work today, filming another movie. Getting his manicured nails dirty. He'd already called D.J. several times, laying out a plan for an after-school facility he wanted to open in Los Angeles. Yep, the man had an amazing work ethic. Maybe Rosa had rubbed off on him more than we knew.

I spent the next hour showering and dressing. Though I took my time, I was aware of the fact that the clock was ticking. A new client awaited. And a new client meant another themed wedding. Southern plantation, no less. How fun would that be?

At 10:30, after double-checking my appearance in the mirror, I turned to Precious. "Time to go outside, little girl."

She wagged her tail—the first sign of movement from her all day—and sprang from the bed. I carried her down the stairs and out onto the veranda, and she ran into the yard to take care of business. I stood on the front porch, looking across the street at Dakota Burton's window. Last I'd heard, Phoebe had grounded him until the second coming. Not that I blamed her. The kid just didn't know when to quit. Still, he had a lot of business sense. I had to give him that.

Walking back in the house, I noticed a rustling sound coming from the living room. I walked in there to find Mama looking through boxes of old photographs.

"Good morning." I sat next to her. "What brought this on?"

"Oh, those people from the Food Network called, asking for some pictures of Rosa as a little girl. They wanted to know if we had any of her cooking as a youngster." Mama held up a couple of black-and-white photos of Rosa as a child in their family restaurant.

I smiled as I looked at it. "Perfect."

"Yes, but look what else I found while I was in here." Mama held up a picture that had to have been taken when she—Mama—was just a little thing. Elementary age, probably. Rosa, who was probably in her late teens in this photograph, looked different back then. Much different. While she didn't have Mama's startling natural beauty, there was something in her eyes . . . a goodness. A kindness.

However, when I looked closer, I could even see a little pain there. Not that I wanted to see pain in my aunt's eyes, but it was there all right. I had to wonder what—or who—had put it there.

"This picture brings back so many memories . . . and not all of them good," Mama said with a sigh.

"When was it taken?" I asked.

"Oh, I can tell you exactly. I remember that day so clearly. My parents were throwing a little celebration for Rosa because she was leaving the next day to join the convent."

"Ah." I'd heard this story before—how she'd joined the convent, thinking it would quiet the ache in her heart over not fitting in with her peers. But how sad to see the pain in her eyes in this photograph, just one day before leaving.

"Looks like she knew even then that it wouldn't work out."

"Well, it wasn't for lack of effort," Mama said, staring at the picture. "I truly believe she wanted to give her life in service for the Lord."

"Mama, she *did* give her life in service for the Lord."

My mother looked at me with wrinkled brow.

"Rosa has the most wonderful servant's heart in the world," I said. "She takes care of all of us from morning till night. And I never hear her complain about working so hard."

"True." Mama sighed. "I'm ashamed to admit I'm not as good with cooking and housekeeping as Rosa. Before she came to live with us, I did all of the cooking. But from the day she walked in that door, she wouldn't let me touch a thing in my own kitchen."

"Did that hurt your feelings?" I asked, picking up another picture.

"Are you kidding?" Mama laughed. "Rosa had a natural talent for cooking. I did not. Every minute in the kitchen was a chore for me."

"Oh, wow. I didn't know that."

"Yes. I was much more at home taking care of you kids and

helping your father with the wedding facility." She paused a moment and looked at the photograph. "But I think you're right about Rosa serving the Lord. I'd never thought about it like that, but everything she's done, she's done for others. And she's done it all out of a deep faith in God. So, in that respect, I guess you could say she's lived her life in service for him."

"Definitely. And you have to admit"—I pointed to her downcast eyes—"you never see her looking like this."

"Unless Laz has hurt her feelings," Mama said. "And to be honest, I'm pretty sure that's what happened the day this photograph was taken. His family had come to our home for the celebration, and he made a snide remark to her about having to go to the convent because nobody wanted her."

I gasped at that news. "Mama! That's awful."

"I know." She sighed. "But sometimes we say things we don't mean."

"Who says things they don't mean?"

I looked across the room at Laz, who had entered while we weren't paying attention.

"Oh, well, we . . ." Mama quickly gathered up the photographs she wanted to send to the Food Network, then put the lid on the box. "We're just talking about the old days."

"Oh? Looking at pictures?" He drew near and extended his hand. Mama sighed as she put the photographs of Rosa into his outstretched palm.

Laz took a seat on the sofa, looking over the photos. He didn't say a word, but I could practically see an entire novel running through his head. Something about those photographs was touching him, making him a little misty.

Mama and I eventually tiptoed out, leaving him to his own devices.

"He's acting a little strange lately, don't you think?" I whispered once we reached the foyer.

"Yes. I think he's just torn. That kiss was the first sign we've seen that he has feelings for Rosa. But now he's back to normal, acting like it never happened."

"I will never understand the two of them." I sighed. "But maybe it isn't mine to understand. Maybe I'm just supposed to love them and pray for them."

"Right." Mama shrugged. "But I'm a firm believer that love can't stay hidden for long. It's got to come out in the open for all to see. Like a flower opening up."

Talking about flowers made me think of Marian's wedding. Thinking of Marian's wedding made me think of my new client. Thinking of my new client made me glance at the clock: 10:45. Yikes! I'd better get back to doing what I did best—making people's dreams come true!

37

Fly Me to the Moon

The week after the wedding, Rosa received a surprise call from someone at the Food Network offering her a weekly show. I had a feeling we had Brock to thank for this. The news both thrilled and horrified everyone in the Rossi household. While we wanted Aunt Rosa to become an international cooking sensation, we didn't want to lose her. She was simply too much a part of the family.

Not to mention being our family chef! What would we do without her nightly meals? Surely everyone in the household would drop ten pounds the first month if Rosa went away!

Laz took the news especially hard. It was written all over his face. He was in anguish over potentially losing her, but as usual, he didn't say a word.

On the day we got the news, D.J. and I watched Laz pace the living room, his jaw clenched tight. Though I could almost read his thoughts, he didn't share them. With anyone. Why couldn't he just come out and tell Rosa how he felt about her? That would fix everything. He'd managed to kiss her in front of the masses. Was he trying to convince himself, perhaps? Why couldn't he say a simple "I love you" when she needed to hear it most?

I finally approached him, trying to work up the courage to broach the subject of Rosa's leaving. "Laz?"

He exhaled sharply, then turned to me. "Not now, Bella."

I drew near, determined not to give up. "Laz, it's okay. You can talk to me about this. Your secret is safe with me. I won't tell a living soul."

He turned, and I saw tears in the man's eyes. Crocodile tears, no less.

"Oh, Laz." I gave him a hug. "I knew it!"

He drew in a deep breath, and I could hear the catch in his voice as he whispered, "What am I going to do without her, Bella Bambina?"

"Do without who?"

We both looked up as Rosa's gentle voice caught us off guard. She stood in the doorway with a hopeful look on her face. "Did you say what I think you said, old man?"

For a minute, I thought Laz would clam up. Deny he'd said anything at all. It wasn't in his nature to soften, but that's exactly what he did. What I witnessed next was a miracle of biblical proportions, ten thousand times better than the stunt he'd pulled in the kitchen when the Food Network guys were filming him.

Tears rushed down Laz's cheeks. He opened his arms, and Rosa ran—well, if you could call it running—into his embrace.

He kissed her—not just once but a thousand times. On the lips. On the cheeks. On the eyelids. In her hair. He released all of the kisses he'd been holding inside all of those years.

And Rosa didn't fight it. Oh no. She was like a stick of butter that had been left sitting in the sun too long. She melted in his embrace, the happy recipient of all his affections.

I stepped back, mesmerized. My heart beat so fast, I thought it might explode. Turning to look at D.J., I mouthed, "Wow!" He nodded in response, and I was pretty sure I saw tears in his eyes. For that matter, I had tears in mine.

When the kissing finally stopped—and that took awhile—Rosa lingered in Laz's embrace for a good minute. Or two. Or three. Finally, when I realized neither of them was going to make a move, I cleared my throat.

"Laz doesn't want you to go, Rosa."

She looked up at him, eyeball to eyeball. In the gentlest voice I'd ever heard her use, she whispered, "Is that true, Lazarro Rossi?"

He drew in a breath, then nodded. "N-nothing will be the same if you're gone. The house won't be the same. Meals won't be the same. I . . . I won't be the same."

She laughed—a great icebreaker. "Are you sure you're not just worried you'll have to take over the cooking?"

Laz shook his head as he reached with a fingertip to brush a loose hair out of her face. "Trust me. I don't mind cooking. It's not that."

"Well then, what?" She stepped back and put her hands on her hips. For a minute, the magic spell appeared to have been broken. Would this one defiant move on her part undo everything I'd just witnessed?

Nope.

My eyes widened as Laz grabbed Rosa, tipped her backwards, and planted a passionate kiss on her lips—one for the record books.

Okay then.

Precious chose that moment to start one of her leaping up and down episodes. Either she didn't like the idea that Laz had his hands—er, his lips—on Rosa, or she was just plain jealous that someone else was getting attention and she was not. At any rate, I scooped her into my arms and touched my finger to her nose, cautioning her to be still. "Leave them alone," I whispered. "Not everything is about you!"

Rosa came up smiling and looking a little woozy.

"Does that answer your question?" Laz gave her a knowing look.

"Yes." She grinned. "But I wouldn't mind a little more convincing."

He tipped her back and kissed her again. This time when she came up, she started laughing. Three minutes later, she was still laughing. In fact, tears were pouring down her face. Before long we all had the giggles.

When things finally calmed down, Rosa looked at Laz and smiled. "I was pretty sure that day in the kitchen, but I just needed a little reassuring. You know how women are."

"Yes, I know how women are." He shook his head and sighed. "And I know how men are too. We're slow to admit what we're feeling. Will you ever forgive me for waiting so long?"

"Of course. If you'll forgive me for all of the mean things I've said to you over the years." She gave him a sheepish look. "Can we just start with today and go from there?" Rosa gave him a little kiss on his cheek, and he flushed.

"Of course."

"And . . ." She released a long, slow breath. "Can I just tell you one more thing, to get it off my chest?"

"Sure, Rosa. Anything."

She gripped his hand and gazed up into his eyes. "I've loved you since I was twelve years old. That means I've loved you over fifty years."

"Wow." I whispered the word, knowing how difficult this must be for her to confess.

"I'm a coward and a fool," Laz said, holding her close. "Otherwise I would've told you how much I cared for you years ago. I think the older I get, the more stubborn I get. But that's not the only reason. I've been a little worried about something."

"Oh?" she said, looking somewhat nervous.

"Rosa, you have to admit, we're as different as night and day."

"We are," she whispered.

"If I say it's black, you're going to say it's white. If I say it tastes good, you're going to say it tastes bad. If I say it's gravy, you're going to call it sauce."

"Oh no!" She put her hand up. "I'd never say that."

"Still. We have a history of arguing just for the sake of arguing."

"It's how we communicate." Rosa gave him a kiss on each cheek. "And I'm pretty sure we have quite a few arguments ahead. Being different isn't a bad thing."

I felt compelled to interject something. "Rosa's right, Laz," I said. "Being different is a good thing. Take D.J. and me. We're as different as night and day, but it works for us. Life would be pretty boring if everyone was the same."

"True." Laz slipped his arm around Rosa's waist and held her tight.

I turned to Rosa, dying to ask the next question. "So, are you going to take the gig on the Food Network?"

She paused a moment, then shook her head. "Don't think so."

"Really?" I could hardly believe it. "You'd give it all up for love?"

"Oh, Bella . . ." Her eyes filled with tears, and she reached to take Laz's hand in hers. "Don't you see? I wouldn't be giving up anything. To have the love of a good man . . . well, it beats every other joy life could offer. I've waited over fifty years for this. Fifty years."

I smiled as she stressed the words. Truly, she had waited. She'd never married, never known a honeymoon night. Probably never even been kissed until that day in the kitchen.

And now . . . I looked across the room at Laz, who beamed like a Cheshire cat. I wanted to sing his praises from rafter to rafter. Wanted to run and tell the others that Rosa was staying put and we wouldn't all starve after all. Wanted to call Brock Benson in Hollywood and let him know I'd just witnessed one of the greatest love scenes of all time, one that even the best actors in Hollywood could never emulate. Unrequited love was now . . . requited. And I'd witnessed it firsthand.

D.J. and I backed out of the room and gave them the privacy they needed, the time to whisper the words they'd been denying all these years. I wouldn't spoil that moment, no matter how badly I wanted to shout to all within hearing distance.

D.J. took me in his arms and gave me the cutest smile. "Sometimes life surprises you," he whispered.

Yes. No doubt about that.

We made our way out onto the front porch and took a seat on the swing. After a few moments of blissful silence, D.J. squeezed my hand.

"So what comes next, Bella? A pirate wedding? A shootout at the O.K. Corral? A planetarium extravaganza featuring the sun, moon, and stars?"

"I'm open to all of those ideas, but I have the strangest

feeling I'll be planning an impromptu wedding of a different sort. No doubt it'll be filled with lots of Italian food and the very happy croonings of Dean Martin and Frank Sinatra."

Oh no! Even as I spoke the words, it occurred to me—Laz and Rosa had never resolved their ongoing conflict of who was the better singer. Would their relationship come unraveled over this one question?

Nah. From what I'd witnessed in the living room, their hearts—and their lips—were safely joined. And what God had joined together . . . well, even Ol' Blue Eyes and Dino couldn't put asunder.

38

I Wish You Love

Less than twenty-four hours after their kiss-a-thon, Laz and Rosa announced their engagement to the family. Less than twenty-four hours after that, we had the whole thing planned out. They wanted the 1940s swing package, complete with a live swing band. Wow, was that ever going to be a fun one to coordinate!

But, December? Could I really get it done that quickly? It was already October, after all. Still, as Rosa was quick to tell me, when you'd waited fifty years for the man of your dreams, there was no point in waiting longer than necessary for the wedding night. She'd blushed at that revelation.

I spent the second Friday in October making plans for their big day. The menu? Italian food, of course. Though we'd argued against it, Laz and Rosa insisted they would prepare the food themselves. The locale? The wedding facility, naturally. But it would be transformed into a 1940s wonderland. I knew it would take a lot of work to pull off, but I figured that after all I'd been through, I was up for the task. Seemed the longer I worked at Club Wed, the more secure I felt.

Well, unless you counted that incident with the police. But I'd almost put all of that behind me. In fact, I'd done one better. I'd actually gotten in contact with my cellmate, Linda, and met her children. They would be coming to dinner one day soon. After that . . . who knew!

With the busyness of the wedding behind me, I was finally free to relax. Take it easy. Late afternoon I headed up to my room to take a nap before dinner.

Tucked under the covers, I reached down and patted Precious, who rolled over on her back for a tummy tickle. This raised that age-old question, the one that often plagued me in the night. What happened to one's dog when one got married if, say, that dog was accustomed to snuggling under the covers at night? I sighed as I looked at the naughty little Yorkie-Poo. She might be a handful, but she was my handful. And if D.J. loved me, he had to love the dog, right?

I reached out to rub her little belly, and she made that contented sound I loved so much. See? She was a good girl!

Just then a knock sounded at the door, and Precious came flying off the bed, growling at the back of her throat, ready to save me from harm. If you could call a chat with my younger sister harm.

Sophia rolled her eyes as she came in the room. "You've got to do something about that dog, Bella."

I picked up Precious and nuzzled her against my cheek as I sighed. "Yeah. I know."

Maybe tomorrow.

Or the day after that.

Sophia came in and stretched out on the bed, then let out a dramatic sigh.

"What is it, honey?" I asked.

"Laz and Rosa are getting married."

"Right."

"That's just weird. I wonder which bedroom they're going to move into."

I hadn't thought about that, to be quite honest. Things were moving so quickly, likely they hadn't either. "Good question," I said. "I wonder if they're going to stay here at all, or if they'll get their own place."

Sophia sat straight up at this revelation. "No way! You don't think they'd really do that, do you?"

"Maybe. They're going to be honeymooners, you know."

She shuddered. "That's another thing. Can you picture . . . I mean, can you imagine . . . ?" She giggled, and I laughed in response.

"No. I can't. I have a hard enough time imagining my own honeymoon night, let alone someone else's, especially Laz and Rosa."

"Me too." She rolled over onto her stomach and stared at her nails. "I guess I'm not ever getting married."

"Oh?"

"I hardly ever hear from Brock anymore. He's only called me once since he left—and that was to ask my opinion about decorating that new after-school facility of his. He's too busy saving the world to remember that I exist. So I'm destined to remain alone for the rest of my mortal life. Maybe I'll become a nun."

"But you're not Catholic."

"Yeah." She sighed. "Maybe I could get a job on a cruise ship and sail the world. Put things behind me."

"Don't you get seasick?"

"Yeah." Another sigh.

"I think it's admirable that Brock's starting the after-school facility. Don't you?"

She nodded. "Yeah. I'm just being selfish, I guess." A sigh erupted. "It sounds like a great place, and I'm sure the kids are great too. But he's so busy that he doesn't have time to call me anymore, and that stinks."

"What about Tony?" I asked.

"What about him?"

"Does he call?"

Sophia shrugged. "Yeah. We're going to the movies tonight. He's a great guy."

"Yes, he is."

"Still, I have to wonder if I'll ever get married."

"Oh, I have a feeling you will. So don't join the convent just yet. And I wouldn't plan that cruise anytime soon either. I think you just need to take a deep breath and remember that God's got your love life under control. No worries. He wants you to have your happily ever after."

"You think?"

"I do."

We both giggled at that one.

Sophia stretched out on the bed once again, looking a little dreamy-eyed. Even her voice took on a faraway sound. "It is fun to think about getting married, isn't it? If I ever do, I'd like to have a traditional ceremony. Nothing too frilly. Maybe have the ceremony at the church, then have a small reception at the wedding facility. What about you?"

"What about me?"

"Have you thought about your wedding day?"

"Have I thought about it?" I couldn't help but chuckle. "Only since I was seven! Where were you?"

"Falling in love with all the wrong guys."

I laughed. "Well, I've definitely given this some thought. Would you like to see the pictures I cut out of bridal magazines and the fabric samples I started collecting when I was thirteen?"

"Maybe later." Sophia grinned.

"To answer your question, I've spent as much time thinking about the wedding as I have thinking about love itself."

"What do you mean?"

I did my best to explain. "From the time I was a little girl, I've thought about what it would be like to fall in love. And we have plenty of examples in our family. Just look around you. We're surrounded by love on every side."

"I guess you're right." Sophia nodded. "Never thought about that before."

"Take Mama and Pop. They have that 'I'll rub your back with mentholated ointment, you rub mine' kind of love. Steady. Sure. The kind that says it's okay to let your guard down and just be yourself."

"I never thought about that before, but you're right." Sophia paused a moment, and I could tell she was thinking. "I love that kind of love. It's so comfortable. So easy."

"Yes, but we also have the 'I'm too scared to tell you how I feel' version with Rosa and Laz. It's basically the same thing, only in reverse. They've been as uncomfortable as Mom and Pop have been comfortable, if that makes sense."

"What would you call Nick and Marcella's brand of love?" Sophia asked.

"Hmm. They have the tempestuous 'Did you pay the light bill today?' kind of love. It's just as real as the other versions. Maybe more real." I grinned.

"So what about you?" Sophia gazed at me with a hopeful look in her eye. "What's it like for you and D.J.?"

"Oh . . ." I paused, trying to figure out how to explain it.

"Well, we're not at the light-bill stage yet. That's for sure. It's still so fresh. I have the butterfly kind of love. When he comes into the room, my heart starts working overtime. But the longer we're together—and I realize it's only been a few months—the more it's turning into that comfortable sort of love."

We sat without saying a word for a few minutes. Likely Sophia's thoughts were running as deep as my own. We'd both known love all our lives. I couldn't recall a time when I'd ever been without it, in fact. And I thanked God for it in all its varieties. The brother-sister kind. The mother-daughter kind. The guy-girl kind. I loved love. Period.

Most of all, I had to say, I loved the one who'd created love. None of it would make any sense without him. And he'd done a pretty good job of creating the universe, so he must understand the workings of my heart.

And Sophia's. I offered up a silent prayer that God would show her what to do about the whole Brock-Tony thing. I wanted my sister to experience the kind of love I'd found with D.J. The real deal.

The silence held us in its grip for a moment longer, but the sound of music playing downstairs broke the spell.

"What is that?" I asked. The melody was faint but familiar.

Sophia's brow wrinkled as she listened. "I don't know. I can't make it out."

"Let's find out." I rose from the bed and walked out into the hallway. I could hear the strains of a familiar song wafting up the stairwell. Only when I got to the halfway point on the stairs did I realize what it was: "Someday My Prince Will Come," the theme song from Cinderella. Weird. Either Rosa had completely changed her taste in music, or . . .

I never had a chance to finish pondering the what-ifs. As I landed on the bottom step, I was greeted by D.J., who was dressed in a tuxedo complete with tails.

"W-what in the world are you doing?" My heart did a little flip-flop. "Are we headed back to the opera?"

"Nope." He extended his hand and, with a twinkle in his eye, made an announcement. "Madam, your carriage awaits."

39

Our Love Is Here to Stay

I stared at D.J., completely confused. By now everyone was gathered in the foyer. Mama took one look at my sweetie's getup and gasped. I'd never seen her in such a state.

I wasn't doing much better myself. For some reason, everything went to sepia tone when I saw D.J. dressed like that. It was kind of like one of those moments when you think you're dreaming but you're not sure. If I could've pinched myself, I would have, but that would have required thinking clearly. Completely out of the question at the moment.

Rosa turned her sights to the front window, a stunned look on her face. "Why are those horses in front of our house? And what's that man doing in such a funny costume?"

Horses? Costume?

Everyone rushed to the window, and I got lost in the crowd. D.J. took me by the hand and led me out onto the veranda, where I caught a glimpse of the Cinderella carriage Marian had ridden in to her wedding. Under the setting sun, the twinkling lights looked prettier than ever.

"W-w-what have you done?" My heart was now thumping out of control, and I was having a little trouble breathing. Maybe this was what hyperventilating felt like—I couldn't be sure.

He gave me a boyish grin. "I just thought you might like to go for a ride. If you don't already have plans, I mean."

"Looking like this?" I gestured to my jeans and T-shirt. "If I had known . . ."

"If you had known, then it wouldn't have been a surprise. But if you want to change into that gown you were wearing at the wedding, I'd be happy to wait."

"Really?"

When he nodded, I didn't hesitate. I raced back inside and bounded up the stairs with Sophia on my heels. We didn't have time to do much with my hair and makeup, though my sister took a stab at both. I focused on changing into princess attire, the whole thing feeling rather surreal. What in the world did D.J. have up his sleeve?

Five minutes later I sprinted in unladylike fashion down the stairs in the same dress I'd worn to the wedding.

D.J. met me at the bottom with extended hand. "Come ride with me, Bella Bambina. I want to spend some alone time with you."

"O-okay."

Moments later, with my entire family looking on—and likely with Dakota taking pictures from his roof—I climbed aboard the Cinderella carriage. The driver, an older fellow with white hair and an upturned moustache, tipped his hat at me and smiled. I grinned when I saw his coachman's attire. Very fairy-tale-like. Just my cup of tea.

He offered me his hand and helped me aboard. Then D.J. climbed in behind me. We settled onto the leather bench seat next to each other, grasping hands. Sweet. The feelings that washed over me reminded me of the conversation I'd just had with Sophia about love. Dwayne Neeley Jr. was a gift straight from heaven, one I was truly thankful for. And when I held his hand . . . when I looked into his eyes . . . I was that little girl all over again, dreaming of what it would one day be like when my prince came and swept me away.

In a carriage.

Like this one.

The evening skies were just turning that sort of orangey-purpley-pink that I loved so much. Very pretty against the twinkling lights of the coach. As the coachman took his place, I waved at my family—my wonderful, awesome, quirky, wacky family. They waved back, never moving from the veranda. I had a feeling they'd still be waiting there when we got back.

If we got back.

I had the weirdest feeling that D.J. was really going to fly me to the moon. Or, at the very least, take me on an adventure I'd never forget.

He slipped his arm over my shoulder and held me close as the carriage moved down Broadway. We garnered a few looks from passersby, mainly folks in cars who paused to point and stare. One woman even took a picture.

Turning to D.J., I giggled. "So, what's this about? Are you about to break some big news? Maybe you're moving to Hollywood to take a part in a movie? Or maybe you've decided you've had enough of me, and you're moving back to Splendora where life was . . . splendiferous?"

"No, silly." He placed a kiss on my forehead. "I told you before . . . I just want to spend a little time with my girl. That's all. No big deal. Just relax and enjoy the ride."

"Okay." I drew in a deep breath, doing my best to relax.

Not an easy task for a girl like me who rarely relaxed. Still, I gave it my best shot.

If you have to think about relaxing, are you really relaxing?

Though it was only early October, the evening had turned a bit cool. I shivered, and D.J. smiled. "You cold?"

"No." I shivered again, and he held me a little closer. Perfect.

For a while neither of us said anything. I didn't want to break the spell. It was like we'd drifted into our own movie scene, complete with Hollywood backdrop. Only I had no idea how this particular scene would end. I had a feeling D.J. did.

He wasn't talking, however. We rode in silence for so long, I finally felt compelled to say something. I was reminded of something that had happened earlier in the day. "D.J., you're not going to believe this."

"Believe what?"'

"This morning I heard Rosa tell Laz something shocking."

"What's that?" D.J. asked. "She's decided to take the Food Network up on their offer?"

"No."

"She's investing in some mascara and lip liner?"

"Definitely not." I paused, then delivered the punch line. "She can't stand Frank Sinatra."

"W-what?" D.J. looked at me with disbelief in his eyes. "You've got to be kidding me. She loves Ol' Blue Eyes."

"Apparently she *used* to love his music years ago. So this whole thing didn't start out as a lie. But somewhere along the way, she apparently just got sick and tired of listening to Sinatra tunes day and night."

"No way."

"Yep. Can't say I blame her. That's kind of how I feel about Guido and 'Ninety-Nine Bottles of Beer on the Wall.'"

D.J. laughed. "So why did she do it? She could've just turned off the music and dropped the argument. Why make such a big deal?"

"That's not how she is." I grinned as I pondered the real reasons behind her attachment to Sinatra. "She might've been sick of his music, but something about him still linked her to Laz. If she let go of the illusion of loving Sinatra . . ."

"She was letting go of her love for Laz?"

"I guess so. Maybe on some subconscious level."

"So she was toying with his emotions." D.J. grinned. "That part doesn't surprise me, now that she's come clean."

"Exactly. But there's more to this story. It turns out Laz never cared for Dean Martin at all. Ever."

"What?" At this revelation, D.J. sat straight up in the seat, a stunned look on his face. "No way! Parma John's is filled with Dino posters. And every pizza on the menu is named after a Dean Martin song. The Mambo Italiano. The Simpatico. Pennies from Heaven. You name it, it's a Dino song."

"I know. But it turns out he only *said* Dean Martin was the better singer to get Rosa riled up. Of course, that was eons ago. But once he got that ball rolling . . ."

"It was hard to stop."

"Yeah. Can you imagine? What in the world was wrong with those two? They used every means, every method, to keep from telling each other how they felt. Isn't that just . . . silly? Think of all the years they wasted stirring up trouble when they could have been, well . . ." I giggled.

"Doesn't make much sense to me." D.J. kissed me, then leaned back against the seat. "I'd rather just get things out in the open."

"Exactly."

"Which is exactly why I decided this carriage ride was the right thing. This is the perfect place to get something off my chest."

"O-oh?" I looked at him, mesmerized by that last statement. "What is that?" My mind reeled with the possibilities.

D.J. let out a whistle to get the coachman's attention. The carriage drew to a halt directly in front of Parma John's, which was just closing up for the day. D.J. slipped out of the seat, dropping to one knee on the tiny floorboard. My heart leaped into my throat. I could hardly breathe.

"W-what are you doing?"

"Oh, I think you know." He gave me a boyish wink, one that sent my heart fluttering.

For a second I thought I would faint again. I was getting pretty good at that, after all. Instead, I found myself giggling . . . and even more so as passersby began to cheer.

"Say yes!" one man hollered out as he walked by.

I would. Once he asked the question. *If* he asked the question.

D.J. reached into his pocket and came up with a box. "I've been carrying this around for quite a while now," he said. "But I wanted the perfect moment."

"This is pretty perfect." With my hands now trembling out of control, I gestured to the Cinderella carriage and the twinkling lights.

"Thanks." He paused a moment, then looked into my eyes with a soul-piercing gaze. "Bella . . . I told you awhile back that I'm not very good with the fairy-tale stuff."

"You're better than you think."

He grinned. "Thanks. But it's probably a good idea if I get right to this. I've been practicing these words for weeks and don't want to blow it." His cheeks turned crimson, and in spite of the cool evening air, I saw little beads of sweat pop out on his brow.

How cute is that?

D.J. looked at me with such love that I wondered what I'd ever done to deserve him.

"Bella, I love you with everything inside of me."

"I . . . I love you too," I whispered in response, fighting to get the words out over the lump in my throat.

D.J.'s eyes filled with tears. "I can't think of anything that would make me happier than having you as my wife. Will you . . . will you make me the happiest man on Planet Earth by saying you'll marry me?"

At this point, my heart went crazy. I thought it might leap from my chest. "Will I? Of *course* I will!"

As he opened the box, revealing the most beautiful marquise diamond I'd ever seen, I let out a Texas-sized holler. My robust "Woo-hoo!" must've spooked the horses. They took off galloping, which knocked D.J. from his kneeling position and left him scrambling to keep from falling out of the carriage. The coachman did his best to get the horses under control, but they continued barreling full steam ahead down the cobblestone pavers on the Strand, creating quite a rocky ride. Hanging on for dear life was really the only option at this point. Well, that, or falling overboard.

Great. I'd botched my own proposal. What was next? A patrol car pulling us over to issue a ticket? Paparazzi hiding in the bushes? Aunt Rosa chasing the carriage with a broom in her hand? Why oh why couldn't I get anything right? Why did every event in my life—good, bad, or otherwise—have to end in chaos? And why did this angel of a man want to spend the rest of his life with a goofball like me? Surely he could see that I was a walking disaster.

In that moment, I half expected the trio of sisters from Splendora to appear on the sidewalk, singing a perfectly harmonized version of "Call Me Irresponsible."

In all the mayhem, D.J. had somehow managed to make it onto the seat with the box in his hand. The horses finally slowed, though my heart never did. D.J. reached inside the box, took out the tiny ring, and slipped it on my finger. I stared at the diamond, completely blown away. Seconds later, I was wrapped in his arms, giving him a kiss he wouldn't forget anytime soon.

Afterward I gazed into his eyes, happiness settling over me and wrapping me like a blanket. "So, are you *really* sure you want to spend the rest of your life with me?" I asked. "Because I can be quite a handful. That's what they tell me, anyway."

"Oh, don't I know it!" He gazed into my eyes and then laughed.

"I mess things up a lot, D.J., and stuff has a tendency to fall apart when I'm around. I set out to do right, and things go terribly wrong. And I usually blow things in a major sort of way, say, in front of a television camera. Can you really live with that?"

"Yep."

I loved a man of few words.

He took me in his arms and whispered, "Bella, you can argue all you like . . . tell me every flaw you've ever had . . . but I'm not changing my mind. I'm going to spend the rest of my life with you. You're the Juliet to my Romeo. You're the lady-in-waiting to my knight in shining armor. And I'm the one with your glass slipper."

I smiled as I realized he was repeating the line I'd spoken to him days before. Funny. He must've been working on it all this time to get it just right. Turned out D.J. really *was* pretty good at the fairy-tale stuff. He didn't give himself enough credit.

He lifted my chin with his fingertips, gazing into my eyes. "God didn't make a mistake when he brought me all the way from Splendora to Galveston Island, Bella Bambina."

"O-oh?" My heart raced as I pondered his next words.

"I thought I was coming just to build houses," D.J. said, his eyes now filling with tears. "Turns out . . . I was coming to build a life."

Wow.

Now *that* was a line even the Hollywood scriptwriters couldn't match.

Sister Jolene's Top Ten Cruising Tips

1. Be polite to others on karaoke night, even those who don't have the same God-given talents you do.
2. Take advantage of the all-you-can-eat buffet. You may never get this opportunity again.
3. Make sure your pants have elastic waistbands, as you will likely put on a few pounds on the trip.
4. Wear your sequined dress on formal night so you stand out in the crowd.
5. Only fall in love with one handsome stranger per ~~cruise~~ day.
6. When you purchase your pantyhose for the trip, remember one size does *not* fit all.
7. When snorkeling, be sure to use the mask and breathing tube.
8. Take extra makeup. You never know when you might meet a sister in need.
9. Don't be afraid to let your little light shine, especially in the midst of a storm.
10. Travel with your sisters in Christ. Where two or more are gathered . . . there's bound to be a party!

Acknowledgments

I am forever grateful to my editor, Jennifer Leep, who fell in love with Bella and the whole Rossi clan. And how can I ever thank my copyeditor, Jessica Miles? You've given this book a Texas spit shine!

I'm also extremely blessed to have a great agent like Chip MacGregor, who not only champions my work but prays for me as well. And I'm tickled to have some of the greatest critique partners in the world: Kathleen, Martha, Linda, Janetta, and Ane. You ladies buzzed through this one in record time, responding with laughter and helpful comments.

I would be remiss if I didn't mention my awesome cruising buddy, Kay, who endured seven days on the high seas with me during the writing of this book. Many of Twila, Jolene, and Bonnie Sue's antics came from our week at sea on the Royal Caribbean cruise liner.

Finally, to my Lord and Savior—my reason for writing in the first place. Your grace (as Guido sings) is truly amazing.

TELL THE WORLD
THIS BOOK WAS

Good	Bad	So-so

C B

VG! BK

Janice Thompson is a Christian freelance author and a native Texan. She is the mother of four grown daughters, three beautiful granddaughters, and a brand-new grandson. She resides in the greater Houston area, where the heat and humidity tend to reign.

Janice started penning books at a young age and was blessed to have a screenplay produced in the early '80s. From there she went on to write several large-scale musical comedies for a Houston school of the arts. Currently, she has published over fifty novels and nonfiction books for the Christian market, most of them lighthearted and/or wedding themed.

Working with quirky characters and story ideas suits this fun-loving author. She particularly enjoys contemporary, first-person romantic comedies. Wedding-themed books come naturally to Janice, since she's coordinated nearly a dozen weddings, including recent ceremonies and receptions for her four daughters. Most of all, she loves sharing her faith with readers and hopes they will catch a glimpse of the real happily ever after as they laugh their way through her lighthearted, romantic tales.

A Romantic Comedy That Will
Have You Laughing All Day

Don't miss book 1 in the Weddings by Bella series!